the case of the
swamp pirates

DIRT
BIKE IKE

Pursuing the Dream

ROY JENKINS

www.2wheelcommunications.com

ISBN: 1453804463
ISBN-13: 9781453804469

FOREWORD

❦

"Dirt Bike Ike II: Pursuing the Dream" is a very inspirational book that talks about everyone having a purpose in life. Reading this book reminded me of how I became the person I am today — setting goals and having dreams and never giving up 'til I reached them."

TRAMPAS PARKER — Two-Time World Champion and Motorcycle Hall-of-Famer

ACKNOWLEDGEMENTS

∽

This book would definitely not have happened without the team that supported it.

First and foremost, I want to thank my Lord Jesus Christ, who gives me purpose, and power for living. This story has been in my heart for several years. As I sit down to write each book in the "Dirt Bike Ike" series, God gives me a new story each time, as we watch Ike struggle to grow up and achieve his dream.

A huge thanks has to go to my understanding wife, Linda, and my brilliant daughter Lacey, for their patient support and love. And thanks to my son Kyle, who, as of this publication, is fighting with the 2/6 Marines in Afghanistan. He and I took *most* of the pictures in this book. Come home in one piece, Kyle, so you can race Vintage motocross and hunt with me!

I'd like to thank the students and faculty at Abita Springs Middle School (where I work) for allowing me to read "Ike I" and the first half of "Ike II" in some of the classes, and help in the hard work of editing. At first I thought I would take the students along for the journey of publishing a book as part of their education; but they got into the story itself and gave me valuable feedback, making corrections in vocabulary, grammar and content details. I have learned more from these students than they will ever realize – every day!

I could not have done it without the patient, professional editing of David R. Holther, who never misses a deadline, not only in his years of editing for *Cycle News* but for his new website at www.todayscyclecoverage.com.

Special thanks to former motocross champions Trampas Parker, Steve Wise and Chuck Sun for their insightful advice and support.

Also, thanks to Sharon Deloach, Ophelia Fray, Aubrey Jenkins and Jane Bickford for reading and giving feedback on the manuscript, and to Billy Orazio for helping me keep the vintage race bikes running like fine Swiss watches.

Finally, I'd like to thank Morgan Parker and Cody Thomas for being the models for many of the pictures, including the cover shots. Most of the rest of the pictures come from my archives from over a decade of submitting race reports and articles for magazines and newspapers, and my website at www.2wheelcommunications.com.

INTRODUCTION

I wanted to share with the readers the beauty of south Louisiana. The mix of cultures – with our food, music, language, and way of living – is fascinating. Did I mention seafood? Oh, yeah, *now* we're talking – po' boys with fresh French bread, boiled crawfish, shrimp, crabs, fried oysters, or even raw oysters. I love to go hunting with bow or gun for that fresh venison and then smoke, grill, fry or bake it – not to mention fishing for fresh catfish, bass, trout or redfish.

The time I spent hunting and fishing with my father and grandfather in the woods and swamps near Springfield, and also along the marshy coastal areas with my friends, hold fond memories (except for those involving the mosquitoes and gnats). I spent several years living south of Thibodaux and Houma when I was a commercial diver in the offshore oil fields. One of the jobs in which I participated (with Barker's Mobile Diving Service) was to salvage the vessels in Bayou Lafourche, from Larose all the way down below Golden Meadow along Highway 1. These are very beautiful areas, and the ones I picture in my mind as I write about Ike's fictitious home in Calais, and Crip and Doug's home in Springfield, Louisiana. Although there is no Indian reservation there, I wanted to honor the Choctaw nation.

The bad guys in the story are purely fictional and have no basis in fact whatsoever. The good guys are based on real people that I know in the motocross and military communities.

Many people around me grew up in single-parent families, including my own father. I want to encourage single parent families with this tale.

Every person has a God-given purpose, and we must read the clues as we reach for our destiny. This begins in school. However, there are those who would tear us away from our dream, either accidently or on purpose. My goal is to help this generation discover their purpose, grow up into it, and avoid our common mistakes.

Come take this adventure with me as we watch Dirt Bike Ike struggle with the usual issues of being a teenager as he begins to understand – and then pursue – his dream.

Roy Jenkins, *November 1, 2010*

CHAPTER 1

"Where's my helmet?" Ike snapped, with nervous panic rising in his voice.

"Where'd you leave it after practice?" answered Mr. Gonzales in a soothing tone, trying to calm him down.

"I dunno, I put it right here," Ike countered, slipping his chest protector on with one hand and grabbing his gloves off the chair with the other.

"125 beginners to staging," the PA speakers boomed.

"Ike, that's your race!" Rick Abernathy called from behind the trailer.

"I know, I know! I can't find my helmet!" Ike said, his voice betraying the fear of a first-time racer.

"Does it look like this?" Mr. Gonzales asked coolly, holding up Ike's helmet.

"Where was it?" Ike demanded, grabbing it as he rolled his bike by.

"In the trailer. Did you check your air pressure?"

"Yes."

"Chain tension?"

"Yes."

"Adjust your cables?"

"Yes," said Ike, his voice rising.

"Fuel?"

"Yes! Do you have to ask me that every time I ride? I always do it," Ike mumbled through his helmet as he buckled it on.

"Yes I do, until you can..."

"I know, I know, until it becomes a habit. Can I go race now?" Ike asked sarcastically, frantically kicking the starter on his Honda, with no results.

Mr. Gonzales walked over to the bike and turned on the gas, then choked it. Then he stepped back with a smile of a knowing father. Ike rolled his eyes and tried once more. The engine roared to life. In his nervousness, he over-revved it. Mr. Gonzales gave him a look and started to step toward him but caught himself. Ike was busy putting on his goggles.

"Ike, hold up," Mr. Rick said, catching him as he started to pull out of the pits. "Take your goggles off and sling them on your wrist."

"Why?"

"Because you're just gonna have to go up to the staging area and wait, and they'll fog up."

"No they won't," Ike snapped as he pulled out.

Mr. Rick and Mr. Gonzales exchanged glances of frustration.

"I have never seen him this nervous," Mr. Gonzales said.

"Don't you remember your first race, even though it was, what, about 200 years ago?" Mr. Rick chuckled.

"You've got a point, but I surely didn't talk to adults that way," Mr. Gonzales said, with a little anger.

"Well, you're right, but look at it this way: You're not his dad, and his dad hasn't been around since he was really young to enforce respect. Besides, he just wants to win."

"I know, but I hope he's not racing for the wrong reasons. If he tries too hard, he'll get hurt."

"Who of us raced for pure reasons? Didn't we all have something to prove when we were young stallions?"

"He's looking more like a mule to me," Mr. Gonzales quipped. "I'm going to turn two to watch."

"The mechanics' turn is in four."

"But they're going too fast through there. I want him to have more time to read the pit board."

"Aren't you going to the gate with him?" Mr. Rick asked.

"He wouldn't let me. I think it's the cowboy hat," Mr. Gonzales said, pointing to the frazzled, weather-beaten hat he wore, and smiled. He reached down and picked up the mechanic's bag with the extra plugs, wrenches and other essentials, and then grabbed the pit board.

"Are you sure you want to use the pit board?" Mr. Rick asked "This isn't a championship. It's his first race!"

"That's the point — it's his first race, and I want to communicate to him."

"Why not just let him ride, make his mistakes, and learn that way? You know he's only going to get hung up on the gate or fall in the first turn."

Mr. Gonzales just stared at him. Then he put the board down.

"True. But I say he falls in turn nine."

"Why?"

"It's right after the big tabletop, and he won't get stopped in time. I saw him in practice. He's concentrating so hard on trying to time the jump that he forgets about the turn right behind it."

"Then why aren't you going to turn nine?"

"'Cause he's got to learn to pick up his bike in a race," smiled Mr. Gonzales.

"Oooooh, you're so mean," Mr. Rick teased.

"Tough love."

They both laughed, and the PA speakers boomed again: "Open Novice on the gate, 125 Beginner is staging, Senior 45+ and Women's classes get ready."

CHAPTER 2

～

Ike pulled up to the entrance of the staging area. A line had formed all the way out the gate. Other riders had their helmets and goggles hanging on the handlebars and were just leaning against their bikes. He pressed the kill button and fumbled with his helmet strap. He couldn't feel it through his gloves, so he removed his gloves and stuffed them in front of the tank. Now he couldn't see through the foggy goggles, so he took them off and hung them on the bars. When he finally got his helmet off, the line had moved, and the rider behind him bumped his rear tire.

"Hey, keep the line movin', man," he ordered impatiently.

Ike started pushing his bike, but his boot slipped in the mud and the goggles fell off, dropping right into the muck. When he reached down to pick them up, his helmet fell off the other side. As he reached back across the seat to pick up his helmet, he lost his balance and fell over, bike and all, burying his throttle in the mud.

The riders behind him laughed and shook their heads as they pushed their bikes around him, leaving him to pick up the bike by himself. One rider accidentally stepped on his goggles, squishing them into the mud.

"Hey, you jerk! That's my goggles!" Ike spouted as he reached out and tried to trip him.

"What are you gonna to do about it, you little twerp? You won't need to see from last place!" the rider responded angrily, turning around and pushing Ike's head with his hand.

Ike jumped up, but lost his balance and fell backward over his bike, landing flat on his back in the mud. The riders laughed heartily, and the rider in front of him just waved to him and continued on toward the gate.

When Ike finally got the bike back up, he nearly fell again. Now his hands, goggles, boots, helmet and throttle were all covered in the brown ooze. Gas had leaked from the carburetor and was all over the engine case.

"Oh, great, I bet you won't start, too," Ike said to Vinnie.

"Vinnie" was a 1982 Honda Elsinore 125 that he and Mr. Gonzales had built a few months ago. It was old, but it was the newest bike they had. Ike had grown accustomed to it after riding for hours through the back country around his house in Calais, Louisiana. He had only been practicing on the Abernathy track for two months when the opportunity came to race. Sam's dad, Mr. Rick, had to convince Mr. Gonzales to let Ike race. Mr. Gonzales thought Ike needed more experience, but he finally gave in when Ike pestered him enough. Now here they were at the racetrack in New Iberia, just 35 minutes from Calais, and Ike's dream of becoming a pro motocross racer was *finally* about to begin. He had waited all his life for this moment. He had played it out in his mind every night before he fell asleep and while daydreaming in school. Now the dream was about to become reality, and he was ready – or at least thought he was.

The Open Novice class took off, sending dirt clumps all the way back to the staging area; some of them hit Ike in the face. Ike's class quickly rolled their bikes up to the gate, jostling for the best spots, while Ike was trying to wipe the dirt out of his eyes. A rider down the gate saw the motion and announced, "Hey, look at 14 – he's starting to cry! Don't be scared, we won't hurt you."

"Look, a red dinosaur," another chimed in, and then pointed to the port-a-potties. "The antique class is over there."

"Hey, get him out of our class," one rider complained to the starter. "We don't want him getting in the way."

"He's legal, it's been cleared," the starter responded. "Just get yourselves ready."

The riders put their helmets on, then their gloves, and began to start their bikes. Ike just did what they did, but when he started kicking Vinnie, she wouldn't start. He tried turning off the gas, then kicking again. Turn the gas back on – nothing. Mr. Gonzales suddenly appeared from out of nowhere and told him to pull the bike off the line. Embarrassed, Ike refused.

"Pull the bike back off the gate, pronto. Just trust me!" Mr. Gonzales shouted over the noise of the other bikes. Reluctantly, Ike backed it off.

"Now let's push-start it, that way!" Mr. Gonzales instructed "Put it in second, then drop down on the seat and let out the clutch when I say!"

They rolled out away from the gate, then in front of the gate, center stage, where everyone was watching. Ike had never been so embarrassed.

"Okay, drop!" Mr. Gonzales shouted, huffing and puffing as he pushed from behind, his cowboy hat falling off behind him.

Ike plopped down and let out the clutch. Nothing happened; there was no sound but the hum of the dead motor turning over. When they slowed to a stop, Mr. Gonzales ordered, "Push it off to the side, I gotta change the plug."

"We don't have time for that!" Ike protested.

"We've got two minutes. Hold the bike."

Mr. Gonzales ran over to grab his bag. The starter held up two fingers to the riders on the gate, causing some of them to shake their heads in frustration. When Mr. Gonzales got back, he already had the new plug out of the box and the wrench in his hand. He popped the spark-plug cap off and fit the wrench in under the tank. He bumped it with the heel of his hand and clicked the ratchet at warp speed. He exchanged plugs and tightened the new one. He stuck the cap back on, and stepped back.

"Start her up!"

She started on the first kick, but ran wide open.

"Let off the throttle!" shouted Mr. Gonzales.

"It's stuck!"

Mr. Gonzales worked the throttle loose and revved it down. He reached into his bag for the WD-40 and sprayed away the mud, and then wiped it with the rag. He blipped it a couple of times and stepped back. Ike put her in gear and launched over to the gate, taking his position. The starter pointed down the line and the racers nodded, one at a time, including Ike. Then the starter held up the "two" sign, then turned it around to the "one," then sideways. He scurried out of the way as the gate dropped. And with that, Ike launched into his dream of becoming a motocross racer.

CHAPTER 3

⟋⟍

When the gate dropped, Ike let the clutch out too fast and killed the motor. He glanced up helplessly as his entire class roared away. Instinctively he reached down, pulled open the kick starter and gave it a swift kick. But it was in gear. He pulled in the clutch and kicked again, sparking the 125 to life. He tore across the gate and down to the first turn. Two riders who had tangled in the chaos of turn one moments earlier were just getting up.

'Two down, 15 to go,' thought Ike as he laid the bike down low and gassed around the turn. His adrenaline was flowing, and now Ike was fully alive. All the problems of school and home, and his own struggles with identity, were pushed into the recesses of his mind; and in an instant he had changed to "Dirt Bike Ike" – at one with his bike, free as a bird, master of his own destiny.

But he was not yet at one with the *track*, as this was the first time he had ever ridden here. The turns that were similar to Sam's track were easy, even natural, for him. But the jumps – oh my goodness, he was not used to those.

He approached the first double jump and backed way off, which caused him to come up short. He landed into the face of the second jump, springing him off the bike. His legs flew up into the air and over the back of the bike, but he hung on to the bars with all he had. By sheer will power, he stayed on the bike as the back end popped up like a bucking bronco. Bike and rider finally landed, nose first, off balance, on the front side of the jump and veered into the fencing. Spectators fled as he barely regained control, but not before he'd slid into the fence, stalling the bike. After wasting a few valuable moments try-ing to get Vinnie restarted, she finally woke up. He darted back out onto the track. Before the next big jump, the leaders had already completed their first lap and caught up behind him.

'Aw, man, I'm a lap down already!' he thought as he backed off the throttle again. The two front-runners held the throttle on, passing him, one on either side, sailing over his head. 'No! This ain't happening!' He gassed Vinnie and tried to keep up with them. He soon fell into a rhythm and began to keep pace with the leaders. It was a good feeling, riding at the same speed as the fast guys, and he started to settle down and think.

'Okay, I'm okay. I can do this. Vinnie is as strong as these bikes, and I'm not too tired. Let's just see what they do.'

Then came the big triple.

'I know they're not gonna try this. I'll just settle for the double,' Ike thought as they made the turn for the jump. He remembered his practice speed and backed off; standing up, he cleared two of the jumps like he had learned to do at Sam's track, but the two leaders went for the whole thing! The first one cleared the triple, but the second one came up a bit short and cased the crest of the third jump, popping his body into the air, just like Ike had done a few minutes earlier. Ike knew the out-of-control rider would have to slow down to recover, so when he cleared the double, he sped up over the final jump and went around the wounded rider and passed. Ike could hear the crowd moan as they watched that rider crash off to the side of the track.

'Focus on the leader,' Ike thought as he picked up his pace to close the gap. The KTM was almost one turn ahead, but Ike was sharing the same straights with him. That inspired Ike to hold the throttle on a little longer into the turns, like Mr. Gonzales had taught him.

He was picking up a little time on the leader when they approached jump nine, the big tabletop. Ike chose the line he'd found during practice and hit the jump in third gear. The front end began coming up too high on him, and he held his breath. Finally it started coming back down, and Ike looked for the landing. The turn! He had forgotten about the turn right behind it! He locked his brakes and lost control of the bike as it started sliding onto its left side; then it hit a rut and pitched him over the right side, sending him into the fencing for the second time! Right when he tried to get up, another rider cleared the jump, but missed Ike's head by an inch. Ike dropped back down. He turned and crawled off the track. Mr. Rick was there in an instant.

"You all right?"

"Yeah, I think so," Ike moaned. He tried to get up, but he felt a sharp pain in his left ankle. He dropped back down after putting weight on it.

"My ankle hurts."

"Just stay down. Wait for the medic."

The flagger was waving the yellow flag on top of the jump while the medic arrived to check him out.

"Where does it hurt?" asked the first responder.

"My left ankle."

"Let's take off your boot."

Mr. Rick and the medic carefully unbuckled the boot and slid it off. The medic examined Ike's ankle.

"Ouuuuuch!" Ike yelped, trying to hide the pain as he leaned back.

"It's all right, almost there." The medic removed the long sock and began to press gently on Ike's ankle in various places. "Tell me where it hurts."

"Right there!" Ike yelped as he sat back down again in pain.

"Right there?"

"Yes!"

"You're gonna be okay; it's just sprained," the medic stated calmly. "No broken bones, but your racing day is over."

The two men helped Ike up and put their arms around him to help him back to the pits.

"I'm okay, give me my bike!" Ike demanded, throwing off their arms and taking a step toward his bike. But his ankle couldn't hold his weight and he collapsed in a heap.

"You're not goin' anywhere on that bum ankle, champ," the medic stated firmly as he reached down to help him up.

Mr. Gonzales had just arrived.

"He okay?" he asked.

"Yeah, he just sprained his ankle," Mr. Rick said. "Can you grab the bike? I'll help him up."

They helped Ike up, and Ike put his arm around Mr. Rick's shoulder as they headed back to the pits. When they got there, they sat Ike down in a chair and got some ice and put it in a towel.

"Prop it up and put this on it."

"Here, I'll take care of that," Mr. Gonzales said, taking over. "You go watch Sam race; she's on the gate."

Mr. Rick scurried off to take his place in the mechanics' turn. A loud roar from the 13 motorcycles announced the dropping of the gate.

"And they're off!" the announcer shouted. "Raven Regal and Kate Sterling are out front. Where is Samantha Abernathy? She won the first moto in a vicious battle with Regal and Sterling. There she is in midpack; she got hung up in traffic. Samantha is the fastest girl in Louisiana and won't like it back there. Watch the number-63 KTM cut through the pack!"

"You okay?" Mr. Gonzales asked Ike.

"Yeah, you can go watch – I'll hold this," he said glumly as he grabbed the ice pack.

Mr. Gonzales shuffled off to the fence line to watch.

CHAPTER 4

∽

Ike had no choice but to just sit there in pain and listen to the announcer over the PA.

"Samantha Abernathy continues to cut through the pack, picking off riders left and right; while out front it's a dogfight – or should I say 'catfight'? – between Regal and Sterling! Regal shows a wheel to Sterling and Sterling slams the door shut with her Yamaha. Now Regal and Sterling are drag-racing down the back straight and it's a game of chicken into turn eight. Who is going to let off first?"

The announcer took a breath, and then continued to describe the action.

"Sterling sticks just enough of her front tire in to claim the inside line, then takes Regal up to the top of the berm and sends her over! Man, that was a dirty move!" Then the announcer started shouting excitedly, "Regal goes off the track and gets stuck on a hay bale, while Sterling motors off alone! Wait, here comes Abernathy, flyin' up into second place like a cat with her tail on fire. Last lap – can she catch Sterling?"

Ike grabbed a broom and limped over to the edge of the track to watch. Everybody was along the fencing now, watching the best race of the day. Sterling came zipping by Ike wide open on the number-33 Yamaha, railing the top of the berm to take the white flag. Sam whizzed by next on her KTM, her long blonde hair flying straight back. Meanwhile, Regal had finally gotten her Kawasaki back into the race.

The announcer continued: "Samantha Abernathy has her KTM almost within striking distance, as Sterling looks back over the tabletop. Regal is back into the race but fading in third; looks like she's injured – bike, body or pride."

Ike watched Mr. Rick waving to his daughter furiously as she went by, pointing to the leader. Ike wondered what he should yell or signal to her. This was all so different than riding in the woods. It was 100 times more exciting, but he was clearly disoriented at his very first motocross race, at least as a competitor.

He didn't even notice the pain anymore, as he was mesmerized by the action. As the riders approached the number-nine tabletop and turn, Ike wondered how Sam would handle it. She was the most experienced rider in the class and had raced on many different tracks around the country on her unsuccessful run to a National Championship last year. Surely she had something up her sleeve.

The announcer was rocking now: "Sam Abernathy has Kate Sterling in her sights. The Louisiana champ pulls up behind the Oklahoma champ. Something's about to happen! They both launch up the giant tabletop together, side by side! Sterling has the inside-line advantage into the short hairpin right behind the jump. Are they gonna stop in time?"

Sterling was half a bikelength ahead. Ike watched Sam maneuver her bike in the air. She locked the back brake, freezing her rear wheel in the air, and turned her front wheel left into Sterling's bike. That brought her front end down, turning her into the inside line like a gyroscope and giving her a split-second's advantage on braking as they landed on the downhill side of the big jump. Sterling had overjumped slightly and lost time getting her front wheel down to start braking, while Sam had already landed smoothly on the big jump, front wheel first, and she went hard on both brakes.

The announcer was frantically translating the action.

"Abernathy gets on the brakes first, hard! She just misses Sterling's rear wheel and dives inside the hairpin. On the gas first, she uses her back wheel to nudge Sterling, knocking her boot off the peg. Now Abernathy races down the next straight with a bikelength lead while Sterling has to fish for the shifter with her left foot. Two turns to go!"

The crowd went crazy. The air was supercharged with adrenaline. Ike watched with admiration as Sam expertly negotiated the remaining obstacles and cruised to the finish line for the victory.

The announcer was bellowing into the microphone, emphasizing each word: "Samantha Abernathy takes her Calais Motorsports KTM to victory over Kate Sterling from Ponca City, Oklahoma! The 16-year-old 'Bayou Cat' from Calais, Louisiana, wins both motos today to remain undefeated in the Women's class for 2009!"

As she eased off the track, Sam looked back for Kate Sterling and offered her a thumbs-up. Sterling just passed her rudely and gave Sam a thumbs-down and rode away.

Ike hobbled back to the pits, now remembering the pain and muttering an "Ow, ow, ow!" with each limping step, and then dropped into a chair to wait. Moments later, Sam puttered up and parked her bike. She removed her goggles, helmet and gloves. Her face was dirty and streaked with sweat, but that didn't change the fact that she was pretty – very pretty.

"Nice ride," Ike commented.

"Thanks," she replied, playfully slapping Ike on the shoulder with her gloves and then tossing them on the table and grabbing a drink from the ice chest. She took a long draw and then assessed Ike's situation.

"What's wrong with you?" Sam asked, pointing to his ankle.

"It ain't nothin', just a bump. I'll be okay."

Sam wiped her face with a towel and then took another long swig of water. Her dad came running up with a wide grin.

"Way to go, Sammie, you burned 'em! That's my girl," he boasted proudly, giving her a big bear hug.

Mr. Gonzales came up next, hooting and hollering as he ducked under the canopy, clapping his hands.

"Bravo, bravo," he celebrated. "That was some great riding!"

"Thanks," Sam responded, smiling. "I'm glad you liked it."

She dropped down wearily into the chair next to Ike's.

"We should go out and celebrate on the way home – don't you think, Ike?" Mr. Gonzales suggested, turning to Ike.

"I don't know, my ankle is hurting," Ike whined.

"How about a couple Tylenol and some pizza?" Mr. Rick offered.

Ike had to think about that. "Pizza?"

"At Doc's in Morgan City."

"Doc's Pizza? I guess I can tough it out," Ike said, nodding.

Suddenly, Kate Sterling came riding up on her little pit bike.

"That was a dirty move, Samantha," she accused. "I would have won that race!"

"I barely bumped you," Sam retorted defensively.

"Oh, yeah? You almost took me out!" Kate snarled angrily.

"…And what did you do to Raven Regal?" asked Mr. Rick.

Kate just stuck her nose up in the air and motored away.

"I won't forget that!" she threatened over her shoulder.

"I won't either," Sam answered back.

"Yes, you will," her dad warned.

"No, I won't," Sam hissed angrily. "I put a clean pass on her. Didn't you see it?"

"Yep, I saw it," he answered, holding his ground. "It was the best pass you ever made. Just aggressive racing, like I taught you, not dirty. But you've got to let the anger go."

"He's right, Sam," Mr. Gonzales offered gently. "If you don't let it go, it will fester inside of you until it comes out in some other unhealthy way."

"I don't care what ya'll say," Sam fumed. "She's got one coming."

"She's got lots coming, from several riders. Don't let her drag you down into that!" her dad scolded.

"I'm the one out there riding, and I'll ride like I want!" she shot back, angrily turning and storming off to the camper.

"Okay, we need to start picking up," Mr. Rick said glumly, turning to pick up his towel. "I'm gonna go get her trophy, since she's not in a trophy mood. I'll be right back."

"Does this mean we're not getting pizza?" Ike asked.

"It depends on who cools down first," Mr. Gonzales replied wisely.

CHAPTER 5

⟋⟍

The ride home was long and quiet. Neither Sam nor her father cooled down. They weren't talking, although Mr. Rick had tried. Everyone was in a thoughtful mood, replaying the events of the day in their minds. Mr. Gonzales had commented on the positives of the race, but nobody felt like responding. Mr. Rick drove the rig all the way home, while Ike and Sam surrendered to weariness and fell asleep.

The next day at school was a drag for both Ike and Sam, as they were still exhausted, both mentally and physically, from the race. Still, word got around that Sam had won her race, and people began talking. This led to comments about how Ike had fared as well. This was not good news, as far as Ike was concerned. Jimmy Plaisance, who'd missed the race due to a football game, used the reports of Ike's mishap against him, as usual.

"Hey, Ikey, gotta stop for the turns, buddy!" Jimmy laughed, taunting Ike in front of the other students at lunch.

"Yeah, he got lapped in the Beginner class!" Ben announced. Normally Ben was pretty friendly with Ike, but he was desperate for some "cool" points, and since he was jealous about Ike's new racing hobby, he didn't mind trying to take him down a peg.

When Ike and Sam had solved the Gaudet-Piazza crime a few months ago, they were given the status of town heroes, but a couple of the kids felt like that status should be temporary, and they began to work behind the scenes to humble those heroes – especially the girls.

With boys, what you see is what you get. But girls can be sneakier, with their hidden agendas and an ability to manipulate. When it came to Sam, it was almost a conspiracy – and not just because she was pretty, and the new girl, and now a heroine, but because she was stealing the boys' attention. Some of the text messages and e-mails going around about her got downright nasty.

The whole tense situation made Ike and Sam social outcasts in their own school, and in such a small community, there were very few other places to go. This isolation drove Ike and Sam into a kind of "us versus them" mentality. They could not go to the teen hang-outs and fast-food joints without feeling others' jealousy. Among the adults of Calais, they were held in higher regard, as most of the parents understood and appreciated their position. They were still grateful for how these kids had handled themselves during last year's crime investigation that had brought down the crooked chief of police and councilman who were smuggling drugs. But some parents were as insecure as their kids and would do anything to raise their kids' status. It was almost a sickness. More and more, Ike and Sam began to withdraw into their training for motocross. Their interest in school faded and their grades began to drop.

One day, Sam got the idea that they could reclaim their social status at school by going to more after-school functions. She targeted the homecoming dance as a possibility.

"Ike, let's go to the homecoming," Sam suggested one day after a brisk practice session.

"The game?"

"All of it – the game, the pep rally, the dance…"

"Whoa! Hold it right there. I don't do dances," Ike interrupted, with conviction in his voice.

"Why not?"

"I just don't."

"Ike, have you ever, uh, danced?"

"Nope."

"Come on, Ike! It's not that hard," Sam reasoned, as they pushed their bikes off her practice track. "I can teach you."

"When alligators can fly and crawfish can boil themselves."

"We've been frozen out for long enough," Sam said. "I'm sick and tired of it. I want to go have some fun with other people. Uh, not that you aren't fun, but I miss socializing. We need to bounce back into the scene."

"That's easy for you to say," Ike protested. "You have social skills, you're aggressive, you're pretty, you've got personality – you're a champion."

"Are you feelin' sorry for yourself again? You sell yourself short."

"No I don't."

She stopped and grabbed his bike by the handlebar to get his attention.

"Ike, break out of that negative thinking! You've got lots to offer."

"No I don't."

"You do."

"Don't."

"Do.

"Name one thing!" he challenged, looking fiercely into her eyes.

"Okay – you're kind."

"Soft," Ike countered.

"Intelligent."

"Spacey," Ike shot back.

"Intense."

"Hard-headed."

"Strong."

"Dumb."

"Deep thinker."

"Withdrawn."

"Creative."

"Don't follow the rules."

"Crafty."

"Sneaky."

"Committed to your mother."

"She's the only family I've got left."

"There's Mr. Gonzales."

"I'm all he's got."

"Ike Hebert, that *is* enough!" she said, her voice rising in anger. "There are people that love you. You're being obnoxious!"

"Do *you* love me?"

Sam paused.

"You see? You had to stop and think."

"Ike, I do love you."

"You do?"

"Well, not *that* kind of love."

"What kind do you mean?"

"Well, not the romantic kind. I think I'm too young for that."

"No you're not," Ike countered. "I've seen the way you look at Dave Remington."

"Ike, you can't be serious," she said, starting to blush.

"Look, you're turning red. It's Dave, isn't it?"

"Ike, you're trying to make something out of nothing."

"You call sitting near him in every class 'nothing'?"

"Ike, are you... jealous?"

"No. I don't care."

He began to walk his bike over to the hose to clean it.

"You are! You're jealous!" Sam declared, gleefully razzing him.

"Now *you're* making something out of nothing."

"Sam! Time for supper!" Mr. Rick called out, stepping onto the porch.

"I'll be right in, Dad!" She turned back to Ike and said, "This conversation is not over."

"Yes it is."

"No it's not," she teased, smiling.

"I'm outta here," Ike said, trying to hide his smile. He gave up on washing his bike, put his helmet on, and started Vinnie. He revved it loudly and shouted, "Conversation over!"

"No it's not!" she yelled back.

Ike just revved the bike louder and cupped his hand to his ear.

"What? I can't hear you!"

"Not over!"

"What?" he revved it even louder.

"Ike, are you over-revving that bike?" Mr. Rick yelled from the porch.

"No, sir, I was just leaving," Ike replied, putting Vinnie in gear.

"See, you *can* hear. *Not over!*" Sam yelled.

"Whatever!" Ike yelled over his shoulder, gassing the bike and shooting roost all over Sam as he pulled away.

CHAPTER 6

∽

Calais High School was abuzz with the events of early January. There was Homecoming Week, the big pep rally, the parties, the game and, of course, the dance – which Ike was able to talk Sam out of… barely.

A month later, excitement began to grow on campus for the Valentine's Weekend activities. On the Friday before Valentine's Day, students gave out cards. As usual, the popular students got plenty of cards and waved them around in everyone else's faces like trophies. Some of the girls got flowers. Sam got the most from potential boyfriends. This didn't help her position with the girls at all. But it was good for her ego.

There was nothing to help Ike with *his* ego problems. He got a few cards, but he figured they were just "pity cards" to keep him from feeling left out. His mom could not reason with him. It was as if he wanted to be depressed, and couldn't be talked out of it.

Ike and Sam didn't get in much practice during this time because the weather was so bad. Rain and cold, wet cold, and then rain again. The motocross races that were scheduled for late January and early February were canceled, taking away some of Ike's and Sam's motivation to train and practice. Sam began spending more time on the computer, taking special courses to help with the SAT. She wanted to go to LSU and get into pre-med.

Ike had no illusions about going to college. While Sam was in classes for gifted students, Ike was in Special Ed, with all the stigma and baggage that went with it. He could barely read and he processed information slower than the other students, so he missed so much of what the teacher said. He didn't raise his hand to ask the teacher to repeat anything because it seemed to call attention to his slowness, thus giving the class one more excuse to laugh at him. He had stopped asking questions in the second grade. He could not wait to get out of school. He just wanted to get a job, to work with his hands. He was good at fixing things or putting mechanical stuff together.

So Ike puttered around on his BMX track, expanding it into an MX track, with little jumps he could build with his shovel. He worked after school at Mr. Gonzales' junkyard, which was being converted into a motorcycle shop. But when his grades fell, Mr. Gonzales fired him, at least until his grades improved.

"Bring your grades up and you can come back to work," Mr. Gonzales had told him the last time he was there. "That's the deal, remember?"

Ike hadn't been back in a month, choosing instead to sit around and play video games. When the last report card came, his mom had taken away his games. When that didn't work, she took away his bike. Ike still refused to study, but not riding his bike was starting to get to him.

Finally, when he'd had enough, he started working harder, doing some reading for English class and writing a few papers. In math, he started paying closer attention, but it wasn't enough. He finally gave in to Sam's pestering and allowed her to tutor him after school. But it came with a price: He grudgingly agreed to take her to the Valentine's Day dance. With a little homework, he was able to bring up his grades just high enough to get his bike back. But because of the weather, he wasn't able to ride much. He got tired of cleaning the mud off the bike.

On February 14th, a cold front had moved through south Louisiana that brought bone-chilling, wet cold, driven by a fierce north wind. It was as if the frigid air was battling with the humidity of the Gulf for the rights to drive the residents of Calais inside. Ike hated staying inside. He was just not an "inside" person. At least school got him out of the house. But it wasn't that much better there, because, for Ike and Sam, it was almost as cold inside the school as out, as they braved the stares and comments of the popular kids of Calais High School.

Ike dreaded the upcoming dance, but he sucked it up and soldiered on. On dance night, Ike's mom and Ike picked up Sam, and after a few pictures at the Abernathy house, they were driven to the dance. Ike forced his mom to drop them off around the corner so no one would see that she was bringing them. This was way embarrassing for Ike, since most of the coolest sophomores and almost all the upper classmen were already driving, and many had their own cars and trucks.

Ike felt really uncomfortable in his coat and tie. The last time he'd dressed up was for his father's memorial service, when he was only six years old. On this night, he had argued with his mother about what to wear. He'd been holding out for his cleanest jeans and favorite racing T-shirt, but she was having none of it.

Ike had secretly practiced dancing with his mom, demanding she tell no one. But she told Sam anyway. Tricia and Sam were always scheming to help Ike, although he claimed they were only trying to control him. Ike had a real problem with people telling him what to do. He had a real problem controlling his need for freedom. Though he still hadn't grown much taller, he was starting to deal with the new surge of hormones and muscles and a desire for adult freedoms, but he didn't yet have the maturity to handle these things. This was becoming a dangerous combination, and a new sense of rebellion began to creep into his attitude. Then he made the deadly mistake of comparing himself with others. He began to cover his insecurities with disrespect – for others and himself.

With all the baggage Ike carried, it was no wonder he didn't want to go to the dance, where the boys with more maturity – especially the older ones – seemed to be on display for the girls to scheme about. It took all his confidence and self-discipline to walk into the gym.

Sam had cleaned up nicely, thanks to a trip to the hair salon. Her hair was pulled up in the back, with some strands dangling alongside her face. A touch of makeup, along with some of her mother's jewelry – especially the long earrings – turned the tomboy into a doll princess. She wore a red-sequined, black lace dress with a handkerchief hemline to her knees, with matching black stiletto pumps. She was dazzling, and the boys noticed. Boy, did they notice! Ike felt like he had walked into a trap and soon began to resent Sam – for dragging him here, for dressing him up like some kind of formal monkey, and for creating a drama that he didn't understand, making him play a game he wasn't good at. But it was too late now.

CHAPTER 7

Ike's nightmare began right away, as the boys started elbowing their way in to speak with Sam. Ike took it too personally, since he had brought her. Then, when the music started, Ike hesitated in asking Sam to dance, and the competition began. Boy after boy asked Sam to dance, and being the physical competitor that she was, Sam accepted every offer and tried to outdance the other girls. She was in such good shape that she never tired.

"Come on, Ike, let's dance," Sam offered several times throughout the night.

"No. We've had this conversation," Ike argued, drowning in his insecurities and self-pity.

"Ike, I know you can dance. Your mother taught you."

"She told you that?" Ike asked angrily. Someone overheard Sam's remark, and the news spread around. Pretty soon the troublemakers were using it to assert themselves.

"Hey, babe, how 'bout dancing with me?" Jimmy asked in his most manly voice.

When Sam got up from the table and took his hand, Jimmy glanced over his shoulder and winked at Ike, who was fuming. It was a slow song, and Ike watched as Jimmy tried to put his hands in different places on Sam's back; she removed them twice.

'The next time he does that, I'm gonna spring outta this chair and kick his butt,' Ike decided, sliding his chair back and repositioning his feet, not taking his eyes off of Jimmy, who just smiled at him from over Sam's shoulder. But Jimmy didn't do it again. When the song ended, Jimmy tried to move Sam's head in for a kiss, but she turned and walked out of his embrace as if nothing had happened. She walked back over to the table and sat down and looked at Ike.

"Don't even think about it," she warned, her eyes glaring, knowing what Ike was thinking.

"It's too late," Ike said, looking back at Jimmy.

Jimmy just smiled at him and turned away, coolly striding back over to his big group of friends. He said something Ike couldn't hear, and they all looked at

Ike's table and laughed. Ike's face started turning red. He could feel the anger rising inside of him. He was now on a hair-trigger, ready to explode.

"Come on, Ike, let's go get some fresh air," Sam insisted, getting up and taking his arm.

"Good idea," Ike mumbled, responding to her gentle touch.

He proudly walked her to the door, with Sam's hand under his arm. He thought they probably looked like the couple on a wedding cake, all dressed and proper. As they reached the door, Dave Remington was standing there, tall and clean, in a red-and-black suit that seemed to match Sam's.

"Are you leaving?" he asked Sam.

"No, just going for some fresh air," Sam responded with a coy smile.

"It's really bad out there," he added with a look of concern.

"That's okay, we're athletes in top physical condition," she asserted playfully.

"I can see that," he croaked nervously.

Ike noticed that Dave was turning red. Sam brought her hand up to pull a trail of hair behind her ears, and blushed. Ike immediately stepped between them and glared at Dave as he walked by, pulling her along.

"Excuse us, please," he ordered gruffly, as he led Sam outside.

They stopped just outside the door under the porch, in the only spot that was still dry. The cold rain was coming down in sheets. Ike and Sam inhaled the cold air for a few long, silent, tension-filled seconds, not knowing what to say.

"You all right?" Sam asked, nudging up closer, trying to get warm.

"Yeah. It's just that… well, nothing."

"What?"

"Nothing."

"Come on, Ike," she probed. "I'm your best friend. Talk to me."

Ike looked her squarely in the eyes.

"You wouldn't understand."

"Try me."

"This, all this…" he pointed inside the gym, "It's… uhhh… not… cool," he complained, fumbling for words.

"Yes it is, it's very cool."

"To *you*. You're, like, the star attraction."

"No, I'm not."

"You are. Don't you see how the guys are looking at you?"

"No. Well, yes, kinda. But they're just being boys. Besides, they're not used to seeing me dressed up with a little makeup, that's all."

"No, it's more than that."

"Ike, it's your imagination again."

"What's wrong with my imagination?"

"What's wrong is, you work yourself up into a believing something that isn't true."

"I don't do that," he said defensively.

"Yes, you do." Sam changed her tone. "Now look," she said, moving in a little closer to straighten his tie. "You're looking pretty sharp tonight, and I have noticed that you are turning a few heads yourself."

"Those are just guys who can't believe I'm wearing a tie."

"No, silly – the girls," she giggled, giving him a playful slap on the shoulder.

"*They* can't believe I'm wearing a tie."

"Maybe not, but they're impressed."

"No they're not."

"They are. They think you're cute."

"No they don't, and I'm not 'cute.' Don't call me that," he argued.

"Oh, yeah, you're kinda hot."

"Hot?"

"Yeah, hot. You have this quiet strength coming from those blue eyes and a serious, intense look on your face that's attractive," she said as she straightened his collar.

"I do?"

"You do," she said, a little lower.

Ike couldn't hold back any longer. He grabbed her shoulders and pulled her in for a kiss. But she didn't kiss him back.

"What? What's the matter?" Ike blurted, moving back, annoyed by the rejection.

"I… I'm not your girlfriend, Ike."

"You just said you're my best friend. You're a girl. So that means you're my best girlfriend. You just said that seconds ago, and you gave me the look," Ike insisted, voice rising.

"No, no, no. It doesn't work like that," Sam pleaded, as the look on her face changed. Suddenly she was a cross between Ike's mom and his schoolteacher. "Yes, I am your best friend, but not your girlfriend," she clarified. "There's a difference."

"Okay. What is the difference? Explain to me the difference."

She pulled away.

"Friend is friendly; girlfriend is… well, different."

"In what way?" Ike asked, beginning to lose patience.

"In every way!" she countered defensively.

"Name one."

"Okay: They don't kiss like that."

"Why not? They do in the movies," Ike pointed out.

"This is not a movie!"

"I know that. But why won't you kiss me?"

"Because, I... don't see you that way," Sam confessed, turning away.

"What way is that, Sam? Huh? I want to know. I *really* would like to know how you see me."

She turned to face him with fire in her eyes.

"I see you as my friend, my teammate. Kind of brotherly-like, you know?"

"I. Am. Not. Your. Brother!" Ike yelled each word separately, stepping back into the rain without caring.

Mr. Dansberry, the school principal stuck his head out the door.

"Everything all right out here?"

"Yes, we were just coming back in – weren't we, Ike?" Sam responded, turning to look at Ike, who was getting wet.

Ike hesitated. It was too much for him to handle, going back into the dance. There was really no reason to go back in. Not now.

"Ike, you coming back in?" Mr. Dansberry asked respectfully.

Ike took a deep look into Sam's eyes. He saw pity. That was not what he wanted to see. He wanted to see what she showed Dave Remington.

"No, I'm... not feeling that good. I think I have to go."

Sam looked into Ike's eyes and saw hurt, pain, and the sting of rejection. She tried to fix it.

"Come on, Ike," she teased and winked. "I've got something to show you."

That had always worked before. This time, it didn't.

"Why don't you go show Dave?" he spat sarcastically.

Dave stuck his head out, having listened to the whole conversation.

"Did someone call me?" he inquired expectantly.

"NO!" all three snapped at him in unison, causing him to retire quickly back into the gym.

"Come on in, Ike," Mr. Dansberry offered. "It's warm inside. You've got friends inside…"

"No, I don't," Ike cut him off. "Not a single one," he stated slowly, looking directly at Sam. Then he turned and walked away, into the rain.

"Ike, don't... don't do this," Sam pleaded and went after him, starting to get wet herself. She grabbed him by the arm, but he just shook it off.

"Leave me alone," he demanded, and quickened his pace.

She just stood there, looking at him, "You want me to, uhhh..?"

"Just leave me alone!" he yelled, waving his arm without turning around.

"Come on in, Sam," Mr. Dansberry advised, opening the door wider. "Leave him alone. He's got to think things through."

As he walked, Ike started feeling guilty about his words. Also, the cold water was getting through his clothes, shocking him into realizing the reality about what he was doing. He began to have second thoughts, so he turned to try to salvage his position. But what he saw hit him like a bolt of lightning. Through the open door he could see bright lights, decorations, the red hearts hanging from the ceiling, the music, the warmth, the sounds of people laughing – but worst of all, he saw Dave Remington take off his coat and put it around Sam as she entered the gym.

The desire to go back in, to try to break through the social blockade, to belong, to be friends – it all went away in an instant.

"That's a picture of my life, right there," he muttered to himself.

He looked up and saw the rain dropping from the darkness like so many icy missiles. They stung his face in disrespect. He growled at the heavens, then yanked his coat off and tossed it aside, and then pulled his tie off and crumpled it into a ball and tossed it at the garbage can. He missed and angrily kicked the can over, spilling old motor oil all over his pants.

"That's just *great!*" he screamed at the heavens. He jammed his hands into his pockets – and tore his pockets. He just turned into the dark night and began putting the dance as far behind him as he could, trudging wearily toward home.

CHAPTER 8

∾

The cold rain turned into sleet when Ike was about halfway to the house. He welcomed the pain. In a way, it felt good. But the sloshing of water in his new shoes was causing his feet to slide back and forth, forming blisters. He just shivered his way home. He wondered why Sam had turned against him. He wondered why his life was always like this. Why did he have to be so short, so ugly, so dumb, so skinny, so awkward, and so shy? Why wasn't he good with girls? Sure, he'd had a good run last year, when he and Sam had solved the crime and helped clean up the dirty cops for the town. Sure, it was fun riding in the victory parade down Bayou Castine. He especially enjoyed the festival, with the music, the booths, the food – and the newfound respect. He really liked seeing Mr. Gonzales on the stage that night, receiving the key to the town. What had he done with that key? He had cleaned up his junkyard, turned it into a motorcycle shop, and his business was thriving. Riders came from as far away as Florida to have their bikes tuned. And now that Ike's mom was helping him start an online business, Mr. Gonzalez had to hire more help. He was too busy for Ike now. That's what it was: Everybody was too busy for him. They'd forgotten what he had done for them. They'd forgotten about Ike Hebert Day. In just a few short months, he had gone from hero to zero, and nobody cared.

Ike bounded up the porch steps and out of the cold rain. He took off his muddy shoes and wet socks and threw them on the rocking chair. Then he opened the door and walked in. His mom was watching TV, and when she saw him, she froze in horror.

"Ike, what happened?" she gasped, jumping up and coming over.

"I just walked home."

"In this rain? Are you crazy? Son, all you had to do was call and I would have picked you up!"

"I have two legs."

"You're shivering! You're gonna catch a cold if you don't get warm. Let me start you a bath."

Ike didn't argue. He just stood there a minute, feeling like a drowned puppy. He was weak now and resigned to sickness. Maybe he could get some time off from school. He waddled into the bathroom, where his mom had started the bath. She turned on the bathroom heater and pulled out some more towels. When she started drying him off, Ike stopped her.

"Mom, I can do this. I'm 16 now, remember?"

"But you'll always be my baby," she said, starting to unbutton his wet shirt. "You're freezing," she said with alarm, feeling his face. "Oh, baby, why'd you do that?"

"Stop calling me 'baby.' I am *not* your baby!" Ike yelled, fending her off and pushing her out of the bathroom, closing the door behind her.

"Call me if you need anything," she said sweetly through the door. "Are you hungry?"

"No. Just leave me alone," Ike moaned, testing the water and adjusting it. He couldn't summon the energy to undress, so he just stepped into the tub in his clothes. Then he stopped and listened.

"Mom, are you still by the door?"

"No," she blurted apologetically, slipping quietly back into the living room.

The hot water felt good and it warmed his body, but his soul was still numb. He slipped in all the way up to his neck and just stared at the ceiling. Then he closed his eyes. For 20 minutes, he just lay there, letting his mind wander.

"Honey, are you all right in there?"

"Yes, Mom, I'm all right," Ike droned without even opening his eyes.

He had one thing on his mind: escape. *'If I could only get outta here, then I could start all over,'* he thought. *'Get away from school, from Calais, from the kids, from everybody – especially Sam.'* All the insecurities of the last few years were coming back to his mind like flies being drawn to garbage. The memories came from as far back as 10 years before, when his father had left for the final time. It was as if Ike was drawing every negative thought from the deepest recesses of his mind to join in the pity party. First it was the "what if's?" Then the "why me's?" Finally it was the "if only's." His fertile imagination became his torture chamber. When he was finally buried beneath a load of his own shame, he let out a painful moan: "Oh, God…."

Then, mercifully, he fell asleep.

He dreamed he was in a boxing ring, fighting a faceless opponent. A dim light was suspended from the ceiling over the center of the ring. Faces in the crowd were cheering, but not for him. Instinctively, he knew he was losing the bout. He was out of strength and couldn't defend himself. Every time he tried to block a punch, it went through his defenses and landed – on his face, in his stomach, and when he turned, he took blows to his kidneys. The pain was intense.

He was backing into a corner and his hands began to drop. Then came the final blow: an icy, sharp uppercut that rocked his head back. He bounced off the ropes and fell forward. He didn't even try to catch himself. He just let himself fall. He hit the canvas hard. What a relief to just lie there as the referee began counting...

"One."

Ike had no desire to get up.

"Two."

He thought about school and what the kids would say at his funeral.

"Three."

He thought about his track, how he might never ride on it again.

"Four."

He thought about Vinnie, the race bike he and Mr. Gonzales had pieced together from old parts. It was just sitting in the garage, waiting for him.

"Five."

He thought about Mr. Dansberry, how he had helped him through tough spots at school, but then Ike had avoided him when he didn't need him.

"Six."

He thought about Sam and how she had betrayed him and how much faster she was than him on a motocross bike.

"Seven."

He thought about his first and only race, and about how badly it had turned out. Yet, strangely, he had a deep desire to race again.

"Eight."

He thought about the success he'd had planning and carrying out the trap they had set for the Gaudet gang. But people had already forgotten about that.

"Nine."

He thought about his mom and how much she worried and fretted over him, but tried to keep him ten years old.

Then he heard a voice. It was faint at first, but it got louder.

"Ike, get up, son! You're needed!"

It was coming from his corner. It took all his remaining strength to lift his head off the canvas and look through his swollen eyes at his corner. It was his dad!

"Get up, son! You are needed. There is something you *have* to do! *Don't quit now!* You must go there and prepare! *Get up!*"

His dad was waving his arms frantically, but in slow motion, with an intense, worried look on his face. He was *willing* Ike to get up. Ike turned over and faced the light.

'*I want to,*' he thought. *'God, please. Help me!'*

Suddenly something began to rise from deep inside of Ike. It started from his gut and began to come up his throat. It came out of his mouth. It was an eagle, a big, beautiful bald eagle. It unfolded its wings and launched itself up into the air. It flew to the ceiling, looking for a way out. It was darting between the steel girders that held up the roof, hunting, pecking, trying desperately to get out. Suddenly a hole began opening up in the ceiling, as if a giant hand had peeled back the roof, revealing a bellowing storm outside. Crashes of thunder and flashes of lightning revealed the way out into the howling night. A sudden torrent of wind and rain came flooding down through the hole. And with a shrill call, the eagle launched toward the portal. Its mighty wings tore at the invisible enemy, fighting hard against the wind. The driving wind and rain pushed back against the eagle, but the eagle continued to flap its wings. Again and again it gained ground, even though the wind sent it back. It would flap its wings again and move forward, higher, two feet forward, one foot back. With a Herculean effort, the eagle finally forced its way through the hole and out into the stormy night.

The hole got bigger and bigger. Ike watched the eagle. He was mesmerized by the look in the eagle's eyes. There was fire in there, determination. As Ike watched, the struggle went on. He began to will the eagle higher. The more he willed it, the higher it got. Little by little, Ike became one with the eagle. His spirit lifted off the canvas, out of his bloody body, and ascended into the eagle's body. He felt the pain in the struggle and felt the wind beneath his wings. He braced himself against the cold and fought with the eagle against the wind. He noticed that the very storm he was fighting against was giving him lift under his wings, sending him higher. He gained altitude little by little. He grew tired and faint, yet he struggled on.

Then he looked down. He was higher than the trees. It was scary, but the will to climb overcame his fear. He struggled on until he was as high as the clouds. Then he noticed that he *was* the eagle. All of a sudden, he flew into a cloud bank, and he couldn't see. He felt a pounding in his chest. His heart was beating like a big bass drum. The pounding got louder and louder.

He awoke to the pounding on the door.

"Ike, time to get out. Come on, son, you've been in there almost an hour. Are you okay?" his mom pleaded, sounding worried again.

"I'm okay, Mom, I'm getting out now."

He noticed that his hands were clenched tightly into fists. His knuckles were white, his arms and hands were tired. He relaxed his hands and looked at them. Suddenly he realized that these hands would take him to his dream. Ike felt the fire inside of him. It was the fire of desire. The desire was to work, to train, to win. Ike got up out of the tub and back into the race of life.

CHAPTER 9

After a couple of fairly uneventful days at school, during which he kept his head down, focused intently on his work, and avoided Sam, Ike began to feel lonely. He needed to talk to someone. The weather was still too wet for practice, so he rode his bike over to Mr. Gonzales' shop.

What a change from the old junkyard! The old cars and trucks were gone, as well as the fence. There was a new sign out front boldly proclaiming "Competition Cycles." With the help of some of the townspeople, he had landscaped the ground and renovated the main garage and office into a showroom and motorcycle dealership. Business was up, he had hired a couple of employees, and with lots of new help came something that Mr. Gonzales had never had — organization.

Like any mad scientist, Mr. Gonzales was proficient at solving problems, but he had buried himself in his own junk. It took so much time to dig around and find his tools that it made him tired and frustrated. Now that the tools and parts were all organized and shelved, he was more efficient, and he could keep the shop clean as well.

Ike worked his way through the showroom of shiny motorcycles, enjoying the smell of new rubber. There were vintage motocross bikes, modern dual-sport bikes, touring bikes and street bikes. He walked back into the workroom, where three mechanics' stalls were set up, complete with tools and a motorcycle platform. The work benches were clean and organized. Mr. Gonzales was working in one stall, and a new man whom Ike had never met was in another. There was no one in the last stall, although it was completely stocked with tools and ready to go. Ike ducked his head in and saw a poster of Kevin Windham on one side of the cabinet, with a large picture of Ike perched on Vinnie on the other.

"Ike! It's about time you came to visit. What have you been up to?" Mr. Gonzales trumpeted, wiping his oily hands on a shop rag. He was smiling broadly and really looked pleased to see Ike.

"Hey, I've been kinda busy. You know: school, training, eating, sleeping — stuff like that."

Mr. Gonzales extended his hand for a shake, and then pulled Ike closer for a shoulder bump.

"Come over here. I want you to meet somebody," he said.

Mr. Gonzales guided Ike over to the man in the other stall for an introduction.

"This is Ronnie Simon, an old friend. Ronnie, this is the young rider I was telling you about," Mr. Gonzales said proudly.

"Ike? I've heard a lot about you. I'm Ronnie, but everybody calls me 'Crip,'" he grinned, pointing to his right leg; then he knocked on his thigh, and Ike could hear the sound of wood.

"Hi, uhh… Crip. I'm Ike Hebert. I live a few miles down the road."

When they shook hands, Ike felt the man's hand was as strong as an oak as Crip shook, not farmer-style, up and down, but just a firm clasp, in a you-can-trust-me-forever kind of way. Crip had dark features and high cheekbones like an Indian, but with blue eyes. He had no facial hair, but sported the longest ponytail Ike had ever seen on a man. It was held together by leather bands. He was average in size, but wiry-looking, like there was hidden strength beneath the faded denim work shirt. Crip's hands were dark and weathered, with bulging knuckles. Instead of the usual Leatherman folding knife in a pouch on his belt like most men in this area carried, Crip had a hunting knife with a worn animal-horn handle in an old leather sheath with turquoise beads. It was not big, but not little – just intimidating.

Mr. Gonzales saw Ike eyeing his knife and said, "Crip is half Choctaw. He used to be a Marine scout and sniper in Vietnam."

Ike's eyes grew wide in amazement.

"You were a Marine sniper? How many Viet Cong did you cap?"

Crip obviously didn't like where this was going, but he handled it patiently, as if he'd had plenty of practice.

"It's not how many lives you take, son, it's how many you save. I used my rifle to save American soldiers. That was my job. I just did what I was trained to do, and survived. And now I'm here, helping an old friend," Crip said, putting a hand on Mr. Gonzales' shoulder. "I heard you saved his life, Ike."

Ike glanced at Mr. Gonzales, who just nodded, giving Ike the go-ahead to tell the story.

"Uhh, Mr. Gonzales has a tendency to exaggerate," Ike replied, looking into Mr. Gonzales' eyes as if asking him not to put him on the spot like that.

"Well, exaggeration is not bad in the hands of a man like that," Crip said, nodding toward his old friend. "He uses exaggeration to encourage others."

"I never thought of it that way," Ike said. "But that's true."

"So, Ike, what brings you here today?" Mr. Gonzales inquired.

"Oh, I dunno, just came to visit."

"When do you want to come back to work?"

"Doing what?"

"Are you willing to sweep floors, pick up tools, take out the garbage and keep the place clean, like before?"

"Sure. I'm on top of that. I need some cash."

"Good. Then you're now my new mechanic. You'll be working with Crip. He's a wealth of information. He's the only one I know who has more experience with motorcycles than I do. He can teach you a lot about life, too," Mr. Gonzales said, turning to Crip with a wink and a grin.

"Wait – I thought you just wanted me to sweep floors and do the dirty work," Ike asked, confused.

"No, I just wanted to know if you were *willing* to do that work. And since you aren't too proud to do that, then you are ready to be promoted to mechanic. It'll mainly be oil changes and tune-ups at first; and every job will be inspected by me or Crip before it goes out. But this is how you learn..."

"I know, I know, by doing," Ike interrupted. "You've told me a million times. Where do I work?"

"Come see."

Mr. Gonzales led him over to the empty stall.

"This one is for you," he smiled. "It's ready to go."

Ike was astounded. He felt almost as excited as when Mr. Gonzales showed him his first dirt-bike project.

"I, uh, I mean... this is way cool!" Ike gasped, walking over to the bench.

"Look, in this box are your metric tools. Allen wrenches, feeler gauges, pressure gauges and small specialty tools in the top drawer. Punches, cold chisels and drift pins in the right drawer, and in this one," Mr. Gonzales opened the left drawer, "micrometer, precision tools and spoke wrenches."

He opened the first big drawer.

"Screwdrivers, flat-head and Phillips."

He opened the next drawer.

"Wrenches, box end, open end and adjustable, but don't get too happy with those crescents; you know what I told you about those."

"I know: last resort. They round the bolt heads."

"Good. Now here is the pliers drawer: channel locks, vise grips, needle-nose, circlip pliers, and dikes," he explained, closing the drawer and opening the next. "And here are your sockets, ratchets, breaking bars and torque wrench. In this bottom drawer are your hammers, pry bars, tire irons, big punches and hand impact."

He walked Ike over to the rolling cart.

"In here I'd keep my most-used tools in the top so you can grab them quickly, for whatever job you're working on. In this display stand on this side, you'll see the T-handle wrenches. If you look down on the bottom of the cart, you'll see the air impact gun and sockets. The standard tools are in the red box. Any questions?"

"Yeah – where are the lubricants?" Ike asked, looking around.

"Good question. Look in this cabinet," replied Mr. Gonzales, opening the cabinet door to reveal shelves filled with brand-new cans. "Up here are your cleaners and solvents. Next are your spray lubricants. Then your oils, premix, fork oil, crankcase oil, etc. And finally, down here, your spray paints."

"Where are the rags? I can't work without rags. Gotta keep the nails clean, ya know?" Ike teased, holding up his hands.

"Are you being smart with me?"

"I'm always smart."

They both laughed.

"That you are, that you are," Mr. Gonzales smiled, pointing to the rag bin. "Put your dirty rags over there when you're done."

Just then the intercom buzzed and the receptionist said, "Call for Mr. Gonzales on line two."

Mr. Gonzales just smiled and answered the phone on the shop wall.

"Competition Cycles, Victor speaking."

Ike tuned him out and began exploring the rest of the shop. There was a bench with the acid for filling and charging batteries. He saw a parts washer, a sand blaster, a tire machine, and a wall full of small drawers. He began opening the drawers and discovered the best collection of nuts, bolts, screws and washers he had ever seen.

Mr. Gonzales hung up the phone and turned again to Ike, indicating the small hardware.

"How you like *them* apples? I'm tired of digging all over the shop, then robbing another bike to get a bolt."

"Man, you've got it goin' on," Ike said. "When do I start?"

"You're already 15 minutes late. Can you get those clothes dirty?"

"Sure, I don't care," Ike shrugged.

"No, I mean does your *mom* want you working on greasy motorcycles in those clothes?"

"Oh… Yeah…. I'd better go home and change."

"Here, I have something that should fit you. That should tide you over until the uniforms come in next week."

"Uniforms! *Uniforms!* Victor Gonzales is issuing *uniforms?* Now I've seen everything!" Crip shouted, and gave out the deepest laugh Ike had ever heard. But then he started coughing, and coughing and coughing. He slipped into the bathroom, coughing up congestion. Ike could hear him hacking and spitting.

"He's smoked too long," Mr. Gonzales whispered under his breath. "Between that and the Agent Orange from the war, his lungs are in bad shape."

"What do the doctors say?"

"He refuses to go to doctors. He always goes to his friend, a corpsman."

"What's a corpsman?"

"It's a Navy medic assigned to the Marine Corps. He's the only doctor Crip trusts. But if you ask me, I think he's just scared of what the doctors will say."

"Ain't skeered," Crip said with a raspy voice, having sneaked up behind them.

"Hey, how'd you get there so quietly?" Ike blurted, surprised.

"You know, that's the thing about training: Once you get it, you always got it. Get it?"

"Got it," Ike reacted, looking at Mr. Gonzales with a look of apprehension.

CHAPTER 10

❦

Ike had begun to feel much better about himself since he started his new job. His long talks with his two mentors had straightened out some of his wrong thinking. Mr. Gonzales had made a sign and put it up in Ike's stall; it read: "Fall down six times, get up seven!"

Ike began to feel a new self-respect as he hung out with these wise and experienced men. He felt valued by them. He looked forward to going to work after school, and in a couple of weeks he had saved some money. Eventually, Sam and Ike starting talking again, and they were able to patch over the problem they'd had at the dance. They started practicing together about twice a week. Ike trained at home on his workout bench and on the chin-up bar mounted in his doorway to his room. He rode his bicycle to school. When he was teased about it, he would just say, "Gotta train."

When he was with Sam, they just talked about motocross or school, but never about the dance or relationships. Ike had put up an emotional wall between them, and as for Sam, she just didn't want to hurt him again, either. They were almost becoming friends again, but in a guarded way. Still, Ike didn't trust her.

"Are you coming with us to the race up in Kentwood this weekend?" Sam asked one evening after a brisk ride on the test track.

"Nope, I'm gonna ride up with Mr. Gonzales," Ike said. "I'm kind of riding for his team now."

"You're still riding for Calais Motorsports, aren't you?"

"Sure, I wear the gear and still have the decals, but I added Competition Cycles to my sponsor list, too."

"I see. When are you guys goin' up to the track?"

"Sunday morning. What about you?"

"We're taking the camper up Saturday. I want to get some seat time in on that track. It's big, fast and rough. You sure you don't want to come up with us and get a good look at the track?"

"No. Gotta work. I got three jobs I have to finish before we close on Saturday."

"Okay. Well, I'll see you up there. Are you gonna pit with us?"

"I don't know. We'll see," Ike grunted noncommittally.

"Ike."

"Yes."

"Why are you being this way?"

"What way?"

"This – you know, distant to me."

"I'm not distant."

"Yes, you are. You've withdrawn from me."

"No. I'm standing right next to you."

"You know what I mean."

"We're friends. Isn't this what you wanted?"

"Yes, but we could be closer than that. You act like I have the swine flu or something."

"You don't have the swine flu, you have germs. They're worse! You're a girl!" he teased.

"Yeah, well then, I'm gonna get them on you," she teased, and began to wipe her hands on his jersey. He took her hands off. She put them back on. He grabbed her wrists to keep them off of him. She rotated her hands into his and suddenly they were holding hands, face to face. For a brief moment they just looked into each other's eyes. Invisible sparks flew, but both pretended that nothing had happened. Ike let her hands go and walked away.

"Gotta go."

"What, homework?"

"Something like that."

"Ike?"

"What?" he barked, turning around.

"That was the first question I ever asked you and you answered the exact same way," she explained in a sweet voice. "Remember, at the Bayou Kitchen, when we raced home from school?"

"So what's your point?"

Ike just waited, showing no emotion. He wasn't about to go there.

Sam was stunned. She just stood there, trying to think of what to say.

"So I'll see you Sunday," he said, and he turned and walked away.

This time Sam let him go.

CHAPTER II

The next day, Ike felt a little guilty about the way he'd treated Sam the day before. Then he thought, '*She had it comin',*' and he felt much better, and thought no more about it. Today was Friday, and he tried to concentrate on his weakest point – taking tests. He tried pulling out his notes and studying, but his mind drifted again and again to racing. He was excited about the upcoming race this weekend and thought about going up a day early with the Abernathys for practice. It was true that he needed to get in some time on that track. He had never even seen it before. It was the roughest and most feared track in the state. They said the jumps were bigger than houses, that they sent you as high as the trees. He heard there were fifth-gear straightaways and serious elevation changes, which was unusual for Louisiana. It was known as a Pro-style championship track.

He turned his attention back to school, trying to keep his mind off the distractions so he could finish the tests. He had one in every class, but he had studied for them. He was doing fine until third period. That's when he saw it happen.

Sam walked into the room holding hands with Dave.

Ike couldn't believe his eyes. He had heard the rumors and had been able to deal with it, but seeing it flaunted right before him was a different matter. And she looked right at him when she walked in!

'*Now she's playing hardball!*' he thought.

He looked down and continued to study his notes, pretending that he didn't see. But out of the corner of his eye he saw Dave linger at her desk, holding her hand, until he took a seat behind her. Ike's hand started shaking, and he had no earthly idea why.

The teacher walked in, drawing Ike's attention back to the task at hand. Then he heard the most dreaded words a student can ever hear: "Okay, students, clear your desks and take out a pen and a cover sheet."

Ike broke out into a cold sweat.

'*What am I doing? I studied – kind of... I can do this.*'

He had thought about making a cheat sheet, like some students did, but Mr. Gonzales had warned him: "If I ever hear of you cheating, on the job or at school, you'll be fired, immediately. Do you understand?"

'Why was Mr. Gonzales like that? Didn't he ever have to take tests?'

Ike cleared his desk and put his head down to think. But all he could think about was Sam. He sneaked a sideways glance at her and caught her sneaking one at him. They both looked back down at their paperwork.

After school, Ike tried to slip away quickly before Sam could flaunt her new boyfriend before him. As he was unlocking his bike, he heard Dave's voice: "'Bye, Ike, have a good weekend." And he drove by in his shiny, powder-blue Mustang convertible, with Sam sitting right next to him.

Then Jimmy Plaisance drove by right behind him in his big four-wheel-drive wannabe-monster truck and stopped, his four friends poking their heads out of the windows to jeer.

"Hey, Ike, need a hand with that lock?" Jimmy needled. "Hey, wasn't that your girlfriend I saw in the Mustang with Dave Remington?"

"Shut up," Ike snapped as he pulled the chain through the bike stand. But his bike just fell over on his foot, and he let out a yelp of pain. Jimmy and his buddies just laughed as the truck sped away, rap music blaring.

Ike kicked his bike in frustration. Then he picked it up and threw it down again. Mr. Dansberry drove by in his Jeep and stopped to check on him.

"Hey, kind of rough on your bike today, huh, Ike?"

Ike just looked at him.

"Girls," he finally spat. "I just don't get it."

"And you never will," Mr. Dansberry promised. "That's part of the fun, the mystery. Just buckle up and enjoy the ride."

"I think I'll stick to motorcycles."

"Do that for as long as you can. Are you racing this weekend?"

"Yes, in Kentwood."

"You keep it up on two wheels!"

"Thanks, Mr. Dan – you, too. I mean four wheels – uh, for you, I mean," he stammered sheepishly.

"I know what you meant. Have fun."

"Oh, that I will, that I will."

When Ike got to the shop, he went right to work. He had to change the oil and service two street bikes and a four-wheeler. He knocked the jobs out quickly and then began to gather his things.

"Are you coming in tomorrow, Ike?" Mr. Gonzales asked.

"I was thinking about going to Kentwood to practice."

"Well, that's a good idea, but I'll pay you overtime to take on a special job."

"What is it?"

"Come see."

Ike followed him into the showroom. There was a modern Honda with a "for sale" tag on it.

"Ohhhh… Ahhhhh… tight!" Ike proclaimed, his eyes wide with excitement.

"It's a 2006 Honda CRF250 four-stroke. A guy traded it in this morning. Want to ride it?"

"Sure. I've only ridden Sam's 250F twice. But it's a KTM."

"It's not as peaky as your two-stroke. It's got a wider powerband, and the best part is, it has much more suspension. Go ahead, take it out."

He didn't have to be asked twice, and in 15 minutes Ike had his gear on and had motored out to the field behind the shop, where they had cut a little track. He went through the gears a couple of times and was amazed at the Honda's power. And the ride was so plush.

Mr. Gonzales and Crip came out to watch. Ike rode over to them and killed the motor.

"Well, what do you think?" Mr. Gonzales asked.

"It's way stronger than Vinnie, and the brakes almost put me over the bars."

"It should be better; it represents 25 years of improved technology," Crip explained. "And, it has more stability."

"Ike, I'll make you a killer deal on this bike," Mr. Gonzales proclaimed, "if you want it."

"Like what?"

"Five hundred dollars, plus A's on your report card," Mr. Gonzales proposed.

"I don't have that," Ike complained.

"He'll give you more overtime and side jobs and we'll take it out of your pay," Crip added. "If you work hard, you'll have it paid off in two or three months."

"So by spring it'll be mine?" Ike guessed.

"Yep, if you play your cards right," Mr. Gonzales answered with a nod and a smile that was contagious.

"I've got $127 saved already!" Ike proclaimed, lifting his arms in victory.

Crip stepped up and grabbed his handlebars to get his attention.

"You'll have to get used to two main differences: starting and jumping."

Ike's heart sank when he heard jumping. It was his Achilles' heel.

"What do you mean, 'jumping'?" Ike asked, folding his arms defensively.

"Listen carefully: Never – I mean *never* – chop the throttle going up a jump," Crip cautioned, pointing a finger in his face. "If you do, the back pressure from the four-stroke motor will grab the jump and send the front wheel down. You might not recover."

"Okay. Sounds simple. Don't chop the throttle on a jump," Ike acknowledged.

"…And don't grab the front brake in the air," Crip continued, touching the front brake. "Keep your fingers off it; otherwise you'll end up with your face stuck in the dirt."

"Got it: Don't chop the throttle or grab the front brake in the air."

"Easier said than done," Mr. Gonzales said, adding firmly: "Now you have to practice on it to get used to the different ergonomics. I recommend you don't go race tomorrow."

"What? You know I've been waiting for this race since January," Ike whined.

"I have two words for you: *New. Bike.*"

"…And new track," Crip chimed in "Deadly combination. One is bad enough. But trying to race with a new bike on a new track is like going to a gunfight armed with a knife."

"I can handle it," Ike protested.

"I know you can handle it," Mr. Gonzales replied. "What I'm worried about is your fierce, competitive nature getting you in trouble."

"I thought that was good," Ike contended, with palms upraised.

"It is, when it's controlled, but you're still a beginner," Mr. Gonzales warned.

"I'm not a beginner!" Ike crowed. "I've been riding for almost six months." Both men tried hard not to laugh.

"How many times have you raced?" Mr. Gonzales said, challenging him.

"You know the answer to that."

"There's your answer. Now if you want to ride the modern bike, you need to change the oil, tires, and clean the filters. But you can't bring it up to Kentwood tomorrow."

"That an order?"

"That's an order," Mr. Gonzales stated with finality.

"Can I race Vinnie?"

Mr. Gonzales looked at Crip and then nodded.

"I don't see why not. But remember: You don't have near the suspension that the modern bikes have. It hasn't been a problem so far, but now you're gonna race on a real track with giant jumps. You can't jump with the modern bikes."

"Whatever you say, chief," Ike mumbled, and he began to roll the modern bike inside.

Mr. Gonzales looked at Crip.

"Was that a 'yes' or a 'no'?"

"I think that was a 'whatever.'"

"That's what I thought," Mr. Gonzales conceded. "What do you think?"

"About what?"

"About Ike."

Crip paused, and then began to walk toward the shop.

"He's just like we were when we were younger."

"Oh, no," Mr. Gonzales sighed. "We're in for a bumpy ride."

"I wouldn't have it any other way," Crip replied, and they laughed all the way back inside.

CHAPTER 12

Ike was totally intimidated by the Kentwood track. They were right. The jumps were huge. The track was fast and rough. There were two serious injuries during practice. He had followed a few riders around during the practice session, just to get a look at the track, but he still didn't have it memorized. To make matters worse, half the sophomore and junior classes and some of the seniors from Calais High School had shown up to watch Sam race. Now they would see what a goon he was. He wanted to crawl under a rock. But there weren't any rocks around.

"What's wrong, Ike?" Mr. Gonzales probed, sensing trouble brewing.

"I don't like the track," Ike whined.

"It's not a beginner track."

"I'm not a beginner. I told you!" Ike said, his voice rising.

"Okay, which jumps are you not clearing?"

"All of them!" Ike reacted in a frantic tone, as he tossed his goggles down and dropped into a chair.

"Hold on – wrong attitude to race with," Mr. Gonzales observed.

"Well, give me another one," Ike retorted sarcastically.

"Okay. First and foremost, I'll be praying for your safety."

"What else?"

"I'll give you a strategy I used when I was outclassed or uncomfortable, but you're not gonna like it."

"What is it?"

"Will you follow it?"

"You tell me what it is and I'll tell you if I'll follow it."

Mr. Gonzales thought for a moment and then said, "Let everybody take off from the gate."

"What?!"

"You heard me. Just let them go. Wait a split second for them to clear, then you take off in last place."

"Thanks a lot, 'Mr. Wisdom.' Got anything else in your bag of tricks?"

"Hear me out," Mr. Gonzales insisted. "If you don't think you belong in the front, then you wouldn't last long in the front, even if you got a great start.

If you start in the pack, they'll push you faster than you want to go over the jumps. So let them go. Then go after the guy in front of you. When you catch him, you go after the next one, and on down the line until you find where you belong in the pack. You can then ride your own race at your own pace and hit the jumps like you want. No pressure. You'll gain confidence that way without riding over your head."

"Wait a minute, I think you've got something there," Ike conceded, his tone changing as an idea formed in his mind. "I can come from behind to win."

"Theoretically, if you go fast enough."

"What? Don't you believe in me?" Ike challenged.

"Oh, I believe in you. But you're just not ready to go full out yet – not on *this* track, anyway."

"I hate it when you say that."

"Say what?"

"'Not ready yet.'"

"Hey, we're all a work in progress. Don't rush it. You'll win. Believe me, you will win, and soon. Just do me a favor."

"What's that?"

"Don't show off today."

Mr. Gonzales held his eyes firm, waiting for an answer.

"Is that an order?"

"No, that's a request, from a friend."

"I'll think about it."

"Good. Now get dressed."

Ike took Mr. Gonzales' advice and let everyone take off. He pretended to have motor problems, because the kids from school were watching him. Then he tore away from the gate like a jet taking off from an aircraft carrier. He caught the first rider in turn two, and he caught three more in the next turn.

'This isn't so bad,' Ike thought, 'and all I have to do is just ride my own race.'

He caught four more riders by the end of the first lap. On lap two, he passed three more, and on lap three he passed four more riders as they began to tire. But now they were getting harder to catch. He had no idea what place he was in until he saw Crip standing in a turn, holding up three fingers.

'What? I'm in third place? Can't be!'

Ike was going faster approaching the jumps and becoming more comfortable with his lines. On the next big jump, he looked ahead on the track and saw the two leaders. He put his head down and went to work. He tuned out the crowd, the photographers, the flaggers – everything. He hyper-focused on the track. Everything else faded away. He didn't have to think about Vinnie because he was already one with the bike. He was glad he hadn't tried to race the new bike today.

At the white flag, he had caught up with the second-place rider. He found even more speed and soon was right on his rear fender. The pass came easily, because when the rider heard him, he overshot the turn, and Ike went by.

'*Use both brakes, knucklehead,*' Ike thought, silently lecturing the rider who hadn't even touched his front brake.

By the last turn, Ike was within sight of the leader and was bearing down fast. But time ran out and he had to settle for second.

"Now, that's what I'm talkin' 'bout!" he shouted through his helmet, oozing with newfound confidence.

When he arrived in his pit, Sam, her dad, Mr. Gonzales and Crip were all waiting for him. They all applauded. Sam handed him a towel and water as soon as he took off his helmet.

"*Now* you got it! That was *magnifico!*" Mr. Gonzales shouted proudly.

"Yeah, you didn't even look like it was your first ride on this track," Sam declared.

"I just can't wait for the second moto. I'm gonna race him straight up this time!" Ike predicted.

"Now you feel like you belong in front. So now, if you get a good start, you can hold the lead – unless you make a mistake, of course," Mr. Gonzales warned.

"Not gonna happen. No mistakes. The race is mine to win," Ike boasted.

"I believe you," Mr. Gonzales seconded. "I predict a win."

"I'll go a step further: I'll *guarantee* a win," Ike proclaimed.

They all looked at one another, wondering if Ike had gone too far.

Ike saw the worry on their faces and added: "Don't worry. I don't have to push it. I'm only gonna go out for a Sunday ride, and I'll probably end up at the finish line first."

They all breathed a sigh of relief.

Ike watched Sam win her race easily. Sam knew this track well. She had simply secured the holeshot and checked out, in both motos, thrilling the students of Calais High School with a wheelie at the finish line. Kate Sterling had crashed while trying to keep up with Sam in both motos and had tried to start trouble afterward in the pits, but Sam kept her cool. Sam's other serious rival, Raven Regal, was at a race in California.

Now it was Ike's turn. His classmates were gathered along the fence and invigorated after Sam's big win. Now they were expecting the same thing from him, and he wasn't about to let them down.

When the gate dropped, Ike was off in a flash, but he missed a gear, allowing three riders to beat him to turn one. So he settled into fourth place and went to work. He had the track dialed in — or so he thought. He was faster than the other riders, having learned to enter the turns and get back on the gas faster than these beginners.

By the second lap, he had passed the two riders in front of him and begun to watch the leader. It was a Suzuki RM-Z with a wild rider on it. The Suzuki rider was riding the ragged edge and was out of control on the rough straightaways, but he managed to stay in front of Ike by outjumping him.

By the last lap, Ike was tired of getting the Suzuki's roost in his face, and he was determined to take the lead. He planned to change his line on the big ski jump; up until now, he had been letting off and rolling it, and then jumping the second jump. On the last lap, Ike pushed hard to the outside and cut back to the inside approaching the ski jump. He pulled alongside the Suzuki as they launched into the air, flying high — higher than Ike had ever been. It was exhilarating, and Ike braced for the landing. But Vinnie was not built for this type of jump, and when she landed, she revolted, bottoming out the suspension and bouncing back up into the air, sending him flying off the bike and into the woods. As if in slow motion, Ike began to realize that he was going to crash, and he started yelling, "Ahhhhhhhhh!"

And that was the last thing he remembered.

CHAPTER 13

Ike was awakened by the voices of nurses as they fussed over his covers. His head felt like a tank was sitting on it. He looked up at the IV pole that held the clear bag of drip and followed it down to where it entered his left arm through the needle inserted into and taped to his skin. Then he made the mistake of moving, and a sharp pain shot through his right side.

"Ahhhhgggg," he groaned, wincing as he tried to settle back into a comfortable position.

"Settle down, flyboy," one of the nurses said, smiling, as she stepped closer to the bed. "Let me check that bandage."

"Bandage?"

"Yes, the one on your head," she said softly as she gently adjusted something on his head. "I hear you took a nasty spill."

"I remember having to step off my bike and then going into the trees," Ike recalled.

"You hit your head pretty hard, so you need to stay as still as you can for a while. My name is Linda, and I'll be your nurse. The doctor will be in to look you over in a little while."

"How long have I been here?"

"You were brought up from the ER last night."

"What's wrong with me?"

"Well, you've got a laceration on your right side and some serious bruising there, possibly broken ribs, and a concussion. You've also got a gash on your head and a possible concussion. You're scheduled for a CAT scan and X-rays this afternoon."

"Can I sit up?"

"The doctor has ordered you to lie still and rest."

"Why can't I sit up if I'm still?" Ike pressed.

The nurse just put her hand on her hip and looked at him and shook her head.

"So you're going to be one of *those* kinds of patients, huh?" she scolded, but with a smile. "All right, if you don't mind the pain."

"Oh, I can handle pain," Ike bragged.

"Okay, here's the control for the bed," she replied, digging it out from under the sheets and handing it to him. She started to show him how to use it, but Ike stopped her.

"I know how to use a remote," Ike protested, and he took the remote from her hand and pressed a button. The TV came on. He pressed another, and the channel changed. He finally found the one that rotated the bed up, and he heard the hum of a little motor under the bed and he began to rise. Suddenly the pain increased with the height of the bed, and he had to stop.

"Uh, I think this is high enough," he said through clenched teeth.

Nurse Linda just smiled that knowing smile, with her hands on her hips.

"There are a couple of people here to see you, so let's get your blood pressure and take your temperature."

After the nurse was done, she stepped outside the room and, after some mumbled conversation, in walked Ike's mother, Mr. Gonzales, Sam and Mr. Rick. They had concerned looks on their faces, especially his mom, who made her way to his bedside first.

"Ike, honey, how are you feeling?" Tricia asked with all the nervousness of a worried mother, as she touched his hand.

"I'm okay. Just a little... dizzy."

The others nodded to him but kept their distance at the foot of the bed.

"The doctor says you hit your head pretty hard, and might have broken ribs," she added, looking at the bandage on his head.

"I'll be okay, Mom. Don't worry," he said, grimacing as he tried, unsuccessfully, to reposition himself in the bed.

"Do you want to sit up?" his mother asked with a nervous glance, looking for the nurse.

"Just a little bit, right here; my butt is tired of being in this position," Ike complained, trying to move, but he was stopped by the pain.

"I'll help," Sam volunteered, stepping to the other side of the bed. Between Sam and Tricia, they got him repositioned with a minimum of moans from Ike, as he again tried to hide the pain. When he was finally situated, he looked at Sam.

"Have you ever been in the hospital?" he asked her.

"Once or twice," she replied. "One time was for a broken arm and the other was a broken femur."

Ike's mom looked at Sam with horror on her face and then cast a glance of accusation at Sam's dad. Mr. Rick just raised his hands and shrugged.

"Hey, I can't talk her out of racing," he explained. "It's what she wants to do, and it teaches her about the consequences of her decisions."

"I'd say. So it's the old 'tough love' huh?" Tricia shot at him, disbelief in her voice. "Ike, I think you've done enough racing on those motorcycles."

"Aw, Mom, I'm just getting started," he pleaded. "It's what I love. It's who I am."

Tricia stepped back and pointed to the hospital bed and around the room.

"And this is what you love and who you are?" she countered, accusingly.

"No, this is the consequences of not listening," Ike admitted, looking at Mr. Gonzales, who just raised one eyebrow and looked out the window nonchalantly.

"What? What did you not listen about?" Tricia demanded, digging deeper into the issue.

"You want to tell her or should I?" Ike asked Mr. Gonzales, trying to shift the pressure onto him.

"Oh, you're doing fine," Mr. Gonzales answered, gesturing for Ike to continue.

"He warned me that I should not jump Vinnie on those big jumps," Ike said, trying to cover the pain of the throbbing in his head.

"Did you?" Tricia probed.

"Yep." Ike shrugged guiltily. "But I needed to make a pass."

Mr. Gonzales and Mr. Rick swapped knowing glances. Tricia noticed the silent exchange between them.

"What? You can tell me," she said.

"Well, Ike is, uh, how should we say…"

When Mr. Gonzales paused, Tricia interrupted him.

"Too wild? I can see that!" she snapped angrily.

"No, not wild, just competitive," Mr. Gonzales explained. "He wants to win. All champions have that drive to succeed. That's what drives him to train, to practice, to do his schoolwork…"

"Well, he hasn't been succeeding in *that* area too well lately," Tricia complained.

Just then there was a knock on the door, and Dr. Denton came in. He was a short, African-American man with a rounded face and sparkling, lively eyes.

"How is Evel Knievel doing?" he asked with a smile as the others stepped back from the bed.

"I'm okay, I guess. Just tired of this same position," Ike answered, gently moving his lower body into a new position on the bed.

"Well, that is the hard part – staying in one position all day. But you can turn over as much as you need to, as much as your ribs allow. May I check that bandage?" he asked, setting his clipboard down on the table.

"Sure," Ike mumbled, as he sat up a little.

Dr. Denton peeled back the bandage over his left ear, revealing a cut with sutures. Part of his hair was shaved off where the bandage was taped. It was leaking a little blood, which caused his mom to cringe.

"Well, we're doing okay here; nothing that a little bed rest can't cure," Dr. Denton explained, putting the bandage back. "How are the ribs?"

"They hurt," Ike replied, patting his side softly.

"They're supposed to. That's your body telling you to slow down so it can heal," Dr. Denton said matter-of-factly. "Good thing you were wearing a helmet."

"How'd he get the cut on his head?" Tricia asked.

"The helmet broke," Mr. Rick said. "He landed against a big pine tree."

"What was a pine tree doing on the track?" Tricia asked in alarm.

"It wasn't near the track," said Mr. Rick, glancing at Mr. Gonzales. "He came off the jump and went off the track."

"So if he wouldn't have been wearing a helmet..." Tricia said, her voice trailing off.

"He'd be dead," Dr. Denton finished her sentence with finality. He picked up his clipboard and turned to leave the room. When he got to the door, he paused and added, "You should find a safer sport."

"He is," Tricia replied, looking at Ike.

"No, I'm not," Ike argued.

"Yes, you are," Tricia countered.

"Mom, I am a motocross racer. Dad would approve, and you know it!" Ike said, his voice rising.

"But he's not here now, is he?" Tricia said, her voice, like her anger, edging up another notch. The others excused themselves from the room. "Ike, can't you see what you're doing to yourself?"

"It's my body, and I want to race," he argued, trying to hide the pain as he moved too sharply.

"See? That's my point. You are hurt, Ike. *Hurt!*"

"Not that bad."

"'Not that'...? '*Not that bad*'? Ike, do you *hear* yourself?"

The nurse came back in and got between them, shuffling the sheets.

"How are you feeling?" she asked.

"I'm okay," he said, glaring defiantly at his mom.

"You need to rest now. Okay, visiting time is over," the nurse said, turning to pull the curtain around him. Tricia got the hint.

"'Bye, honey. I love you. I'll talk to you later."

Tricia turned and left the room.

When they were alone, Nurse Linda handed him a little cup with a pill and instructed him, "Take this and wash it down with water. Sounds like you're in trouble."

"No trouble. She's not taking motocross racing away from me," he stated in a firm, steady tone.

"But she's your mother."

"But I'm a world champion motocross racer."

"The world champion wouldn't have let his bike buck him off the track and into a tree."

"National champion?" Ike tried.

Nurse Linda just nodded "no."

"*State* champion?"

Nurse Linda just stared at him, unconvinced.

"A swamp panther?" Ike tried, raising his fingers into an imaginary paw and hissing like a cat.

"Uh, no."

"An alligator?"

"An alligator wouldn't have ended up in the hospital with broken ribs."

"A raccoon?"

"Well..." she paused and thought. "You *do* have some darkness under your eyes, and a tendency to forage food from visitors in here."

They both started laughing. That's when Ike really, *really* started to hurt.

"OWWWWWWW!" he exclaimed, grimacing, and grabbed his side.

"No more laughing for you," Nurse Linda scolded him. "Now let's put the bed back down and get some rest."

"Yes... ma' am," Ike sounded out the words slowly between gasps.

CHAPTER 14

∽

Tricia Hebert brought her son home later that week, and on the way she gave him an earful in the car. They went at it, back and forth. Forth and back they went, all the way into the house. Tricia had all the arguments one would expect a mom to make: "You'll get hurt worse; we can't afford the doctor bills; what about your future?"

Ike countered with typical teenage rebellion: "You can't make me; Dad would have let me; it's safer than football; it was just a freak accident."

And then it turned ugly.

"You don't care about my dream! You're trying to take my life away. You're just scared and don't want to have to worry!"

Tricia and Ike began to drift apart. It seemed that almost every time they talked, it would end in an argument. Ike's desire for independence, combined with his raging hormones was sometimes more than he could handle. He wasn't used to being a man-boy, and Tricia wasn't used to dealing with teenagers. The climate in the Hebert house grew icy – almost as cold as the climate at school, at least for Ike, who now hated being at school *and* being at home. His last two refuges were the motocross track and Mr. Gonzales' shop. But Mom had hinted that she might make him quit working there so that he would stop racing.

'If she tries that, I will definitely run away,' Ike thought.

The only two people who seemed to understand him were Mr. Gonzales and Crip, and he got to see them every afternoon. It was as if they were his *real* family.

The next Monday afternoon, when Ike came into work, he walked right up to Crip's stall and announced, "I'm quitting school."

Crip just kept working, as if he hadn't heard.

"Hand me that pry bar, please," Crip asked, in his usual deep, raspy voice.

Ike turned to look on the bench.

"Where is it?"

"Just hand me the pry bar," Crip asked again, his tone getting more intense.

Ike whirled around and looked in the toolbox.

"Hurry up, I can't hold this engine up much longer," Crip said, his voice rising with impatience.

"Where is it?" Ike pleaded, opening and closing drawers all the way down the toolbox.

"Ike, I need it now!"

"I can't find it!"

By now, Ike was into the other box, opening and closing drawers, starting to slam them.

"Hey, easy on my boxes! Just get me the bar!"

"How about a breaker bar?"

"Did I ask for a breaker bar? Don't make me drop this motor!"

"What about a big screwdriver?"

"That's how you ruin a good screwdriver. If you don't hand me that pry bar in 10 seconds, I'm gonna kick your butt!"

"But I can't find it!" Ike blubbered, his voice getting louder as he started digging through boxes and tossing shop rags out of the way.

"Five seconds!"

"I'm trying!"

"Okay, that's it. Get out the way!"

Crip dropped the motor on the stand and came around the bike. He brushed past Ike and opened the bottom drawer. He reached in, pulled out the pry bar and shook it in Ike's face.

"What good are you if can't even find a tool?" Crip snapped, his eyes full of fury.

"I didn't know where it was," Ike said defensively, and a little fearfully.

"You didn't know? You didn't know? So you don't know everything, do you?" snapped Crip, reaching up for the rope hanging on the wall behind his toolbox. "Turn around," he ordered Ike.

"What are you gonna do?" Ike protested, but before he could utter another word, Crip had tied his hands behind his back and run the rope around his waist and between his legs.

"Crip, stop!" Ike cried out, trying to get away, but he was no match for the strength and speed of Crip's hands. In five seconds, Crip had tossed the rope over a rafter and hoisted Ike six feet off the ground. Then Crip tied it off, picked up the bar and raised it back as if to beat Ike.

"Crip, no!" Ike was near tears. "What are you doin'?"

"What is nine times seven?"

"What?"

"You heard me. What is nine times seven? How about seven times eight?"

"I, uh, 56? No, I mean 63! I think. Get me down! This hurts!"

"You *think*? You don't know? How about a noun, what's a noun? How about a verb?" Crip demanded.

"A noun? Uhhh – a person? Wait, it can be a thing, too. Can't it?"

"You don't know? How about the capital of Florida? Where does the Mississippi start? What are the time zones in America? Who makes the laws in our country? Who are our representatives? What's the difference between an appellate court judge and a Supreme Court judge? Huh? You think you're ready to be a man in this country? Do you?"

"I, uh, don't…" Ike stammered.

Crip continued: "How old do you have to be to sign a contract, vote, drink? Do you know how to write a check, balance your checkbook, where to pay your bills? Do you know how much it costs to run a household, to pay property taxes, sales taxes? Huh? You think you're ready to be a man? Can you write a simple business letter? Huh? *Answer… now!*"

"I, uhhh, I can write," Ike answered with confusion in his voice. He knew he was beat.

"Do you know the differences between Democrats and Republicans, North America and South America, carbon monoxide and carbon dioxide?"

"I know that one," Ike offered quickly.

"How about the difference between a warm front and a cold front, the North Star and Venus, a hurricane and a typhoon, a balance sheet and an income statement, AC and DC current, Shakespeare and Thoreau, Hitler and Stalin, a city councilman and a mayor, where our taxes go? Well? *I'm waiting!*"

Ike was fighting back tears, and he was hurting. Mr. Gonzales walked in and looked up at Ike.

"Crip, what are you doin'? You cut that boy down!"

Crip whipped out the knife so fast Ike didn't even see the motion. He just stared at the big blade. Ike tried to use humor to disarm him: "Is that thing sharp?"

Crip just stared at Ike, then looked at the knife. He slowly moved it to his arm and shaved off a patch of hair. Then he looked at Ike, and in one swift motion he slashed the rope, which severed like a thread, dropping Ike to the floor like a bag of potatoes.

"Oh, all right, I guess he's got the point." Crip conceded, sheathing his knife.

"What's the point?" Mr. Gonzales asked Crip as Ike struggled to sit up.

"He wants to quit school," Crip spat out.

"String him back up," Mr. Gonzales stated angrily. Then he looked at Ike sadly, shook his head, and then turned on his heels and walked out.

Crip smiled and retied him, hoisting him back up.

"No! Don't do it, Crip!" Ike protested with all he had.

"You gonna quit school?"

"No, I said I was *thinking* of quitting school!"

"No, you said you were quitting school. I know what I heard," Crip replied, raising him higher.

"Okay, okay, I meant to say I was *thinking* of quitting. I was just thinking of it!"

"Well, you let me know when you finish *thinking* of quitting school."

"Okay, I'm not quitting, honest. I won't quit school."

Crip started lowering him. When Ike's feet touched the floor and he started untangling the rope, Ike added, "At least not until next year."

Crip quickly wrapped the rope around Ike's leg and hoisted him back up again. This time Ike was dangling upside down, swinging his arms, trying to pull himself upright, to no avail.

"Okay, okay, I won't quit until I'm a senior!"

"No," Crip corrected him, "you won't quit until you graduate from high school. That's what you need to be a responsible man in our country today."

"Okay, okay, no quitting. Just get me down!"

"You're gonna graduate?"

"Yes, I'll graduate!"

"You sure?"

"I promise. I promise!"

Crip started letting Ike back down. Right before Ike touched the floor, Crip started tickling him.

"No, quit! Not that! Crip! Help! Mr. Gonzales!" Ike yelled hysterically between squeals of laughter.

Mr. Gonzales came back in and saw what was going on.

"Crip, let me help you with that," he said, and then he pulled off Ike's shoes and started on his feet. Ike went wild. He started squirming like he was being electrocuted. They all were laughing so hard, they were crying. They finally let Ike down, and he collapsed into an exhausted puddle on the floor. Crip went into a coughing fit and had to go to the bathroom and spit up his congestion.

Mr. Gonzales sat down on the floor next to Ike and looked at him, seriously.

"Do you understand why you can't quit school?"

"Yeah, I guess so."

"How much do you have left in this school year?"

"Oh, about two months."

"I'll tell you what: If you give 110-percent effort for the next four weeks and bring up your grades, I'll send you on a vacation."

"Where to?"

"It's a surprise."

"With who?"

"It's a surprise."

"For what? Wait, I know. Let me guess. It's a surprise?"

Mr. Gonzales just nodded with that "I know something you don't know" look.

"Can you give me a hint?"

"I'll say this: It will do you good, the place will do you good, the person you're going with will do you good, you need them. You need this experience."

"But… what? I mean, where…?" Ike stammered.

Mr. Gonzales just put his finger to his lips and shook his head "no."

"It's a surprise."

CHAPTER 15

Ike had never been so focused in his life. He rose out of bed at 6 a.m. to jog a mile. Then he showered, ate a healthy breakfast, and packed his schoolbag with the homework he'd completed the night before. He rode his bicycle to school and got to every class on time, with all his books and papers ready to go. The only thing sharper than his attitude was his pencil. For the first time, school became more than a dreaded prison; now it was a mission to be accomplished. He asked to be moved to the front of the class, where he could pay better attention. He even began asking questions. Some of the classes even became interesting, as he focused on the subject matter instead of what was going on in the back of the classroom.

After school, he'd ride the long way home, even using some trails through the woods to simulate motocross racing. After doing two hours of homework, he'd go to work at the shop. There, he worked with focus and intensity, finding he did less daydreaming. After work, he'd practice on his modern dirt bike, riding two 20-minute motos on the shop's test track. There was only one thing that wouldn't come together for him: jumping. After the crash, he had a fear of launching off a big jump. He had lost an edge in speed as well. Every evening, after the shop closed, Mr. Gonzales and Crip would come out and watch him practice.

"What do you think?" Mr. Gonzales asked Crip.

"Something's wrong," Crip replied, with his hand resting on his chin as he studied Ike's riding.

"You mean his fear of jumping?"

"Well, that's obvious, but there is something deeper. You can see it in his entry speed into the turns."

"He's lost 'the edge,' hasn't he?"

"Yep, but it's even deeper than that."

"Have you tried to talk to him about it?"

"Yep, but he just doesn't seem to understand," Crip replied. "It's like an unseen enemy. I've seen it in battle many times."

"Can you name it?" Mr. Gonzales asked, turning to look at his old friend.

"Yes," Crip said, nodding toward Ike. "But it won't change a thing until *he* names it."

"How can you get him to name it?"

"The only way to get him to name it is to have him confront it, head on," Crip said. "For that, I'll have to put him in a position to discover it for himself. Then he has to be motivated enough to conquer it."

"How do you make him motivated enough?"

"He has to be so angry or sick and tired of it that he is willing to put his pride away and ask for help."

"How do you do that?"

"Put him in a position of desperation. Let him use up his own strength and see his weakness, his need for help. Usually, life has to do that over a period of years, or through trials, for men to see their need, before they are willing to look up for help, depending on how prideful they are."

"But we don't have years," Mr. Gonzales noted.

"Then I'll have to put him in a situation to break him."

"You're not gonna crush his spirit, are you?" Mr. Gonzales gasped, alarmed.

"No. I already made that mistake before with someone." Crip paused, a distant memory capturing his thoughts; he gazed up at the purple and pink streaks the setting sun was painting in the sky. "It's like breaking a bronco. You've got to break his strength without putting the fire completely out. Then, when he has given over control, the fire can be rebuilt and his passion can be sent in the proper direction. After that, success will motivate him to keep going in the right direction – *his* direction."

"You learn that in boot camp?"

"That was my first exposure to it," Crip admitted, "but Marine boot camp was kind of extreme. They would crush your individuality so they could rebuild you into a team that thinks together. Ike isn't quite ready for that. He needs a softer version that doesn't go so far."

Just then, Ike crashed. The two men went running over to him. He was lying on the ground, trying to catch his breath. He held up his hand to tell them to hold on a minute, since he couldn't talk. The men stooped down to examine him.

"Are you all right?" Mr. Gonzales asked, panting.

"I… uhhh…. wait," Ike gasped, trying to catch his breath.

Mr. Gonzales and Crip just looked at each other and then back down at Ike and waited. After a few moments, Ike's breath came back and he could talk.

"I… got the wind knocked out…." he said, sitting up and unstrapping his helmet.

"What happened?" Mr. Gonzales asked.

"I tried to hit that jump right there and I guess I let off near the top of the face. Then the front end dove down and sent me over the bars."

"You chopped the throttle on the jump face?" Crip asked harshly.

"Not chopped, but, well, kinda backed off."

Ike just looked at them. They looked at each other and then back at him.

"What?" he asked, casting a questioning look at them. "You said not to chop the throttle in the air."

"Ike, you can't jump that way," Crip warned.

"What way?"

"Half-hearted. You have to commit to the jump, first with your heart, then with your head," he explained.

"What? What are you talking about?" Ike mumbled.

"You throw your heart over first and the rest will follow."

A look of confusion crossed Ike's face. Crip tried again.

"Let me put it another way: You have to have the will, then apply the proper knowledge."

"How do I, uh… get that?"

"By learning to jump the little ones first. Then, step by step, you take on the bigger ones as you grow in confidence. That's your heart. And knowledge, that's in your head."

Ike just looked at him with a puzzled expression on his face.

"Come on, let's go put the bike away," said Mr. Gonzales, as he helped Ike to his feet. "I think you've had enough for one day."

Crip went over to pick up the bike.

"Bent your bars," Crip called out. "Broke your clutch perch, too."

"You can fix it tomorrow," Mr. Gonzales told Ike. "Did you finish your homework?"

"No, I have to write a book report."

"Do you have the book picked out yet?"

"No."

"Can it be any book?"

"'Within reason,' she said."

"Mrs. Fisk?"

"Yeah."

"I've got a book for you to use. I'll clear it with her myself," Mr. Gonzales offered confidently.

"What if she won't allow it?"

"She will."

"What is it?"

"*Against All Odds.*"

"Who wrote it?"

"Chuck Norris," Crip interjected. "Good read."

"You mean 'Walker, Texas Ranger?' Isn't he an actor?"

"He was in the Air Force in Korea, where he learned karate from the masters – old school. Then he taught himself more, not just about karate, but life. He was the undefeated six-time World Professional Middleweight Karate Champion. I used to train with him in the '70s. He's a champion, and not just in karate – a real straight-up dude."

"So this book report is a... kind of a setup, huh?" Ike guessed slyly.

"That's right. We're setting you up for success. Got a problem with that?" Crip asked, challenging Ike.

"No, just asking," Ike conceded in a cooperative tone.

They looked the bike over carefully until they were convinced nothing else was broken.

"I'll get right on that book," Ike announced.

"Tonight!" both men echoed.

"Tonight," Ike agreed, and they all started walking back to the shop as the sun was setting.

"Who's the champ?" Mr. Gonzales challenged, ducking down into his fighting stance.

"I am?" Ike guessed, giving the bike to Crip and hanging his helmet on the handlebar. They stopped walking as Ike sparred with Mr. Gonzales. They boxed around a little as Ike probed his defenses with darting jabs and crosses. Mr. Gonzales just bobbed and weaved while casting smiles at Crip.

"Who's the champ?" Mr. Gonzales snorted again.

"I am!" Ike responded, sending an overhand right that clipped Mr. Gonzales' ear. He just turned and blocked.

"Hey, you're just letting me win!" Ike protested.

Suddenly Mr. Gonzales let loose a volley of left jabs to the gut that brought down Ike's arms and then planted a knuckle thump on his forehead. The tap was a little too hard, and it put Ike on the ground. Ike immediately grabbed his head.

"Hey, that hurt!"

"Sorry, I meant to pull it, but you moved your head right into it," Mr. Gonzales clarified apologetically as he reached down to help Ike up.

Ike clasped his hand but sent out a ground kick to his knee, and with a tug he put Mr. Gonzales flat on his face!

"What?" Mr. Gonzales spat out as he went down.

"What!" Ike shouted back at him, his arms raised in victory.

"What!" Crip shouted. "Nice move, Ike. Now who's the champ, Victor?" Crip howled at Mr. Gonzales, who took his time getting up.

"Uh, he just hit my bad knee, that's all."

They laughed as Ike helped Mr. Gonzales back to his feet.

"Who's the champ?" Ike said smugly to Mr. Gonzales.

"You are!" Mr. Gonzales conceded with a grin, looking first at Ike, then at Crip.

"Only one little problem now," Crip cautioned.

"What's that?" Ike asked, proudly taking the bike.

"Payback!" Mr. Gonzales hooted loudly. "And it's comin' from the boss!"

They all laughed again as they continued back to the shop.

CHAPTER 16

Ike had a good week in school, making A's and B's on his quizzes and tests. He was starting to feel good about himself and his schoolwork, but he couldn't get used to seeing Sam and Dave together – holding hands in the hallway, talking closely near the lockers, sitting together in the courtyard during lunch; Ike was beginning to feel like a man without a home. His closest friend was his dream of racing, and sometimes he wondered if that was really enough.

On Wednesday, he was getting some books out of his locker when he noticed in his peripheral vision some of the older guys gathering around behind him. The girl next to him had her locker open, and he checked the mirror she had hanging on the inside of the door. He could see the face of Jimmy Plaisance nodding and smiling that cocky grin to the other guys as he drew up behind Ike. At least Ike had a split-second warning before he turned to face him.

"Hey, rookie," Jimmy taunted as he turned around.

"Me?" Ike asked.

"Yeah, you. Do you see any other rookies around?" Jimmy said, turning and smiling to his friends.

"Well, the reason I asked is because I'm not a 'rookie,'" Ike responded confidently.

"Sure you are," Jimmy said, badgering him. "You think you're a motocross racer, but you're just a little beginner poser."

The "bad boys" were chuckling and nodding in agreement. The crowd was getting bigger.

"I'm not a beginner," Ike noted, disputing Jimmy's claim. "Anyway, everybody had to start somewhere. You were a beginner once."

"Nope. I was never a beginner. I was born to roll in the Expert class, after a very, very small learning curve," Jimmy boasted with a prideful nod to his friends.

"So, what's your point? I'm late for class," Ike said impatiently, turning and grabbing another book out of his locker.

"Point? He wants to know what the point is," Jimmy echoed to the crowd of onlookers, buying time to think up something else. "My point is that not only are you a beginner rookie, now you're turning into a nerd."

Jimmy knocked the books out of Ike's hand, glaring at him, trying to pick a fight. Ike resisted the temptation to take a swing at him. The first thing that went through his mind was the vacation that Mr. Gonzales and Crip had promised him. He was already in trouble, and a fight would probably get him kicked out of school. He coolly reached down and picked up his books. Jimmy put his foot down on his math book before Ike could pick it up. Just then the tardy bell rang, and some of the students turned and rushed into the classrooms.

"Get your foot off my book," Ike demanded.

"*You* get it off," Jimmy said, challenging him.

Ike snatched the book out from under Jimmy's foot and then sidestepped the push he knew was coming. Jimmy was slightly off balance, but he attempted the push anyway. When Ike's body wasn't there to catch his push, Jimmy fell against the locker. Unfortunately for him, his fingers curled around the opening of Ike's locker right as Ike slammed it shut.

"Ahhhhhggggggg!" Jimmy wailed, causing heads to peek back through open doorways.

"What's the matter?" a teacher demanded from two doors down.

"Nothing," Jimmy growled painfully, holding his hand and glaring at Ike.

"Jimmy keeps putting his appendages where they don't belong," Ike announced.

The kids laughed; even a couple of Jimmy's buddies couldn't help but chuckle. Jimmy stepped in front of Ike, blocking his escape.

"I'll see you after school," he swore under his breath, just low enough so the teachers couldn't hear.

"I have more important things to do than wrestle around with you on the playground," Ike quipped, turning and walking away.

At 3:15, as Ike was walking to his bicycle, he noticed a crowd of students gathered around it, with Jimmy's little gang right in the middle. Jimmy had his feet up on Ike's bike.

"Why am I not surprised?" Ike groaned, walking up and unlocking his bike as if they weren't there.

"You're not surprised because you know you have this coming," Jimmy warned, as he took off his letter jacket and handed it to one of his boys.

"Oh, and what is it that I've got coming?" Ike replied, turning around with his backpack on his shoulder.

"*This!*"

Ike turned just enough for Jimmy's punch to glance off Ike's backpack. His fist landed with a thud on the corner of one of the books. Jimmy shook his fist in pain.

"It pays to bring your books home to study," Ike stated coolly. "I'm going to work; you finish your fight without me."

"What? You don't want to fight?" Jimmy blurted out, turning to face him. "Scared? You *are* scared. Everybody knows you're afraid!"

"I'm not scared!" Ike countered.

"Yes you are," Jimmy accused, with a mocking attitude. "You're afraid, a chicken!"

"Name something I'm afraid of!" Ike challenged him.

"You're afraid to jump! You're afraid of me. You're afraid of Sam's boyfriend. You're afraid to go out for football…"

"I'm not afraid of anybody!" Ike interrupted, his voice rising.

"All right, that's enough!" Mr. Dansberry commanded, walking up to the scene.

The crowd of students quickly dissipated as Mr. Dansberry faced Ike and Jimmy.

"What is going on here?" he demanded.

"Ike hit me with his backpack," Jimmy accused.

"In the hand?" Ike shot back, glaring at his accuser.

Mr. Dansberry looked at Jimmy's right knuckle and saw it was bleeding.

"Who started this?" he asked.

They both pointed at each other.

"Let me remind you boys that there is a camera right over there," he cautioned, turning and pointing to the top of the light. "Now, you wanna tell me what really happened?" he repeated, this time looking squarely at Jimmy.

"Ike smashed my hands in his locker today," Jimmy complained.

"I already know about that. Saw it on tape, as a matter of fact. I think after what you've been doing to Ike, you owe him an apology," Mr. Dansberry advised, looking Jimmy in the eyes, expectantly.

Jimmy knew he was cornered. He was a lot of things, but dumb wasn't one of them.

"I'm sorry, Ike," he offered half-heartedly.

Ike just looked Jimmy in the eye and studied him. Then he extended his hand.

"Apology accepted," Ike responded cautiously.

Jimmy looked at Mr. Dansberry, who was watching him closely, so Jimmy shook hands, but Ike noticed a sharpness in the shake and a fierceness in his eyes that communicated that Jimmy was only sorry about being caught, and that the trouble was not over.

"Okay, now don't you boys have some homework to do or something?" Mr. Dan hinted pointedly.

They took the hint and turned and went their separate ways.

Ike straddled his bike and began to peddle home. His mind was in high gear.

'Man, that was close. He's comin' back for more from another angle, though. Maybe I am scared. How can I get rid of this fear? Can people see it that clearly? I'll show 'em. No, they'll discover for themselves. Wait a minute – I don't have to prove anything to them. But I want to. Why does it always have to be something? Why can't they just leave me alone? I just want to race. Maybe Jimmy's just jealous. Of what? He's a star on the football team and an expert motocrosser. He has a nice truck, friends and girlfriends. I've got none of that. Why would he be jealous of me? Oh, well, can't let that distract me. I've got more important things to do.'

The next day at school, Ike heard that Jimmy had been suspended for three days. This confirmed what Ike already knew: He had done the right thing by not being lured into a fight. Jimmy's friends were mad at him, though. One even pushed Ike into the locker with his shoulder, but Ike just rolled his eyes and let it go. One good thing came out of it, though. His old friend Ben came over to sit with him at lunch.

"Hey, Ike, mind if I join you?" Ben inquired, as he put his lunch tray down next to Ike's.

"If you can elbow your way through the crowd," Ike responded sarcastically, making fun of his isolation.

"Uh, Ike, I've been meaning to say something to you," Ben confessed.

"Shoot," Ike replied, opening his milk.

"I'm sorry for what you've been going through. I think most kids are just jealous of the attention you and Sam got when ya'll solved the crime."

"Maybe so," Ike muttered while chewing on a roll.

"Think I could come practice with you sometime?" Ben proposed, with a piece of turkey hanging from the corner of his mouth.

"Sure, anytime," Ike agreed with a smile. "Well, anytime after five; that's when I get off work."

"Hey, you gonna eat that?" Ben pried, eyeing Ike's brownie.

"Nah, you can have it. I'm in training anyway," Ike explained, picking it up and tossing it on Ben's tray.

"Training? For what?"

"Racing. I'm trying to get myself ready to move to the Novice class."

"You're not going to the National Championship this year?"

"Didn't qualify."

"Oh, yeah, the crash," Ben remembered.

"Yeah, but I'll be ready for next year. I've got to work on my jumping."

"I know the feeling."

They both stared ahead and chewed.

Suddenly Sam and Dave came walking up.

"Is this seat taken?" Sam asked.

Ike just looked at her, then at Dave.

"No, help yourself," he replied, moving his milk and napkins.

"Hi, Ike," Dave uttered cautiously.

"Hi, Dave, Sam," Ike returned the greeting courteously.

"Ike, I like the way you handled yourself with Jimmy yesterday," Sam offered cheerily. Ben and Dave both nodded.

"Yeah, you were so cool about it," Dave mumbled.

"You didn't get all caught up in the male-ego trap," Sam declared.

"What exactly is the male-ego trap?" Ben asked.

"That's when a guy's scared somebody's gonna think he's a wimp, so he kind of goes off and does stupid stuff, so nobody will think he's scared," Sam explained. "Then sometimes, when it starts working for him, he turns into a bully. Then he goes after guys he thinks are scared so he can get easy 'cool points' to impress others, so people will think he's tough." She looked around and then continued. "But, he's the scaredest one, because he goes to the greatest lengths to establish himself in a position of power over others."

She waited for their response.

The boys just sat there, trying to process what she'd said. Finally, Ike broke the silence.

"So, where'd you read that? In one of those teen magazines?" he asked mockingly.

"Simple observation," Sam stated, matter-of-factly.

"Can you, uhhh, run that by me again?" Ben gulped, clearly confused.

"Please, I'm tryin' to let food digest here," Ike choked gruffly, while chewing a mouthful of meat.

"Sam, you are so smart," Dave sighed, clearly kissing up.

Ike turned and mimicked Dave's words to Ben sarcastically. Then he turned back to the food on his plate. There was a long, uncomfortable silence. Then Ike looked up from his plate and decreed, "There will be a test on the male ego tomorrow."

Ben snickered. Sam narrowed her eyes at Ike. Dave tried to hide his chuckle with a cough.

"Read chapter 12 in your 'Girls Are So Much Smarter Than Boys' text-book," Ike razzed with a smile as he got up while gathering his milk carton and fork. "I'll see you ya'll tomorrow." Ike finished off his milk and wiped his mouth as he got up to leave. "I gotta go hit the books."

Then he turned back to face Sam.

"Sorry, Sam," Ike added, "I couldn't resist."

Sam just sat there, fuming under a fake smile.

"You done with that?" Ike asked, reaching for Ben's lunch tray.

"Sure," Ben answered with a surprised look, leaning back out of the way. Ike reached for Sam's trash, too.

"I'll get that," she objected.

"No, I got it, I'm on my way to the trash anyway," he insisted, picking it up.

"You done?" Ike inquired about the crumbled-up paper bag in front of Dave, and reached for it.

"Uh, yeah," Dave answered in a confused tone, "but I'll get it."

Dave picked it up before Ike could reach it.

"No, really, allow me," Ike retorted good-naturedly, making a quick stab for it, catching a piece of it.

"No, no, I got that," Dave insisted, pulling it back, causing a little game of tug-of-war over the trash. They smiled at each other momentarily; while Sam and Ben looked on, their heads moving back and forth as if they were watching a tennis match. Finally Ike tore off a piece of the bag, and the sudden slack caused Dave's hand to recoil and he popped himself in the mouth with his own fist. Sam and Ben flinched, their expressions echoing the look of pain on Dave's face.

"Sorry, Dave," Ike lied. "I'll see ya'll tomorrow."

Ike gave them an over-the-shoulder smile as he headed to the trash cans.

From that moment on, Ike had friends. Not just hangers-on, or acquaintances, or people with hidden agendas who wanted something from him – but real friends he could rely on; all for just putting away his pride and being himself and being friendly.

CHAPTER 17

The next week, Ike crashed again, this time breaking his wrist. At least it was his left wrist, which did not affect his writing hand. This sparked a major argument with his mom. She had given him a new rule: No more motocross racing. Not now, not ever. He had countered with his usual arguments, but to no avail. She was not going to budge. She was like that; once she got an idea in her head, nothing on earth could make her change her mind. So Ike tried something different: He stopped arguing with her and began to think about it as he got back into his routine. He prayed about it. He searched for the answer – hard. He decided to ask advice from Mr. Gonzales and Crip.

"What do you think I should do?" Ike inquired one day after they locked up the shop.

"She's your mother, and so she has responsibility for you," Mr. Gonzales pointed out. "In her mind, motocross racing is bad for you. You have to respect her authority, even if you disagree."

"True," Crip added. "So you're not gonna 'argue' her out of it, no matter how passionately you make your case. She's gonna have to change her mind about racing, when she sees how it benefits you."

"How do I do that?" Ike pleaded.

"You're gonna need help. We'll have to go talk to her," Mr. Gonzales answered.

"Whoa! I'm not good at talking to women," Crip protested.

"Not 'you and me' we, but 'Rick and me' we," Mr. Gonzales clarified. "Rick is a single parent, too, and uses racing to help parent Sam and keep her out of trouble. He's a great example for how motocross can be used to help kids grow up."

"I think you've got something there, Victor," Crip smiled.

"Totally. Let Mr. Rick *and* Sam talk to her. She loves Sam," Ike added.

"It's settled, then," Mr. Gonzales said. "We'll go do something with her that she likes to do, like, uhhhh…"

"Eat," Ike interrupted. "She loves to eat. Seafood – let's have a crab boil!"

"A crab boil, with a barbecue. I'll grill some of my famous chicken," Crip declared.

"Oh, you guys have never experienced pure nirvana until you've had Crip's barbecued chicken," Mr. Gonzales smiled, licking his lips.

"That's slow-roasted, hickory-smoked, secret-recipe barbecued chicken," Crip clarified, boasting, "The generals used to fly me into Saigon just to grill on my custom-built 55-gallon drum pit. They said the war would stop when it was time for Crip's smoked chicken."

"Ask him to tell you the story of how he used his grilling prowess to escape from a Hanoi prison camp," Mr. Gonzales suggested.

"Uh, that's classified," Crip stated flatly. "I can't discuss that."

"Aw, come on, Crip," Ike pleaded. "I won't tell anyone."

"You don't need to know everything that happens in war. Let's just say I softened 'em up with the food, then zigged when they thought I would zag."

"Okay, so it's settled then," Mr. Gonzales interrupted. "How about this weekend?"

"Fine with me," Crip agreed.

"We'll be there," Ike said. "Just need to check with Sam and Mr. Rick."

"I'll give him a heads-up call and let him know the lay of the land," Mr. Gonzales said.

"But what if she still won't let me?" Ike asked worriedly.

"Ike, there are no rewards without risks," Mr. Gonzales said. "She is your mom and you'll have to obey her until you move out of the house."

"Until I move out of the house? So that means if…"

"Don't even think about movin' out until after you graduate," Crip ordered. "You don't run from problems. You solve them."

"Yes, captain," Ike said, standing and saluting briskly.

Instantly, Crip was on him before Ike could blink his eyes. Crip took advantage of Ike's arm being up on his forehead and whipped Ike around and pinned the other arm up into a full nelson. He just held him there while Ike struggled.

"Crip, let me out," Ike gargled, in pain.

"Speak up, I can't hear you!"

"Let me go!"

"I won't let you go until you learn your lesson."

"What lesson?"

"What lesson do you think?"

"I don't – ouch! – I don't know!"

Crip tightened his hold.

"You'd better come up with something!"

"I, uhh, I need to quit saluting?"

"Try again."

"I need to listen to my mom?"

"Close."

"I need to show respect to adults?"

"Are you sure?"

"Yes, I'm sure!"

"What about your teachers?"

"Yes, even my teachers!"

"What about us?"

"Yes, of course!"

"Of course what?"

"Of course I need to show respect to you guys!"

"Do you know what you'll get back?"

"No, what?"

"It starts with an 'r'…"

"I don't know… uh, rain, rings, rest, ravioli?" Ike chortled.

Crip's grip tightened again.

"Owwwww! Okay, *respect!*"

Crip loosened his grip and let him go. Ike dropped his arms and started rubbing his neck.

"That hurt!"

"Pain is the best teacher in the world. As you get wiser, you can learn the easier ways. But with that immature foolishness you've got right now, pain is the quickest teacher," Crip scolded.

"Maybe I don't want to learn that much," Ike quibbled.

"When you stop learning, you start dying," Mr. Gonzales added. "Now you'd better go home and pray that God softens your mom's attitude, and we'll do what we can."

"I don't know if I can even lift my arms to pray," Ike whined.

"It's not the position of your body, it's the position of your heart that counts. Now go do your homework and we'll take care of the rest," Crip ordered.

"But what if she doesn't go for it?" Ike asked.

"You must learn to walk in faith, not fear," Mr. Gonzales replied. "You are focusing on your fears and will bring them down upon you if you believe the worst. Now, instead of looking at what bad *might* happen, look at what good *could* come of it — expect it, act on it. Let go of fear and think in faith. Here, I'll show you."

Mr. Gonzales disappeared into the back room and came out with a box. He handed it to Ike.

"Go ahead, open it," he said.

Ike just looked at him, then at Crip, then at the box. He popped the cardboard lid off and pulled away the packing. He smiled as he pulled out a brand-new full-face Shoei helmet.

"What's this for?" Ike asked.

"That's for you to wear," Mr. Gonzales answered. "You are starting to go faster and need more protection."

Ike just stared at it in disbelief.

"Well, put it on," Crip suggested.

Ike looked the colorful paint job over carefully, checking the little vents in the front and sides. Then he pulled the helmet on over his head.

"Looks good," Mr. Gonzales observed.

"It will look better when he's going fast," Crip answered.

"I like the cool designs on it," Ike mumbled with a muffled voice from under the helmet.

"I like that it's the best helmet made and will protect that great mind of yours," Mr. Gonzales said.

"Great mind? Yesterday you said he was hard-headed," Crip said, turning to look at Mr. Gonzales quizzically.

"That's why God gave him a hard head: to protect that great mind," Mr. Gonzales answered.

"Can I take it home tonight?" Ike asked excitedly.

"Uh, no. I don't think your mom is quite ready to see that just yet," Mr. Gonzales remarked. "We've got to give prayer a little time to work on her. We don't want to jump out in front of God. It's a mistake I've made way too many times."

"Me, too," Crip agreed, taking the helmet from Ike. "How about you leave that in your stall for a few days and just look at it to keep you focused on what can be."

"And I've got something for *you*," Ike announced.

Crip and Mr. Gonzales just looked at each other and shrugged.

Ike pulled a folder out of his book bag. Then he slipped a report out with red ink markings on the top. He proudly presented it to Mr. Gonzales, who looked it over and flipped through the pages. Then he showed it to Crip, who took the report and read the teacher's note on the top:

"Very good work, Ike. I've noticed a vast improvement in your attitude and work the last few months. I hope you stop by and tell me about it. I always thought you were capable of work like this. Good choice of book, too. Take Chuck Norris' advice and you'll see more success come your way. Good luck with the racing. I think it's done you good."

Mr. Gonzales and Crip stood up and high-fived.

"Well, now, I think your mom is ready for *this*!" Mr. Gonzales exclaimed excitedly.

"That's just what we needed," Crip echoed with a grin, "an ace in the hole."

CHAPTER 18

The barbecue went well, except for one thing. Ike's mom refused to agree to let Ike race, despite the best efforts of all involved. Mr. Rick and Mr. Gonzales reasoned with her about how it was good for Ike and showed her the teacher's notes and even had the teacher call her while Crip boiled crabs and grilled his magical chicken. But she was dead-set against it. It was as if there was an unseen enemy lurking deep inside her that they couldn't get to.

Ike got into another argument with her and then stormed out of the house. All the guests picked up and left. Now there was only one person left that might talk some sense into her – Sam. She had missed the barbecue due to a track meet.

Everyone fell into their routine again as the weather began to warm with the coming of spring. A dark cloud of depression began to cover Ike again as the thought of not being allowed to race began to sink in. Tricia still allowed him to ride, though. So he practiced on his modern bike and Vinnie every chance he got. It seemed to help his mood. But as he tried to keep his grades up, he had trouble concentrating.

The arguments in the Hebert household became more frequent and more volatile. At best, there was an uneasy truce between mother and son. At worst, it was like two enemies trying to live in the same house. There was no end in sight except one: the end of the school year.

Sam had been busy with school and racing. She made the honor roll at school, won some gold medals at the track meets, and continued to win every motocross race. But everything was not well with her. Someone had started rumors about her and Ben, her and Dave, and her and Ike – even her and Jimmy Plaisance! If that wasn't enough, Kate Sterling had bad-mouthed her in a magazine interview that became the talk on motocross message boards around the nation. Kate had accused her of using performance-enhancing drugs and cutting the track during races.

Sam soon become discouraged and began to make excuses to get out of going to the races or to school. At the last big race, someone put sugar in her fuel tank and the bike stalled on an approach to a jump, sending her over the bars. She landed on her right shoulder, dislocating it and breaking two fingers.

After two days in the hospital, Sam made a decision. When Mr. Rick came to visit, she just came right out and said it.

"Dad, I'm quitting motocross."

"But why?"

"Because it's not fun anymore," she admitted. "You told me yourself: When it's not fun anymore, I should quit."

"Yes, but that meant if you wanted to pursue something else or if you got burned out, not quit when it gets hard. What you're doing is quitting because it's getting tougher, and that's just wrong."

"But it's my body, my career, and I'm tired of you pushing me. I'm tired of training. I'm tired of having to eat the right foods and sacrifice other things. I just wanna be a regular teenager like everybody else."

"Honey, listen," her dad said. "When you start comparing yourself to others, you are making a mistake. Because that's a game you'll always lose. It's human nature to compare your worst side with their best side, or your best side with their worst side. And even if you do come out on top, it will only lead to conceit and arrogance."

"But I just want to be normal," she whimpered, as she tried to move into a more comfortable position in the hospital bed.

"What is 'normal'?" he asked. "Do you mean 'average'? Because most people settle for just being average out of laziness. They don't want to pay the price it takes to reach their dreams. They want to do just enough to get by or get what they want. You can be average if you want. We'll sell the bikes and trailer and gear and you can just concentrate on the little stuff that other teenagers concentrate on – getting people to like them, going out to party on the weekends, staring at themselves in the mirror and worrying about blemishes, gossiping, fighting with parents..."

"Okay, Dad," she interrupted. "I get the picture. But aren't we fighting now?"

"No, we're discussing."

"Arguing."

"Okay, arguing. But arguing is healthy if we stay on the topic and don't attack each other personally."

"All right, back to the topic. I'm quitting racing."

"No, you're not."

"Yes, I am."

"No, I've got too much invested in you to quit now," he said, his voice rising. "Besides, you are only two races away from qualifying for the National Championship."

"I don't care about that anymore," she whined.

"Yes, you do. You're just tired of the sacrifice and now you want to quit right before the finish line."

"Dad, I'm tired. I'm just so tired!"

She couldn't hold back any longer; she began to sob. Mr. Rick reached over to grab the box of tissues. He pulled a couple from the box and kneeled next to the bed, getting level with her tear-stained face.

"I know, honey," he said tenderly. "Just promise me one thing."

"What's that?" she sniffled, as she took a tissue to wipe her eyes.

"That you won't make an important life-changing decision while you are tired and hurting, okay?"

"Okay."

"Those are some nice flowers you got here. Who sent them?"

"Ike."

She wiped her eyes and began to regain her composure.

"Ike? What about Dave Remington?"

"Oh, he's a jerk," she blurted. "We broke up when he heard the rumors. He just wanted some of my popularity anyway. So when it was gone, so was he."

"So he wouldn't believe you?"

"No one would, at least not if they wanted to kiss up to the 'cool kids.' Ike was the only one."

"I think you've got a good friend there. But he's having struggles, too."

Mr. Rick got up and went back to his seat.

Sam thought for a moment and then asked, "Dad, why won't his mom let him race?"

"Because she loves him and wants to protect him," said Mrs. Hebert, answering Sam's question as she entered the room. "I can't stand to see him get hurt."

She looked at Sam with concern.

"Are *you* all right?" Tricia asked.

"I'm just tired," Sam replied, "tired of everything: tired of school, tired of racing, tired of being me."

"Are you really thinking of quitting racing?" Tricia prodded, a shocked look on her face.

"Yes, I've had enough. It's a rough sport anyway. I might try something like painting or cheerleading."

There was a long silence as Tricia and Rick just looked at her and glanced at each other, trying to hide their chuckles. Everyone in the room knew the obvious, but no one wanted to say it. So it went unsaid.

CHAPTER 19

༄

Things had gone downhill for Ike since he'd had to stop racing. The weeks dragged on, and he'd begun to isolate himself. The walls he put up caused the destructive thinking to come back. By May, he was in a full-blown depression.

Ike just stared at his mashed potatoes. He knew he should eat them, and the banana, but since he wasn't in training anymore, he just picked up the cookie and stuck it in his pocket. He got up, took his tray to the window and dropped it off. He trudged out of the cafeteria alone, as usual.

In his depression, and with Sam out of school, Ike didn't care to pursue any new friendships. It took too much energy, which he didn't have. He had to concentrate on just putting one foot in front of the other in his now pointless routine. The only thing that kept him going was the thought of getting his own truck. It made work seem worthwhile. He needed to have some wheels under him, and he had outgrown the bicycle. This summer he would have freedom: freedom to go where he wanted, when he wanted, with no one telling him what to do. He wanted to get away – away from school, away from home, away from Jimmy Plaisance and his bullying goons, and away from Calais. Maybe he could start all over in New Orleans or Lafayette.

When school was over, Ike got the job of telling his mother he had failed 10th grade. She had already known, but she wanted him to tell her. They didn't fight about it; they were too tired of fighting. Tricia was weary of being a parent of a teenager and Ike was ready for a change. But there was no way out and they were at an impasse. That's when Ike quietly packed his backpack and walked out. He didn't really intend on coming back. He left a note that simply read: 'Sorry about being a bother to you. I love you, Ike.'

Ike hitchhiked to New Orleans. When he got to town, he walked into the French Quarter and began the darkest two weeks of his life. It only took three days to run out of money. Then he got beaten up by another homeless man who stole everything, even his backpack and wallet. He resorted to digging in trash bins behind restaurants for his food. He learned to panhandle the tourists for pocket change and began to hang with a lower-level street gang that seemed to like him. His mood began to improve as he finally felt a sense of belonging, camaraderie – like the family he'd always wanted.

But the fun didn't last long. One dark, rainy night, the gang was arrested when they set off a car alarm while trying to jack a stereo. Ike went to jail. For the first time in his life, he had *really* lost his freedom. With his one phone call, he contacted Mr. Gonzales.

"Mr. Gonzales?" Ike asked as the call went through.

"Yes? This is Victor Gonzales."

"Hi, this is…"

"Ike? Is that you? Where are you?" Mr. Gonzales grilled Ike frantically.

"I'm in the juvenile detention center."

"For what?"

"Burglary."

"What? You?"

"Yes sir."

"Why?"

"I gotta eat."

"But not that way. I'll be right over."

In two hours, Mr. Gonzales was there, talking to Ike.

"Now what happened?"

"I, uhh, don't really know," Ike confessed. "I guess I was just tryin' to grow up."

"Are you done with your experiment, or should I leave you in there to see if your hypothesis is correct?"

"My hypothesis was wrong," Ike admitted. "This was not the way to live. Maybe there's a better way."

"You know there is. What do you want to do now?"

"Well, I don't really want to go back to Calais, but I don't want to stay here."

"What do you suggest?"

"I don't know," Ike said, and then paused. "Can I stay at your place until I figure something out?"

"You'll have to apologize to the judge and work off your bail and fines," Mr. Gonzales insisted. "But I think we can work something out."

"Can I go home tonight?"

"No, you'll have to spend a night or two, but I think I can have you out by Tuesday."

"Tuesday?" Ike groaned.

"Yes."

"But… why not tonight?" Ike stammered.

"Because sometimes the wheels of justice take time to roll," Mr. Gonzales said. "Just sit tight. You'll be okay."

"I guess I don't have a choice," Ike sighed.

"I guess you've put yourself into a position where your choices are very limited," Mr. Gonzales scolded. "I'll see you tomorrow, one way or the other."

It took Mr. Gonzales two days to get Ike out of jail, and it took meeting with the judge and agreeing to have Ike released into his custody. By the time Ike was able to walk out into the street and look up into the daylight, he felt like a new person. The feeling of freedom was like none he had ever had in his life. His mom, Crip and Mr. Gonzales took him to a restaurant to discuss his future.

"Ike, we've been talking, and we've decided it's time for you to take your trip," Mr. Gonzales began.

"My vacation?"

"It's not going to be a vacation," his mom corrected him. "It's going to be an 'attitude-adjustment' trip."

"I don't mind what you call it, I like going on trips with Mr. Gonzales," Ike pressed, excitedly.

"I'm not going with you," Mr. Gonzales stated steadily, looking into Ike's eyes with sadness.

"Then who am I going with?" Ike asked, perplexed.

They all looked at Crip, who was looking Ike dead in the eyes. Suddenly Ike realized who he would be traveling with.

"Oh, no, not Crip," Ike objected.

"Why not Crip?" Tricia countered. "He loves you."

"You mean like lions love rabbits?" Ike snorted.

"Crip has something planned that you're gonna love," Mr. Gonzales explained.

"Like getting beat up or hung upside down?" Ike argued, his voice tinged with fear.

"No, like a visit to his people in Springfield, to get a fresh perspective," Mr. Gonzales replied matter-of-factly.

"Louisiana?" Ike groaned.

"Yes," Mr. Gonzales replied.

"For what?"

Finally, Crip spoke up.

"To help you grow up. Son, you need to learn discipline, and I'm gonna help you."

"You mean like 'Marine Corps' grown up or 'Indian' grown up?" Ike asked sarcastically.

"Both," Crip stated crisply. "Now let's get goin'. We're burning daylight."

"But what if I don't want to?" Ike debated, folding his arms defiantly.

"Oh, you'll want to. We'll make sure of that," Crip barked with authority.

"Who's 'we'?" Ike challenged.

"Me, Crip, your mom, and the judge," Mr. Gonzales responded firmly.

Ike looked from face to face. He knew he was cornered and out of options. The trip was better than jail, and better than going back to Calais.

"I'll agree on one condition," Ike negotiated.

"No conditions. You just go," Crip ordered.

"Wait," Tricia said, and then asked Ike, "What's your condition?"

"That I can bring my modern bike. I want to ride while I'm there."

Tricia and Mr. Gonzales looked at each other, and then at Crip, who nodded.

"Okay, we'll agree – on one condition," Crip countered.

"What's that?" Ike retorted, distrustfully.

"You'll do everything – I mean *everything* – I say, when I say it, without whining or complaining," Crip proposed.

Ike thought for a moment, looking at each of their faces, measuring their will.

"Okay," Ike conceded, trying to hide the reservations he felt.

"Wait, I'm not done. If you don't, you'll face consequences. If you step out of line, you'll face consequences. I'll be legally responsible for you, and your butt will be mine for one month," Crip said, looking over at Tricia.

Tricia looked at Mr. Gonzales with alarm. Mr. Gonzales slowly began to nod.

"That's the ticket that will take you to the next level, Ike," said Mr. Gonzales. "Tricia, I know you're not completely comfortable with this, but I would trust Crip with my life, even my own son's life. His techniques are sometimes a bit… barbaric, but his heart is true and his mind is sharp. He's helped me out many times, and he'll help Ike, too."

Tricia looked from one man to the other, but she saw no signs of anyone backing down.

"Okay," she consented reluctantly, "do what you need to do."

"One more thing. I'll need power of attorney. Just a precautionary measure in case he needs medical care or anything," Crip explained.

"What do you mean 'if he needs medical care'!?" Tricia gasped.

"What he means, Tricia, is that it's time to cut the apron strings," Mr. Gonzales clarified.

She studied Mr. Gonzales in disbelief, but he stared her down. Then she looked at Crip, who nodded. Finally, she looked at Ike, who just shrugged.

"I see," she said, bristling defensively.

"It's okay, Mom, I can take anything he wants to dish out," Ike pledged, patting her arm. "I'll be all right."

Tricia looked again at Ike, then Mr. Gonzales, then Crip, and then back at Ike.

"You'll bring my boy back to me?" she asked Crip softly.

"No."

"What?" she exclaimed.

"I'll bring a man back to you. We'll leave the boy somewhere in the swamp," Crip vowed with a smirk.

A smile began to form on Mr. Gonzales' face. Then one appeared on Ike's face. The smiles turned into laughter. The laughter finally rubbed off on Tricia, who just shook her head.

"Men," she groaned, rolling her eyes.

CHAPTER 20

Ike stared out of the window of Crip's pickup truck as they ambled north on Highway 1, past the docks and boathouses along Bayou Lafourche. The morning sun was cresting the trees, and most of the shrimp trawlers and crabbers were out in the marshes and the Gulf of Mexico by now.

Ike's mind began to wander.

'*Some of my cousins and uncles are already offshore, workin' in the sun. What are Crip's relatives like? What kind of work do they do? What kind of work would Crip be doing if he hadn't gone to war? Why did he choose to make a living fixing other people's motorcycles?*'

Ike leaned his head against the window and drifted back to sleep.

Two hours later, Ike was awakened by the slowing of the truck. They pulled up to a little country convenience store in a clearing in the woods, just off the asphalt road.

"Gotta get some gas," Crip said. "You want anything?"

"No, I'm good," Ike mumbled, repositioning his head on the door and closing his eyes.

"Crip! Long time, no see, cuz," said a tall, muscular Indian, greeting Crip with arms extended.

"Too long, dog, too long," Crip replied with a wide grin as they embraced, finishing with a forearm shake and broad smiles. "How's everybody?"

"Same ol', same ol' – hangin' in there. They all been askin' about ya', especially Ziptie."

"Funny you should mention him. I'm on my way to see him now. Where is he?"

"Where he always is: at his dirt pit. He'll be happy to see ya'. Hey, who's the young buck?"

"Oh, that's Ike. I think he's bein' a little shy."

"You takin' him in there, too?"

"Sure, why not?"

"Don't you remember what happened last time you brought a stranger in?"

"Hey, how was I supposed to know he was a low-down mule for that drug lord? There's still hope for this one. He isn't spoiled yet."

"How do you know this one will be any different?"

"You gotta try."

Crip finished pumping the gas and replaced the pump nozzle, and then screwed the gas cap back on. He reached into his pocket, pulled out a wad of bills, counted out the thirty-six dollars and handed it to the attendant.

"This one is different," Crip explained. "I know him. And it's a personal favor for a friend."

"Oh, boy, here we go again. Crip tryin' to save the world. Good luck with that."

"It's not luck I need, it's Him," Crip smiled, pointing up.

"Always. Semper Fi!"

"Ooh-Rah!" Crip added as they shook forearms again.

Crip limped around to the driver's door and opened it. He had to drag his wooden leg in behind him and physically place it on the clutch. He carefully closed the well-oiled door and started the motor. It hummed the tune of a big V-8 with headers and glass packs.

"Man, I love that sound," Crip uttered, closing his eyes and relaxing his head against the headrest.

Ike opened his eyes and looked over. "What sound?"

"If you have to ask, you wouldn't understand," Crip chuckled with a sly grin.

"Oh, *that* sound. It's pretty cool," Ike nodded. "But not as cool as a Yamaha R6 at 10,000 rpm in sixth gear."

Ike turned to look at Crip for his reaction.

"Son, you'd be going 130 miles per hour, and you'd better be on a race-track," Crip said, turning to look at Ike. "Does Mr. Gonzales know you did that with one of his bikes?"

"Not yet. And he doesn't have to, does he?"

"That depends on how you act the next few weeks. Yep, it depends on you."

Crip put his glasses on and stuck a piece of gum in his mouth. Then he started snickering.

"What?" asked Ike.

"An R6 at 10,000. You're lucky you didn't blow the motor."

"Hey, to each his own. I like fast and you like old... what is this truck again?"

"A 1967 Ford F-100," he announced proudly.

"I bet it doesn't even have a hemi, does it?" Ike teased.

Crip stared at Ike in disbelief. Then he nodded as if arriving at a decision.

"Buckle up," Crip ordered.

"What?"

"Buckle up."

"Why?"

"It's the law."

Reluctantly, Ike buckled his belt. Immediately, Crip downshifted and punched it. The tires tore up the asphalt and burned rubber for five long seconds, fishtailing down the old road. When Crip shifted into third gear, Ike's head was plastered to the headrest, his eyes wide in terror. Ike tried to peek at the speedometer, but he kept a tight, white-knuckled hold on the door handle.

"How fast are we goin'?" he gasped in fright.

"Take a look," Crip calmly replied as he shifted into fourth and let the tach wind up to redline.

Ike leaned over and stared at the speedometer, which was topped out at 110.

"I don't think so," he shot at Crip with disbelief; then he turned and watched the trees blur past his window. "Looks like 130."

"Guess again," Crip said, looking over at Ike.

"Don't take your eyes off the road, Crip! And slow down, for God's sake!"

"For *whose* sake?" Crip snapped. He glanced at the road ahead, and then back at Ike with a mean look.

"Okay, for *Pete's* sake. You're gonna get a ticket!"

"Might. Might not."

Crip started slowing down, bringing a sigh of relief from Ike.

"If you like speed so much, why were you so afraid?" Crip asked.

"I wasn't afraid."

"Sure you were. But why weren't you afraid when you had that R6 up at 130?"

"'Cause I… I don't know," Ike shrugged.

"Well, I'll tell ya, since you don't know. It's the same reason your mom wouldn't let you race. It's all about control. You were afraid because you weren't in control of the wheel, and you don't trust me yet. You're gonna have to trust me — with your life, if need be."

"'If need be'?"

"If need be."

"Is 'be' gonna be 'needed'?" Ike asked, looking questioningly at Crip.

"Might," Crip cautioned.

"'Might'?" Ike questioned, studying Crip's face, wondering what he meant.

"Might," Crip repeated with finality.

There was a long silence.

"What do you mean, 'might'?" Ike pressed.

"Well, I got this here big, modern motor in this old truck for a reason."

"Oh – 'if need be'?"

"Hey, you're a fast learner."

Crip eased the truck back down to within the speed limit.

"So does this thing have a hemi?"

Crip laughed.

"Don't need no hemi when you got lots of supercharged ponies that are trained to fly!"

They rode silently for a few minutes, each considering his own thoughts.

"Well, here we are," Crip announced, pointing to a sign on the right that read, "You are now entering Choctaw tribal lands."

Suddenly a police car pulled out from a little side road and turned on its lights. It came up on them in seconds.

"Who's that?" Ike yelped in alarm, sitting up.

"My brother. Well, my half-brother," Crip answered as he pulled the truck over onto the gravel shoulder. He took off his sunglasses and looked in the rearview mirror to watch the cop get out of his car.

CHAPTER 21

❡

The uniformed patrolman stepped out of his car and approached the truck. He took off his sunglasses and peered through the window. Crip rolled the window down and asked, "What can I do for you, officer?"

A look of recognition dawned on the patrolman's face and a smile began to crease his lips.

"Well, you can start by following me to the station and getting finger-printed."

"Fingerprinted?"

"Yeah, get those greasy fingerprints on my Harley. It's hard to start and runnin' rough."

"Uh, officer, may I ask you a question?"

"Sure."

"Why didn't you fix it yourself?"

"I'm too busy."

"Too busy? On a reservation with less than a thousand people, mostly family, and you can't find time to fix your bike?"

"Well, that, and I don't have the touch, like you."

"True," Crip agreed and stepped out of the truck and embraced the officer the same way he had the other Indian at the gas station.

"What's up, bro'? It's been way too long," Crip announced with a broad grin.

"Way, way," the officer concurred. "You been keepin' yourself lean and mean?"

"Less and less as I get older."

"Been keepin' yourself clean?"

"Yep. Finally figured out the secret," Crip answered.

"What's that?"

"The company you keep. And I've settled down into a steady job."

"I've been telling you to do that for years."

"Hey, Ike, I want you to meet somebody," Crip called, turning and peering into the car. "This is my brother, Doug."

Ike jumped out of the truck and came around to face the tall officer.

"Doug, this is Ike, a friend of mine. He's a motocrosser."

Doug looked at Ike intently, measuring him up as he extended his hand.

"So you're the one," he smiled as he grasped Ike's hand firmly.

"I'm the one?"

"The one that's coming here to train."

"To train? Yeah, I guess so. I mean, Crip hasn't exactly explained everything to me yet."

"He's like that. Everything's on a 'need to know' basis," Doug chided, casting a wink in Crip's direction. "It's one of his leftover bad habits from the war."

"Hey, I've cleaned up pretty good. Better than most," Crip defended himself, with a push to Doug's shoulder that sent him off balance. Doug just gave him the eye.

"At least you came back," Doug responded.

"Well, *most* of me came back," Crip smiled at Ike, tapping his wooden leg.

Doug walked over to the bed of the truck and studied Ike's bike.

"What year is this 250?"

"2005. It runs good, but we gotta tune the suspension," Ike said.

Doug looked at Crip.

"Did Crip tell you what you'd be doin'?"

Doug looked back and forth from Ike to Crip as if he knew something Ike didn't.

"Uh, no, I haven't told him yet. Look Doug, we'll see ya at the house this evening. Is the camper ready?" Crip asked, trying to change the subject. He reached back into the bed of the truck and unzipped Ike's gear bag. He pulled his race boots out.

Doug took the hint and put his sunglasses back on.

"Yeah, it's ready. Got the stuff you asked for all laid out in there. Well, I guess I gotta get back to work. You're havin' dinner with us tonight. Lacey is cooking your favorite meal."

"Seafood gumbo?"

"No, peanut butter and mustard," Doug stated, trying to keep a straight face.

"Oh, now you're talkin'!" Crip celebrated, high-fiving Doug. Ike just stared at the two in disbelief.

"What, you never tasted peanut butter and mustard? You have got to get out more, Ike," Crip said, faking shock.

"Especially when you put tuna fish on it," Doug seconded.

"And lima beans," Crip added, nodding.

"And don't forget the jalapeno peppers and anchovies," Doug called over his shoulder as he walked back to his car.

"And don't forget the stale bread pudding for dessert!" Crip laughed.

"Your feast should be ready at about sunset, but you can come hang out earlier," Doug declared as he paused at his door.

"We'll be there. Hey, is the peanut butter old?" Crip asked, raising his hands questioningly.

"Oh, yeah, probably over a year," Doug countered. "It's been sitting under the house with the lid off. Probably raised 25 families of flies in there."

"Then we'll definitely be there," Crip said with excitement in his voice, celebrating with a jubilant fist in the air. "Won't we, Ike?"

"Uh, yeah, sure. I can't wait to eat that," Ike said, slowly and sarcastically.

The men laughed and waved to each other as the police car pulled away.

"You guys are weird," Ike noted flatly, shaking his head.

"Son, you'll learn that humor is the spice of life. Without it, we'd all go crazy. Now here," Crip said, tossing his racing boots to Ike. "Put these on."

"Right now?"

"Right now."

"Why?"

"The next time you ask me that question you're gonna do 30 push-ups," Crip warned, his tone changing. "Do you or do you not want to train?"

"But, not the... this is not... the Marines," Ike offered weakly.

"Don't knock the Corps. They have the best program in the world. Why do you think a recruit doesn't have to go back through basic when he transfers to another branch of the service from the Marines?"

"I dunno."

"Because we do it right the first time! Now, you've got two minutes to get your socks and boots on."

Ike sat down and pulled off his tennis shoes. He reached into his boots and grabbed his long racing socks.

"Do you want me to put my race pants and other stuff on, too?"

"Nope. Just your boots."

"Why, uhh, I mean, what will I be doin', ridin'?"

"Nope. Running."

"Running?"

"Running. You've got 20 seconds left."

Crip turned and got into the truck. He started it up and looked behind him out of the window.

"Throw your shoes in the truck. You got it easy today."

"Easy?"

"Yeah, it's not dusty."

Crip began to pull away.

"Wait, I'm not…" Ike slapped the last buckle closed and jumped up, grabbing his shoes and socks. He took off after the truck and tossed them into the bed of the truck. Crip increased the speed and opened up a distance of 50 feet between them. And with that, Ike began a new training program that would take him to the next level of racing.

CHAPTER 22

After two slow miles of jogging, Crip turned down a gravel road under a sign that read, "Lejeune Dirt and Gravel." Ike was sucking wind and slowing to a snail's pace as the boots began to feel like big chunks of concrete on his feet. Then he caught the sound of motocross bikes ahead, which gave him just the boost he needed to follow the truck through the gate and up the driveway. Crip stopped the truck under a shade tree in front of a little mobile home overlooking a big dirt pit. He stepped out of the truck to wait for Ike to cover the last 200 yards to a much-deserved rest. Crip reached into the ice chest and drew out two bottles of water. He opened one and surveyed the scene before him.

There were two dump trucks, a giant front-end loader, a back hoe and a bulldozer down in the pit. Off to the right were various older pieces of heavy equipment dying a slow, rusty death. To the left was an oval dirt track. But Crip's gaze stopped on the field directly behind the pit, where a half-dozen motocross bikes were flying high into the sky like bouncing balls.

Ike trotted and tripped his way up to the back of the truck and collapsed on the tailgate. Gasping for air, he turned his sweat-streaked, sun-scorched face up to Crip, but words wouldn't come out of his mouth.

"Save your breath. Here," Crip said, handing him the water and looking back at the bikes. After Ike had twisted off the cap and sucked down half the bottle, he dragged himself up onto the tailgate and leaned against the inner side of the bed.

The door to the office opened and a tall, thin man with a black cowboy hat stepped out onto the porch of the mobile home. He looked the truck over, noticed the bike in the back, and then gazed at Crip.

"Well, well. Look what the dog drug in," he drawled with a western twang in his voice. "Crip, you ol' chunk of rawhide, why didn't you call ahead? I would've iced the beer and fired the grill."

The man made his way down the steps and up to the truck. Crip turned and held his arms open with a smile.

"And you thought you was rid of me, didn't you?"

"Nah, you're like an old turtle. The only way to keep you outta the pond is to shoot ya'."

They embraced like long-lost brothers.

"That's been tried, many times, and it don't work," Crip joshed, as he stepped back to look at his old friend. "You haven't changed a bit."

"You neither – just frozen in time," Ziptie noted, stepping back to look him over.

"Yep, except I'm gettin' old and tired."

"I hear ya, brother."

They looked at each other for a few seconds. Then Crip spoke.

"Come over here, there's somebody I want you to meet."

The tall cowboy followed him around the back of the truck. Ike was following them with his eyes, but his body was still slumped over in exhaustion.

"This is Ike Hebert, a friend of mine. He's come to train for motocross. Ike, this is Ziptie. He's the owner of this outfit."

Ike dragged his tired body off the tailgate to shake Ziptie's hand. They looked into each other's eyes for a split second, as if looking to see what was really inside.

"Glad to meet ya, Ike."

"You, too, uhh, Mr. Ziptie."

"You can just call me Ziptie. So, you like racing or freestyle?"

"I race, but I like to watch freestyle on TV."

"Well, you can see it live here," Ziptie nodded over toward the back of the pit.

"Ziptie owns three race teams – a flat-track, motocross, and freestyle jumping team," Crip explained.

"Cool. So that's your freestyle team out there?" Ike assumed, pointing to the jumpers.

"No, that's just some of the boys playin' around. Some are on one or the other of the teams, and they just like to play out there."

"It keeps their skills sharp to ride every day with each other, just like iron sharpens iron," Crip remarked, his gaze steady on the riders.

"They'll go from the jumps to the flat track to the MX course like a flock of birds, until they get tired or run out of gas," Ziptie said, and then pointed at Ike's boots. "You been runnin' in those?"

"Not my idea," Ike muttered, nodding angrily over at Crip.

"It's a good one; I taught it to him," Ziptie bragged proudly, taking off his bandana and wiping the sweat off his forehead. "It builds the muscles in your legs so they become used to the boots – and gets your feet used to feeling the ground through the boots. Plus, you get more of a workout. Follow me, I want to show you something."

Ziptie led them around the left side of the pit, past the flat track. Once they got beyond it, they could see the motocross track. Ike's eyes were drawn to the huge tabletops and triple jumps. He started to feel sick to his stomach. Crip noticed.

"Before we leave here," he commented, "you'll be able to clear those jumps at high speed without even thinking about it. You'll also be able to run a 40-minute moto full speed."

"Forty-minute motos?" Ike protested. "Are you crazy?"

"Run 40-minute motos in practice so that when you're in a race, you can handle 20 minutes," Crip explained. "You tighten up in a race, which saps more strength and pumps up your arms."

"They used to run 40-minute motos in my day," Ziptie drawled. "That would separate the men from the boys, especially on the old machines that had only six inches of travel on front and four in back."

"I've raced the old bikes, too," Ike offered.

"Not the *real* old ones, just the Post-Vintage, '82 model," Crip corrected. "He's ridden the '74, but not the real old BSAs and Triumphs. You've changed the track since the last time I was here."

"Yep," Ziptie confirmed. "We copied some of the Texas, Florida and California tracks as best we can on flat ground. But we keep the latest developments in for the guys to practice on. Sand sweepers and rhythm sections are real hot right now, as well as step-ons and step-offs. Supercross keeps making things more technical, and the younger riders love air time."

"Not me," Ike complained.

"That's just 'cause you haven't been taught yet on a modern bike. It's all about confidence," Crip asserted, grabbing Ike's shoulder and shaking him playfully.

"Careful, my legs are still wobbly," Ike whined.

"We gonna fix that, too," Crip forecast, winking at Ziptie.

"You gonna have to force-feed him to get him ready in just a few weeks," Ziptie cautioned.

"We'll just get his confidence up and his technique in," Crip said. "This will be like training camp. He'll have to come back for more practices later."

"Okay, Sean Peyton, let's get those Saints to the Super Bowl!" Ziptie crowed with excitement.

"Hey, I got the talent standing right here," Crip boasted, putting a hand on Ike's shoulder.

The sound of the bikes got louder, prompting the three of them to look over at the jumps. Seven dirt bikes began to make their way over toward the office.

"Come on," Ziptie urged. "Let's go meet 'em."

CHAPTER 23

The riders pulled up under the shade of the moss-draped live oak. They took off their helmets and headed for the artesian well. One by one, they soaked their heads and drank their fill, and then collapsed on the ground. They were pulling off their boots when Ziptie walked up.

"Hey, guys! You have a good ride?" Ziptie queried, to no one in particular.

"It was good. Skeeter threw a chain, though," the biggest one explained.

"Ya'll fix it?" Ziptie responded.

"Yeah, he found a 520 O ring chain in the tool shed and put it on," another remarked.

"How'd the sprockets look?" continued Ziptie.

"They were okay. I think I got a rock in there or something. The chain was old, anyway," Skeeter answered coolly.

"I've got someone I want you to meet. You know Crip," Ziptie said, smiling, and they all greeted Crip warmly and with respect; it seemed they all knew him already. "And this here's Ike. He's come to train with us for a couple weeks."

The riders just looked Ike over, cautiously. Ike nodded coolly. They stared coldly and nodded without getting up. Ike cast a sidewise glance at Crip, who looked back at him with a raised eyebrow, as if to say, "This is gonna be a tough crowd."

Ziptie rubbed his hands together and asked, "Who wants some watermelon?" That brought a raucous roar. "Robbie, go get a big one from the patch," Ziptie ordered.

Immediately a boy got up and went out to fetch the melon while the others stripped down to their riding pants and bare feet. When the boy returned, he dropped the watermelon on the ground, breaking it open to reveal the sweet red meat. There was a fight for the heart; then the latecomers settled for the rest. Soon everyone was shoving pieces in their mouths, the red juice dripping down their chests.

"So, Ike, how long you been racin'?" a rider asked.

"Oh, about two months," Ike mumbled between the spitting of seeds.

"You a beginner?" another boy probed.

"No, I'm a novice."

"So you've raced more than a year?"

"One month."

"But how many times have you raced?" another asked with a perplexed tone.

"Twice," Ike stated matter-of-factly.

The racers just looked at each other and slowed their eating.

"And how'd you do?" another grilled him.

"Crashed twice," Ike responded coolly, continuing to eat. His answer brought a laugh from the boys, with a few nods of appreciation.

"I heard that," one boy chuckled. "That's how I started, too. You get hurt?"

"Sprained ankle the first time, broken shoulder and ribs the second."

"Then why are you still racing?" a boy said, needling him.

"'Cause I'm a racer," Ike asserted.

Crip chuckled. Ziptie dropped his piece of melon and the boys stopped talking and just stared at Ike. When he noticed that everyone was staring at him, Ike felt compelled to explain.

"It is what it is. I'm a motocross racer, that's who I am. I'm going to work hard and one day I'll be National Champion."

Everyone burst out laughing – that is, everyone except Ziptie, Crip and one boy.

"Well, Crip, looks like you got your work cut out for you," Ziptie jested, smiling at Ike.

"So I have," Crip agreed, looking proudly at Ike. "So I have."

They began to clean up at the well and get dressed in their gear.

"Come on guys, let's hit the flat track," the biggest one suggested. Ike looked at Crip, who shook his head "no." Ike looked down, and then got up and washed his hands. One by one, the boys remounted, started their bikes, and rode away.

"Why can't I go ride with them?" Ike pleaded.

"You're not ready," Crip replied.

"When will I be ready?"

"In a couple days, depending."

"On what?"

"On how you respond to the program."

"What program?"

"Your program. You ask too many questions. Let's go get settled in at the camper."

"So you're gonna be a champion?" Ziptie drawled with a thick cowboy accent, while wiping his brow with his handkerchief. "I gotta hand it to you. You talk big. Can you back it up?"

"Sure. Just watch me."

"I will," Ziptie assured him and then tipped his hat to Crip. "See you guys tomorrow?"

"Maybe," Crip answered. "We have a few wrinkles to work out."

Crip and Ike got back in the truck and began to pull up the driveway, stopping at the rim of the hill to watch the riders flat-tracking below them. One of the riders peeled away from the group and rode up to the truck, pulling up on the passenger's side. He took off his goggles and looked at Ike.

"Ike, I like what you said back there. If you need anything, jus' ask for Skeeter. I live just down that road."

Skeeter reached out his gloved hand, and Ike shook it.

"Thanks, I will," Ike returned.

"Gotta go."

"See ya," Ike said, waving as Skeeter pulled away.

"Looks like ya got a friend," Crip noted.

"Yep."

"You're gonna need him," Crip predicted ominously.

CHAPTER 24

Later that evening, they sat down with Doug and his wife for a meal.

"Wow, that was some good meal," Crip remarked, as he pushed back his chair and rubbed his belly.

"Yeah, that was the best Cajun Spaghetti I ever had," echoed Ike, who was already finishing his dessert, scraping his bowl with his spoon while trying to get every last bit of ice cream. "What was in it again?"

"Venison sausage and squirrel meat, with gator sauce piquant," said Doug's wife, Lacey. "Ya'll made short work of that batch. Next time we'll have to clean out a whole corner of the swamp to feed you," she teased.

"So, word is ya'll been havin' some trouble with some swampers," Crip observed. "I heard they're raidin' the outlyin' settlements?"

"I'm not so sure it's swampers," Doug began. "This just started about three months ago. It was about the time there was a big escape from Angola prison. If my hunch is correct, it's either those escapees or some of those foreigners that jump off the ships comin' up the Mississippi."

"What are they takin'?" Ike asked, pushing away his bowl.

"Tools, electronics, jewelry – the usual. Anything they can sell or pawn. But they've been getting more brazen and even mean. Besides stealin' stuff, they've even started killing dogs, cows, sheep, even cats."

"Have you tried to track 'em?" Crip asked.

Doug finished chewing, and then wiped his face with his napkin.

"Yep, but we always lose their trail in one of the pull ditches."

"What's a pull ditch?" Ike asked, hoping he wouldn't look dumb. When they looked at him and then at each other, he added, "Well, I don't know."

"Little canals were dug all through the swamp at the turn of the century to get the cypress timber out," described Doug. "They all connect to main lines. There are thousands of them out there. They've been leavin' hardly any sign, and dogs can't track in the water."

"If you know what to look for, you can track in shallow canals," Crip corrected his brother.

"The conditions have to be just right," Doug argued.

"How did all those canals get there?" Ike pressed, grabbing another roll and the butter.

"You see, the Manchac swamp was purchased by northern speculators after the Civil War," Crip explained. "Folks were in dire need of money and sold out for pennies on the dollar. These businessmen and investors wanted the timber out of here. There were thousands of square miles of huge cypress trees back here."

Doug picked up the story: "Yeah, but the problem was getting it out to Lake Pontchartrain to transport it to market. Then the Illinois Central extended its railroad around the north side of the lake, to pass Manchac. That brought people and supplies in and made a way to get the lumber out. Then a new invention made a way to get the trees out of the swamp. It was a steam-powered skidder. All they had to do was dig canals through the swamp, and they could bring in those skidders on barges to drag the trees out and into the ditches."

"So the logs were then floated out?" Ike guessed.

"Right," Crip replied. "The timber was brought to loading docks, where they were stacked for transport to lumberyards. This virtually destroyed the swamp, causing lots of things to get out of balance, which then killed most of the rest of the cypress trees. So much of the swamp is now open marsh, especially closer to the lake. Then, when the nutria came in, they started eating all the vegetation, which started causing the marsh to disappear. But one thing it left was all those canals over many square miles. Anyone with a boat can disappear back there."

"Don't get us wrong," Doug clarified. "There are lots of good people living back there, living off the swamp. They just don't want to live in civilization, for whatever reasons. Think of the mountain men who lived off the land, hunting and trapping, then coming out once in a while to trade for stuff they need. These 'swampers' are like that, only instead of the mountains, they live in the swamp."

"They love freedom. Ain't nuthin' wrong with that," Crip added, reaching for more milk.

"How do you guys know all this?" Ike responded, clearly impressed.

"Many of them are related to us," Crip explained. "Our fathers and grandfathers worked in the swamps, logging, fixing machines, fishing, trapping and hunting, anything to make a living."

"Sounds like a hard way to live," Ike commented.

"Not if you know what to do, and it's all you know," Doug countered.

"Not if it's in your blood," Crip seconded. "Like you love motocross racing and that's your calling? Same with people who live in the swamp. They love the swamp, they know the swamp, and they take pride in it. They are just part of it."

"They're survivors," Doug stated.

"Like that song from, uhhh, Hank Williams, Jr.?" Ike joshed. "Something about a country boy?"

"'A Country Boy Can Survive,'" Crip chuckled. "I guess it's one of the descriptions of my people. But every region of the country has 'em, except for the overcrowded areas in the big cities. So, how close have these perps gotten to you?" Crip asked Doug, getting back to the subject.

"Actually, they hit me last week," Doug said, bristling with anger. "They stole my four-wheeler, a couple chainsaws and some other tools out of my shed, along with fishing poles, traps and my trolling motor. But worst of all, they killed my best hound. Cut his head off and hung it in the tree. They're gonna pay for that!"

Crip looked at Doug, then at Ike.

"They made a big mistake. Now they've sealed their fate," Crip predicted, as he rose from the table and tossed his napkin onto his plate disgustedly.

CHAPTER 25

The next day, Ike awakened to an empty camper. He stepped outside to look for Crip. He found him walking back from the wooded corner of the homestead, wiping off his knife and sheathing it.

"What you doin'?" Ike inquired.

"Setting up a perimeter," Crip said, pointing to the wood line. "I want to know when anyone comes within 200 yards of us. Whether they are looking or raidin', whether man or beast, I wanna know – and I *will* know."

Crip turned and walked to the opening in the fence.

"Come on, I wanna show you so you won't trip the wires. Don't want you steppin' in the wrong places."

Crip led Ike back across the barbed-wire fence into the woods.

"Step only where I step," he instructed Ike. "I'm intentionally not walking in certain areas, 'cause I don't want to leave any sign."

"Do you think they're good at reading sign?"

"My guess is no. Unless they hooked up with the Choctaw, they will be the kind of men that are lazy." Crip walked on and motioned Ike to follow. "Criminals are used to letting others do the work, then stealin' their goods or benefits. Unless he is starving, a man who is trained to track, used to living off the land, will generally be disciplined enough to have more important things on his mind than stealin' or killin' or other destructive habits. And if he is high-level trained – say, from the military – then he'd have more honor than to just become a pirate."

"But pirates are cool," Ike protested.

Crip stopped and turned around with fire in his eyes.

"No, they aren't. You call hunting down the innocent and stealin' their stuff 'cool'? Look at those Somali pirates in the news all the time. They're just lazy, greedy low-lifes that are trying to get rich off of other men's hard work. And like terrorists, they'll kill anyone who gets in their way. They're just a step above animals."

"But what about that pirate movie? You know, the one with Johnny Depp and all?"

Crip rolled his eyes, looked heavenward, and then began to explain: "Ike, imagine yourself riding your dirt bike through the woods and a guy steps out and puts a gun to your head. He demands you get off the bike and give it to him. He demands your money and anything else you have. Then he rides off, leaving you there. If you argue, he shoots you. Is that cool?"

"Well, no, but it's just a dirt bike."

"What if it's a car or truck that you worked and saved for a couple years to buy? He stops you at an intersection and demands you get out. Then he steals your truck. And you don't have it paid off yet. So not only do you lose your ride, but you have to continue making the payments for a few more years until it is completely paid off. Is *that* cool?"

"But that's a car-jacker!"

"Are car-jackers cool?"

"No, they steal babies and everything. They target women!"

"Hello! What do you think pirates are? They're boat-jackers! And when they kill innocent animals, the next step to give them their high is to kill people. So what we've got here are money-, jewelry-, tool-, bike- and, eventually, *life*-jackers!"

Ike just looked down.

"Listen, let's go back to that group of Somali pirates that boarded the ship and captured its crew. One of the crew members took one of the pirates down into the engine room, then jumped him and disarmed him. *That's* cool. The ship's captain volunteered to go as a hostage so they would let the rest of the crew go. *That's* cool. The pirates took him into a little boat at gunpoint. It only took four hours for a Navy SEAL team to get on the ship with their gear. They came out to tow the boat. When the pirates pointed their guns at the American hostage to shoot him, the SEAL snipers terminated them immediately. No negotiations with their elders, no swap for freedom, no ransom, just justice – swift and true. The captain was able to go home to his wife and children. The pirates got what they were tryin' to dish out. The SEALs did their job and went back home. Good prevailed over evil. Good men stopped evil men. Law-abiding people stood up to law-breakers. Heroes rescued innocents. It's called 'justice.' Now *that's* cool!"

Crip dropped the subject, then turned and pointed.

"You see those ferns over there?"

"Yep."

"I've got a trip wire on that rabbit trail. All of these trails have trip wires."

"Did you put an explosive on it?"

"No. I've just got fishing line tied to a small dead branch or something that will move easily. I'm not trying to kill 'em. I just want to see if they come through. And over there, see those cobwebs?"

"No."

Crip led Ike closer to a sweet gum tree.

"Look in the sunlight from here."

"By those trumpeter vines?"

"Yes."

"Oh, I see 'em."

"I moved those cobwebs from there," he pointed, "to there."

"Why?"

"So when they break them, I'll know someone passed."

Ike just looked at him with a puzzled expression.

"You can do that?"

"You can do just about anything you set your mind to do. If you have enough faith, you can move a giant live oak tree."

"I thought that was a mountain?"

"In south Louisiana, it's live oaks," Crip said, smiling. "Come on, we gotta get you trained."

He started walking back up to the path, pointing out different things.

"Basically, I have two perimeters. The outlying perimeter is just to see if someone is getting close enough to Doug's property to look. This closer perimeter I set to warn us if someone gets close to our trailer."

He pointed to the thin monofilament line that went through the window and into the trailer. When they walked in, he led Ike down the hallway to the bedroom. He pointed to the line tied to a spoon in a saucer.

"Will that wake you up?" Ike asked.

"If the crickets and frogs stop making noise, I'll wake up. That's why I must sleep with the windows open. *This* is just to wake *you* up!"

They both laughed.

CHAPTER 26

After a breakfast of cereal and fresh-picked berries, Crip and Ike threw their gear into the truck and headed out. The midmorning sound of locusts harmonized with the calls of crows overhead as the sun began to heat up the south Louisiana woods. Crip turned the truck up the gravel road past Doug's house; Doug's cruiser was already gone. His beagles barked a boisterous warning as they passed the kennels.

"We'll have to start earlier tomorrow," Crip said, "but I wanted you to see the layout around the camper in the sunlight. You'll have to memorize every tree and bush and trail..."

"I know: If need be."

Crip turned and looked into Ike's eyes.

"You are sharp. It's gonna be fun watchin' you grow."

"Grow?"

"Yeah. You're young. The trainin' and teachin' – if you work hard, you'll grow like a weed."

Ike thought about that as he looked out the window.

'Probably not a bad deal, getting the training of this man, for free. He's obviously got a lot to teach me. Besides his military training and his knowledge of living off the land, he's graduated from the school of hard knocks. Maybe I won't have to take some of the hard hits he has,' Ike thought, looking at Crip's wooden leg.

Crip noticed Ike's glance.

"You can learn from my mistakes," he said; then he looked out his window and drew a breath. "A wise man learns from his mistakes. A wiser man learns from *other's* mistakes." he said, philosophically.

"My dad used to tell me that," Ike recalled, an old memory resurfacing.

"Then he was a wiser man."

"He was."

Ike just zoned out again, looking out of the window. Crip reminded him of his dad in many ways – his toughness, his no-nonsense approach to life, his strength. Some men inspire boys to be like them. Crip was one of those men.

They motored on for a while toward higher ground and the low-lying, swampy cypress and tulip poplar stands gave way to piney forest. Crip turned off down a dirt road. After a few minutes, Crip pulled the truck up under the shade of a big live oak tree. A squirrel scurried up through its large branches and into the persimmon tree next door. He turned and looked once, then transferred to a tall pine, where he climbed up to a higher perch and began fussing at them. While Ike was watching the squirrel, Crip tapped him on the arm with the back of his hand.

"Be careful where you step," he warned and pointed to the ground. A black hog-nosed snake about four feet long slithered between Ike's legs and into the bushes. Ike jumped and yelped.

"Calm down, he won't hurt you. It's the moccasins, copperheads and rattlesnakes you gotta watch out for."

"I know about them, especially the moccasins," Ike said. "They'll attack you."

"That they will," Crip chuckled. "Just don't step on anything you can step over. Help me get these bikes out of the truck."

Crip dropped the tailgate and pulled out an old mountain bike that was leaning against the bed wall, next to Ike's Honda. Crip nodded to the other side, where there was another bicycle.

"Where did these come from?" Ike inquired.

"There are on loan from a friend. Check your air pressure," Crip added, tossing the tire gauge to Ike.

"Where we goin'?" Ike mumbled as he checked his tires.

"On a trail I know. Nothing like a nice bike ride in the morning to get your juices movin'," he asserted as he pulled a bicycle helmet out from behind his seat. "Put your helmet and boots on."

"But don't you have one of those for me?" Ike asked, pointing to his bicycle helmet.

"Nope. You need to ride with your racing helmet and goggles."

"Goggles, too?"

"You need to get used to training with your gear on. It helps your vision during the race. You can see much better if you are used to having it on during training."

When Ike got geared up and mounted, Crip tossed a water bottle to him.

"We forgot to hydrate yesterday. We should start drinking two days in advance of heavy work, because it takes that long for the water to work its way to the cells in your body. But we won't push too hard today."

"How you gonna ride with a wooden leg?"

"Don't worry about me," Crip said with a cunning smile. "You just keep up."

As Crip led off, Ike had trouble peddling in his boots. They kept hitting the frame.

"Wait, this isn't working!" Ike howled.

"Turn your toes in and put them on the pedals," Crip yelled back over his shoulder.

"I guess you're gonna say there's a reason for that, too," Ike spat.

"Yep – trains your feet to find the shifter and brake without having to fish for 'em," Crip replied as he disappeared up the trail and into the woods.

Two hours later, they reappeared from another trail across the road from the truck. Both were sucking air and sweating profusely in the hot afternoon sun. Crip laid his bike down and reached into the ice chest and grabbed two waters. He dipped his kerchief into the cold water in the chest and tossed it on his head.

"That was good," Crip panted, plopping onto the tailgate.

Ike took his water and dropped next to him.

"I've never ridden that far, that fast," Ike seconded, unscrewing the cap from his water and wiping sweat from his brow. Then he teasingly said, "You go pretty good for a one-legged old man."

"Yeah, but you can't fight Mother Nature," Crip conceded. "My body is too old to go that hard. Tomorrow I'll take a shortcut back and you'll take the long way. I'll be timing you."

"Good, 'cause you were holding me up," Ike chided with a huge grin.

"I know – I could feel your bumping. You almost put me down one time."

"Sorry 'bout that. I was getting bored."

"I know. But starting tomorrow, you can go as fast as you want. Think of it as a race and it won't be boring. When you think that way, your mind will constantly be alert, looking for ways to shave seconds, pick faster lines, avoid bumps, soft sand, mud or roots. Motocross is more of a mental game than most people realize. You have to constantly be on the lookout at high speed for line choices and so you can make instant decisions on throttle, balance, brakes and lines. In road racing, the track is pretty much always the same, and even though you are going faster, the decision-making is slower."

"So that's why BMX is good training for MX?"

"That, and the cardio, muscle and stamina preparation, which is more important than most kids who race MX realize."

"What do we do now?" Ike asked.

"Eat our sandwiches, go for a swim," Crip replied. "Then you get to ride."

"My Honda? On a track?"

"Yep. With your new friend."

"Skeeter? Now you're talkin'," Ike hooted excitedly.

CHAPTER 27

Skeeter was excited to have a new riding partner. He was ready when they pulled up in the truck.

"Okay, I'm just gonna drop you off and you go have some afternoon fun with him, like you and Mr. Gonzales used to do – play, you know?" Crip explained as he stepped out of the truck.

"Just play, no training?"

"Just have fun, but push yourself to try new things, jump farther, ride faster."

"Okay," Ike said, and turned to Skeeter. "Ready for a ride?"

"Sure. Where ya wanna go?" Skeeter inquired, while gassing up his bike.

"Oh, I don't know. How about the tracks?" Ike looked over at Crip, who nodded approvingly as he pulled down the tailgate.

"That's what I was thinkin'. Maybe hit some trails when we get tired of that," Skeeter offered, checking his chain.

Ike jumped into the back of the truck and tossed his gear bag onto the ground. He could feel his pulse quicken as he reached for the tie-down straps that held his bike in place. In 10 minutes he was dressed, while Crip had prepped his bike.

"I'll leave the tools, fuel and an extra plug right under this tree," Crip announced. "Oh, and here is the ice chest," he added as he pulled it out of the truck.

"How long do we have?" Ike asked.

"Until you run out of fuel or get tired, whichever comes first," Crip declared with a grin.

"So what are *you* gonna do?"

"Go fishing. I'll be on my cell if you need me. Otherwise I'll meet you back here at dark."

"Sweet! Ya heard that, Skeeter? We got all day. Man, I love summer vacation."

"Me, too," Skeeter agreed as he kicked his bike to life.

Less than an hour later, Crip was paddling down a narrow canal among the palmettos, water lilies, cypress and water oaks, headed deep into the swamp. His breathing slowed as he could feel his whole body relax. He just closed his eyes, leaned his head back and soaked up the atmosphere of the deep woods. It reminded him of the careless days of his youth, spent fishing, trapping and hunting with his grandpa. This always happened to him when he got into a boat, alone, in the swamp. Between paddle strokes, he steered the old canoe along the western bank so he could study the trails. Turtles slipped into the water from their perches as he approached. He paused to let a water moccasin cross in front of him, its squiggling motion moving it through the water as if it had somewhere important to go.

Suddenly a loud splash drew his attention up ahead, and a big beaver disappeared under water. He paused to watch. A large, reddish-brown fox squirrel clambered up a vine-covered, long-dead poplar tree, while a snowy egret flapped its white wings against the patches of blue sky above. Then something caught Crip's eye; he had sensed something was out of place. He paddled over to the eastern bank for a closer look. It was a gator foot, sticking out of the underbrush. He pulled the canoe up onto the bank to examine it. When he pulled back a dead branch, a swarm of flies abandoned their treasure: a good-sized gator carcass that had been butchered recently, its hide missing.

"Interesting," Crip mumbled to himself.

After examining the way the gator had been skinned, he moved on to study the ground. He found four different sets of boot prints. He followed the trail for about a half-mile until it disappeared into the bayou. He went back, got his canoe and continued downstream. The canal widened into a bayou. After a few minutes of paddling, the swamp opened up into marshland. The let his gaze wander out across the grassy prairie to scan the horizon. When he was satisfied there was nothing out of place, he nosed the canoe downstream. Just as he turned the next bend, he found more evidence of poachers – gator-bait. He studied the large hooks with fresh chicken parts hanging from the trees over the water on either side of the bayou.

About 30 minutes later, a movement in the sky caught his attention. Raising his hand to shield his eyes from the sun, he observed vultures circling. He watched them for a few minutes, while letting his senses absorb the other sights, sounds and smells of the swamp. Eventually the vultures descended to a place in the marsh where there was a clump of trees. He resumed paddling until the bayou brought him as close to them as the water would allow, and then he pulled the canoe up against the bank. He pulled the canoe out of the water and into the grass to hide it. He grabbed his knapsack and carefully began to make his silent trek across the marsh. Finally he came to a high, dry area in the midst of a pine thicket.

"*Wood smoke,*" Crip thought to himself, sniffing the air. He circled the thicket and watched it for about 15 minutes. When he was convinced no one was there, he began to move in. Avoiding the trail, he made his approach from the downwind side, stepping on leafy areas to avoid leaving sign.

A sudden movement caught his eye. Instinctively, he dropped behind some cover to watch. Then he heard the flap of wings and saw a half-dozen turkey buzzards tussling over the ribcage of a deer. He got up and walked into the thicket, causing the buzzards to hop away to the edge of the tree line. Suddenly one turned and came toward him, clucking and flapping its wings in warning. Crip reached down and picked up a stick. He waved his arms around to scare him away, but the buzzard just got more aggressive, so he flung the stick at the big bird, hitting it in the chest and knocking it over. The bird took off in flight, sending the others into panicked retreat as well.

Crip turned and resumed reading the signs left by the careless visitors. When he got close to the remains of the campfire, he stooped down to study the area. It was obvious that someone had spent a few nights here and had some kind of party. He investigated further and found a large pile of beer cans, many torn in half.

"*Interesting,*" he thought, picking one up and examining it. He picked up a plastic bag and stuffed the can inside. He scanned around and collected a potato chip bag, an empty can of mosquito spray, and a cigarette butt. Then, stuffing them in the pockets of his cargo pants, he poked around some more. He spent some time studying the ashes of the fire, finding some pieces of burnt work gloves, hinges and a lock. These, too, he bagged. He stood back and scanned the perimeter. Then his eyes stopped on something that caused his heart to skip a beat. He went over for a closer look and found a buck's head, mounted on a tree, with Spanish moss draped over it like hair and a pentagram burned into its forehead.

"So,' he thought, ' *you're gonna be* those *kind of guys, eh?*"

Crip made the sign of the cross and kissed his hand, and then continued his investigation. He kicked around a few more bones and pieces of garbage until he was satisfied he had all the clues. When it was time to leave, he followed the footprints, which meandered in a southerly direction. But they stopped near another small canal. He checked the bank and found the docking point of a boat. He took off his sunglasses and reached into his knapsack, fishing around for something in particular. He pulled out two small glass jars and, bending down near the water's edge, placed the opening of the jars over each eye. Then he leaned his body over the water and pushed the bottoms of the jars just below the surface of the water. Now that he had defeated the refraction of the water's surface, he could study the bottom of the canal. He saw footprints, a Redman chewing tobacco bag, a few more beer cans, and a cigarette lighter. Then he got back up and began to examine the bank where the boat had been pulled up. In the mud, he found the imprint of three seams of a flat boat.

He walked around the canal bank and made another discovery. A few feet away, tossed carelessly into the grass, was a mounting block for a trolling motor. Upon closer examination, he noticed that it still had patches of the boat it had been ripped from, and they were red-painted fiberglass – the same color as Doug's boat!

CHAPTER 28

A few miles away, a huge, barrel-chested, unshaven man turned his overloaded skiff from the Tickfaw river up a narrow opening in the trees and slowed as he entered a hidden bayou. About a mile past the next bend, he slowed up at an isolated camp. Two other boats and an airboat were docked under the rusted tin roof of the boat shed. Three men were fishing off the pier, laughing and cursing. He motored up to the pier, almost running over their lines.

"Hey, we're fishing!" a swarthy-faced man complained.

"Shut up and give me a hand with this stuff!" the giant ordered, throwing a line to one of the other men, who tossed his rod aside and began to tie off the boat. The other two men reeled in their lines hurriedly and stood up to get their legs out of the way of the docking boat. The big man stepped out of the boat and onto the dock.

"You know, I had a bite right then," the first man complained. "You could've pulled up over there."

The big man turned and pushed him hard, right in the chest, sending him backward into the water with a splash that sent waves up and down the bayou. He popped back up to the surface, to the laughter of the other three.

"Jim, I'm gonna get you for this!" he muttered angrily.

"Why don't you start right now?" Jim countered, taking a step toward the water.

The man just treaded water, weighing his options as he looked at the bulging muscles of the man standing over him with a scowl on his face.

"But not yet," he spat as he turned to swim over to the bank. Laughter erupted from the three men again.

"Is the boss here?" Jim barked; one of the men just nodded toward the camp. "Get this stuff unloaded," he ordered over his shoulder as he strode up the steps and onto the screened porch. One of the men mumbled a complaint, but they all slowly made their way to the overloaded boat.

Sitting in front of a TV were two men, eyes glued to a wrestling program. One was young, wearing a muscle shirt that revealed tattoos over his bronze shoulders.

Recognizing a wrestler on the television, Jim announced, "I beat both those guys when they were in their prime. Those clowns shouldn't be on TV."

"Hey, Jim, how come you quit?" the young man asked, turning around.

"I got tired of promoters ordering me to let bums like those guys win."

Jim went to the refrigerator and grabbed a drink. Popping the top, he put the can to his mouth and drained the whole beer in one gulp. He tore the can in half and tossed it into the trash can. He looked over at the men on the sofa and let out a long, loud belch. Then he wiped his mouth with his arm, turned, and walked down a narrow hallway, stopping at the door at the end. He knocked, and then opened the door and entered.

Inside, sitting at a desk with his eyes transfixed to a computer screen, was a short, chubby-faced man with a goatee, with a cigarette dangling from his mouth. He was surprisingly well-dressed for a swamper: white slacks and a tropical-island-print short-sleeved shirt, with a white fedora cap cocked to the side on his head.

"I told you *not* to disturb me when the door is closed!" he snapped in a high, nasal voice as he turned in the squeaky chair to face Jim.

Jim just smiled when he saw the gold chains dangling into his hairy chest and the fingers overloaded with rings.

"I knocked," he answered defiantly.

After a long stare-down, the boss broke the silence.

"What'd you get?"

"Some tools, cash, a stereo, TV and DVD player, laptop, silverware and another barbecue pit."

"I told you *not* to fool with the little stuff, like the pit. We already have one."

"But this one has a smoking chamber, and a thermostat."

"I don't care what *you* thought," the boss said, raising his voice. "You are under *orders!*"

Jim rolled his eyes. "I wanted the…"

"I don't care *what* you wanted. We are *not* simple burglars. We have a mission. I've told ya'll before that we are after the land, and that takes money. Money buys people, power and land. Do you understand?"

"Yeah, yeah, but…"

"I am here developing relationships with the right people, making connections to achieve our goals for a greater purpose, and you're out stealing barbecue pits?"

"You didn't complain when we brought in the *more* valuable stuff!" Jim pointed out, *his* voice rising now.

"That is so we can *look* successful and finance our way back to respectability," the boss said. "We need respect, too. Think Robin Hood, not a street thug. When we own this land, we'll have to keep the lines open with the swampers and the Indians. They are *not* our enemies."

"I know, Doc, but if it's right there, we might as well grab it, too," Jim reasoned. "We had room in the boat."

"But the more you steal, the more heat you'll bring on us. And if the right people start looking for us, they'll eventually find us."

Jim looked away; then he sat down in a chair and ran his fingers through his hair.

"What? Wait a minute, you didn't go back to the Indian cop's place again, did you?" Doc challenged him.

"He's got some nice stuff there."

Doc slammed his fist down hard on the desk and stood up to face him.

"I *told* you not to mess with him! Don't you know that he's one of the few people who can find us?"

"He's not gonna find us. We got such a complex system of travel that he'll never..."

"Listen," Doc interrupted. "Don't you know Doug Simon used to be one of the top trackers in Viet Nam, with the Rangers? And he knows this swamp like the back of his hand. He grew up here!"

"I can take care of him if he gets too close," Jim growled in a deep, guttural voice, his countenance changing as if evil itself had taken over.

Doc studied Jim's face and tried to hide his fear as it crept up his back. He could feel the temperature in the room change noticeably, as if another presence had just arrived. He'd felt this before when Jim was in the room.

"Look, Jim, this outfit will be all yours as soon as I can get back into the legislature," Doc said soothingly. "But until then, you've got to be careful. One mistake and we'll all go back, this time for life. Did you like Angola?"

"I'm *never* goin' back there!" Jim spat in a fit of rage, bounding to his feet. He just stared at the boss, as if trying to burn a hole in his soul.

"Well, I can keep you out – *if* I get into power. Do we understand each other?"

Jim's face softened.

"Yeah, I think we understand each other," Jim said with a warning glare.

"Good. The supply boat will be under the power lines in the lake tonight at midnight. We need to transfer more stuff."

"Okay, I'll handle it," Jim said, turning to leave.

"And Jim?"

He turned around at the door.

"What?"

"Don't throw the captain overboard this time, please?"

"But he…" Jim started, but thought better of it. "Okay."

When the door closed, Doc checked his Rolex, then rubbed the diamonds. He sat back down in his chair and lit another cigarette. Then he leaned back and gazed at the certificates on his wall – a master's degree from Harvard, a doctorate in law from LSU – as well as a giant map of the Manchac swamp. Then he looked at the pictures on the other wall. One was of a beautiful woman, the other was a picture of himself in a dark suit, proudly shaking hands with President Obama. He couldn't help smiling.

"It's only a matter of time," he brooded quietly. "Just a matter of time…"

CHAPTER 29

Crip pulled up into Skeeter's driveway at dusk. The bikes were on the stands. The seat was off Ike's bike and he was squeezing out his air filter. Skeeter was spinning his rear wheel, oiling his chain.

"How'd it go today?" Crip inquired as he walked over to Ike.

"Okay," Ike mumbled, without looking up.

Ike had dried blood on his face.

"What happened to you?" Crip asked, pointing to Ike's face.

Ike reached up to feel his forehead.

"Oh, that. Just a scratch. I face-planted on a double this afternoon."

"What happened?"

"He was doing fine, but had a little trouble approaching some jumps," Skeeter explained. "I told him to save it for another day, but he wouldn't let it go. He turned around and went back when we were almost home."

"So you just couldn't wait," Crip surmised.

"I almost had it, but..."

"You backed off at the last second?" Crip finished Ike's sentence for him.

Ike put his head down and walked back to his bike. He fumbled with the filter clamp, but then tossed it away with a growl of frustration. Crip and Skeeter looked at each other.

"He's been like that ever since he crashed," Skeeter confided in a low voice.

Crip walked over and picked up the filter. He brushed it off with his hand and walked over to the bike. Ike was sitting on the ground, wiping his hands and staring at his box. Skeeter was trying to look busy, working on his bike over near the fence. Crip sat down on the ground next to Ike, which prompted Ike to busy himself by wiping off the filter box.

"When I was a kid, I was afraid of the dark," Crip confessed.

Ike just continued working with a scowl on his face.

"Every night I dreaded going to bed because I knew it would take hours of tossing and turning and hiding under the covers, trembling with fear. It was so intense and I felt so helpless that many times I cried myself to sleep."

Ike glanced at him, then returned to his work.

"The worst part was all the negative, scary thoughts I was bringing upon myself. It was like I was my own worst enemy. Then I'd be angry at myself. My childhood was not good, probably because I made bad decisions – many just from lack of sleep, and some to punish myself. Other times I was just a reckless show-off."

Ike paused in his work to give that some thought, then repositioned the rag to use a cleaner part.

"One night was especially bad," Crip recounted. "There was a storm outside and the wind was blowing stuff against the side of the house. Every time it thundered, I jumped. I thought I saw a shadow move through my room and I froze in terror. The shadow looked like the grim reaper, dressed in black, with the hood, sickle and everything."

Ike stopped working.

"What did you do?"

"I started saying the Lord's Prayer. As soon as I started, the apparition disappeared. Then I threw back the covers, jumped out of bed and began to yell at anything and everything that might be in my room."

"What did you yell?"

"For them to come out and face me," Crip said. "I told them I wasn't afraid anymore. It was kinda comical, because here I was, this little kid, standing there in my underwear, yelling for them to come fight me like a man!"

They both started laughing at the thought. Crip got up and got a screwdriver.

"How old were you?" Ike asked.

"Oh, about three," Crip replied innocently.

"Yeah, right. Like I'm six right now," Ike teased.

"Sometimes you act like it," Crip observed.

"So do you," Ike returned.

"That's beside the point," Crip chuckled.

Ike got up and tossed the dirty rag aside.

"Here, you're gonna need this," Crip said, tossing the filter to Ike.

Ike looked at him, and then he stood there a minute, as if trying to decide something. Then he adjusted the clamp, put the filter on, put the seat back on and tightened the bolts. He tossed the tools into the ammo box and secured the lid. Then he wiped his hands on a red rag and looked at Crip.

"You ready?" Ike challenged him matter-of-factly.

Crip nodded and walked back to the truck.

"See ya, Skeeter," Crip called with a wave as he got into the truck.

"Tomorrow?" Skeeter called.

"How about a little earlier? About an hour?" Ike suggested, looking over at Crip, who just nodded and started the truck.

"All right, nine it is," Skeeter said; he waved and continued to wipe off his bike.

The ride home was silent for a while. Suddenly, Crip pulled over to the side of the road.

"What's the matter?" Ike asked.

"I don't know," Crip said. "I think I pulled something when I was ridin' on the trail. You wanna drive?"

"Sure!" Ike responded, jumping out and climbing into the driver's side as Crip limped around to the passenger side.

"You can drive a stick?"

"Learned on a stick," Ike explained. "Don't even *like* automatics."

"I wish this truck was an automatic," Crip said. "It would make it easier on my leg."

Ike adjusted the mirrors and moved the seat up. He put it in gear, revved it once while looking over at Crip, and then eased the clutch out. After a little lurch, they were back under way. Crip looked out the window and tried to hide his smile.

When Ike stopped at Doug's camper, Crip awoke with a start.

"Here we are, safe and sound," Ike said, smiling with delight.

"Okay, you've got one more exercise before supper," Crip announced.

"Aw, but I'm sooooo tired," Ike moaned.

"One more. Follow me."

Crip led Ike over to Doug's woodshed. He went inside and came out with a maul and a chisel.

"Uh oh," Ike frowned.

"Yep, you need to work on upper body strength."

Crip walked over to the woodpile and picked up a chunk of red oak. He placed it on a stump. Then he wound up and delivered a crushing blow to the center of the piece of wood. It split instantly. Ike watched as Crip picked up the split pieces and split them again. Then Crip walked over and picked up a big, knotted piece.

"For one like this, you'll need the chisel."

He placed the chisel in the center of the stump and tapped it with the maul. Then he stood back, wound up, and swung. The blow landed directly on the chisel, sending it about four inches into the wood. Then he struck again, this time sending the chisel six inches further in, and the side of the wood split around the knot, but didn't separate completely. Crip wound up and swung again, and this time the piece split in two.

"I wanna do it," Ike volunteered, stepping in.

Crip picked up the chisel and handed the maul to Ike. Crip set one of the split pieces back on the stump. Ike stepped forward, tapped the chisel into position, and then stood back. He took a swing, but the maul glanced off the side of the chisel.

"Gotta hit it dead in the center, and the handle needs to be parallel with the ground," Crip directed, grabbing the maul and holding it straight out over the chisel.

"I know, I know. Gimme that," Ike demanded.

Ike put the head on the chisel and then wound up and swung. This time he drove the chisel deep into the wood, tearing it in two.

"So you *have* done this before!" Crip exclaimed, smiling proudly.

"We heat with wood," Ike responded.

"Nothing like a wood stove to warm a house," Crip said.

"Nice, dry heat," Ike jested as he picked up the other piece.

"Free fuel," Crip added.

"How much do you want me to do?" Ike asked, as he paused and leaned on the maul.

"The whole pile," Crip commanded, with a wave to the woodpile. Then he turned to walk back to the camper.

"The whole pile?" Ike gasped. "There must be three cords here!"

"You don't have to do it all tonight," Crip called back over his shoulder. "But when it's done, you'll get paid, and I'll take you out to eat."

"How much? Eat what?"

"One hundred dollars, pizza."

"Oh, it's on now!" Ike laughed, turning and picking up the biggest, knotti-est piece he could see. "It's on now! Hey, Crip, what we doin' tomorrow?" he called after Crip, who was almost to the camper.

"Same exact thing, only put your heart into it, and I want 110 percent!"

"You got it!" Ike yelled triumphantly, and then he turned back to his work.

"And that, ladies and gentlemen, is how we will roll to a championship!" Ike announced to an imaginary audience.

CHAPTER 30

The next day, Crip and Ike were on the bicycle trail at 7 a.m. Crip led until he turned off down a narrow trail. He signaled Ike to continue on, and Ike nodded, picking up his pace. Crip took the shortcut back to the truck to wait. By the time Ike got back, he was sweating bullets.

"One hour, 35 minutes. Try to knock at least five minutes off every day," Crip advised, resetting the bezel on his dive watch.

Ike grabbed a seat on the tailgate while Crip handed him a water.

"How much water are you drinking a day?" Crip asked.

"I don't know."

"About?"

"Probably two gallons."

"Double that."

"Hey, how come you know these trails so good?"

"'Cause this is where I learned to ride when I was a kid," Crip confided. "My dad was always out in the swamp, hunting, fishing or trapping, as long as the sun was up, and sometimes at night. I would get up early and ride my little minibike out here all through these woods."

"A minibike? You mean those little lawn-mower engines with no suspension and the centrifugal clutch?"

"That's the one. I had a good year trapping with my dad and was able to buy a Yamaha DT1, 100, the little enduro."

"Oh, Mr. Gonzales has one of those, with the green tank and the curved pipe?"

"Yep, only I rebuilt it for serious dirt. I mounted knobby tires, removed the silencer and lights, and put number plates on it. I rode that thing for hours and hours. I'd bring a can of gas, a few tools and a jug of water, and drop them right over there," Crip recalled, pointing. "That was before they put this road in. Doug had an SL125 and did the same thing."

"The Honda? Those look cool. Wasn't that Honda's first dirt bike?"

"Well, yeah, the SL70, which I always wanted. Doug always got the first and best bikes. I got his hand-me-downs."

"Ya'll must've had fun out here. Did ya'll race?"

"Every time two or more guys get on dirt bikes, they eventually *have* to race," Crip chuckled.

"Who was faster?"

"At first, he was. He was older and had the bigger and better bikes. But that made me mad and I got tired of getting left behind. So I learned to push my bikes harder to keep up. Then I discovered that passing him made me happy – *very* happy!"

They both laughed.

"How old were you then?" Ike asked.

"Doug was 11, I was 8."

"You beat him when you were 8 years old?"

"No, not until I was 9. But once I started beating him, then I made sure to *always* beat him. Winning is addicting. Plus, you begin to see yourself as a fast rider, so you live up to that reputation. It gave me confidence in everything else."

"So you raced?"

"Yeah," Crip replied, getting up. "Come on, we gotta get you over to Skeeter's."

Ike climbed into the cab and pressed the point further.

"Tell me about your racing career."

"No."

"Why not?"

"Didn't I tell you not to ask why?"

"Yeah, but you told me not to ask you 'why,' not 'why not', right?" Ike retorted with a twinkle in his eyes.

"Okay, new rule: Never ask me about my racing career. I didn't make a career out of it anyway."

"Why not?"

Crip slammed on the brakes and pulled to the side of the road.

"Get out!"

"What? Why?"

"Because of that right there."

"What?"

"The 'why' question. Thirty push-ups, now!"

"In the gravel?"

"Yep."

Ike opened the door and dropped down. When he was done with the push-ups, he got back into the truck with a scowl on his face. They rode in silence all the way to Skeeter's.

Each day was the same. For two weeks they got up early, took the bicycle ride, and then Crip would drop Ike and his bike off at Skeeter's to ride all day. Sometimes Ike and Skeeter would join Ziptie's team riders on the tracks. In the evenings, Crip brought Ike back to Doug's to split firewood. Crip always scouted the swamp while Ike was riding, or so Ike thought. Actually, every once in a while, Crip would borrow one of Doug's dirt bikes to go spy on Ike to check on his improvement. Many days, Crip brought home fish, crawfish and wild plants to eat for supper. Some nights they would eat with Doug and his wife. A few times, Doug took them out on his lake skiff for some fishing and exploring.

On some evenings, Crip took Ike canoeing, setting a brisk pace for exercise, and showing Ike the swamp. It didn't take Ike long to learn the main landmarks: Lizard Creek, Blood River, Rose Mound, and the Old Carter Plantation. Ike began to take longer boat rides with Doug and Crip down the Natalbany to the Tickfaw and out into Lake Maurepas. Then they would explore around Jones Island, through North Pass, Stinking Bayou, Middle Bayou and back through the marsh to Owl Bayou. Some Sundays, after church, they would start at the headwaters of a river and explore it all the way down to the lake: the Amite River, Blind River, Ruddock Canal and Pass Manchac. They fished and ran crab traps, and Doug showed them his trout lines, hoop traps and slat traps. Ike became fond of the time they spent together, and especially of hearing Doug and Crip's stories of how the early swampers had eked out a living and raised their families.

One evening they were coming in from a boat ride to the lake when Ike asked more about the swampers. Doug slowed the boat down as they entered the mouth of the river.

"They usually live in small camps or houseboats," he began. "They work according to the seasons: They hunt waterfowl, rabbits, squirrels and deer in the winter; they trap mink, otter or beaver. They fish in the summer, catching catfish, flounder, trout or bass. They catch crawfish and shrimp in the spring. They have truck gardens where they grow cabbage, okra, tomatoes, beans, squash and cucumbers, then bring their extra produce to the French Market to sell in New Orleans."

"Our grandfather cut cypress trees," Crip interjected. "Our father was a mechanic for the lumber company, keeping the steam skidders running when there was work. They lived on the quarter-boats and worked on the skidder boats. They fished to feed the crew. They could literally do anything with their hands. They'd been bitten by poisonous snakes so many times, they were immune."

After a few minutes of silence; Doug continued, "The hard part has been bringing the Choctaw into the 20th century. It took a lot to retrain our young people to stay in school, learn modern trades and adapt to living in cities. Many never made it. Some stayed in the swamp. Others turned to alcohol or drugs, wrecking their lives. But a few went on to college or trade careers and came back here to invest in the next generation."

"So that's why you live here?" Ike inquired.

"Pretty much," Doug said. "And I just love it here. You can take the man out of the swamp, but you can't take the swamp out of the man. So I have one foot in the past and one in the future; one in the Choctaw culture and one in the white man's culture. When you help others succeed, *you* succeed."

Ike thought for a few moments, then asked, "So how does Ziptie fit in with his racing teams?"

"Motorcycle racing is one of the few activities that hold the attention of the teenage boys. It's a bridge to them, so good men can speak truth into their lives and guide them through the challenges of growing up straight. But there's also other sports that are popular with our tribe. Ken Kelsey has a karate dojo with a team that travels around the country, fighting in tournaments. I have other plans in the works, if we can get the leaders, for a bow-hunting club, a wrestling team, a car mechanics' club, a boat-building program, a scuba diving club, all associated with the high school. One day the football, baseball, basketball, track, rugby, soccer and cross-country teams will all compete at a very high level. I think many of the kids will have an opportunity to cross-train in two or three or even four sports. Our success will be dependent on our leaders. I have my eye on a few good men who could coach several different sports. I'm working on them. I believe leadership development will bring health to our tribe. Other tribes will come and see our programs and use them as a blueprint to help their own kids."

They motored up the river in silence for a few minutes, deep in thought, the droning of the outboard motor breaking the stillness of the swamp.

"I'd like to help," Ike announced suddenly.

"We will need all the help we can get," Doug replied with a smile.

"What would you like to do?" asked Crip.

"Become a coach or a teacher."

"Are you a good student?" probed Doug, who looked at Ike, and then at Crip with a wink.

"Well, not yet."

"How are you doin' in school?" Doug continued.

"Well, I, uhhh, failed 10th grade this year," Ike admitted, hanging his head.

"Ike, you've got to be a good student before you can be a good teacher," Doug tried to explain. "You've got to have some knowledge before you can teach. You can't export something you don't already have. Does this make sense?"

"I guess so. But I'll do better next year."

"Check back with me then. If you graduate with decent grades, we'll put you in somewhere."

"Right now I want to train for MX racing. But in the fall, I'll focus on school."

"You've got something else you need to learn before you go home, before you race again, before you can succeed at anything else," Crip cautioned.

"What's that?"

"You know deep in your heart what it is, you just have to name it," Crip stated with tender authority.

They rode on in silence, engrossed in the pink-and-purple sky they could see through the canopy of the trees above as they snaked their way upriver.

CHAPTER 31

∾

The sun had set, and they were almost back to the dock. With only the running lights on, they were mesmerized by the low, throaty moan of the outboard motor, each absorbed in his own thoughts. Suddenly the boat slammed into a steel cable suspended across the bayou, sending everyone flying forward. Crip was knocked unconscious on the dash, Doug got his arm hung up in the steering wheel while flipping over the console, and Ike was thrown completely out of the boat and into the black water.

Immediately, a man stepped from behind the trees and waded into the water. Another man came over in a boat. They both jumped aboard; one was wearing a gun in a holster, and the other was wielding a knife. Ike scrambled up onto the bank and hid behind a tree and watched helplessly as Doug faced the men alone.

Doug knew instantly that his right arm was broken, but he braced for the fight.

The attacker lunged at Doug with his knife, but Doug managed to twist away at the last second, causing the knife to miss his heart, but it sliced off a piece of his good arm, right at the bicep. Doug scrambled to his feet, pulling his own knife out of his boot with his left hand, his right arm dangling at an awkward angle, the bone showing through his skin, blood already soaking his shirt and trickling down to his pants.

"Move out of the way, Jim," one of the men bellowed. "Let me shoot him!"

"No, this is the one they were talking about. *I* want him," Jim growled, crouching forward, tossing the knife back and forth between his hands.

Doug stared at his opponent, and then repositioned the knife in his hand from offensive to defensive, the blade backward in his hand, along his wrist. He feinted upward, causing the attacker to step back, putting him at a perfect distance for a front kick, which he placed right in the man's solar plexus, knocking him back against the other man, who dropped his gun into the water. They both jumped up to face Doug, who turned and feinted again, this time causing the gunman to fall against the side of the boat.

"Watch him, Jim, he's good!" the man screamed in a panic.

"I got him, Lucius," Jim spat, twisting the knife around in his hand, faking one way, then the other.

Doug studied him briefly and then came down with a slicing blow, which the man blocked with the knife. They started sparring with the knives, blocking and slicing, the sounds of metal on metal echoing off the silent trees. Suddenly, Jim punched Doug in his broken bone, sending him sprawling back across the deck with a groan. Immediately, Jim jumped on him, bringing the knife down for a stab, but Doug blocked it with the sharp side of his blade on Jim's wrist, prompting a wail of pain.

Doug sliced at his knee, opening a deep gash, sending Jim to his knees. Doug kicked him in the mouth, sending him backward and knocking his knife all the way to the riverbank.

Lucius caught Doug from behind in a bear hug, the searing pain from Doug's broken arm sucking strength from his body, causing his legs to buckle as he let out a yell. Then, using his good arm for leverage, Doug pulled up while dropping down out of the hold. Then, turning, he smashed his elbow to his opponent's jaw, knocking him back. Before Doug could finish him with a back slice, the boat's anchor came down on his head, knocking him down and senseless. Doug dropped his knife and clutched at his head, while the man began to beat Doug with the anchor.

"Let's get outta here. Come on, Jim!" Lucias shouted, staring at Doug's and Crip's still bodies.

Ike, who had been watching helplessly, scrambled over and picked up the discarded knife from the bushes and stood there, watching in horror. He just froze. He couldn't move; he just stood there, holding the knife. Jim looked over at Ike on the bank.

"Come here, kid," he demanded, gruffly.

Ike turned and ran. Jim jumped out of the boat into the shallow water with the anchor in his hand. He climbed up the bank and began to chase Ike, who was struggling through the briars. Jim got closer, bringing the anchor up for a blow, while Ike tore at the briar patch furiously.

Right when Jim was about to bring the anchor down to strike Ike, the rope ran out of slack, tearing the anchor out of his hand; which dropped harmlessly to the ground. When Jim looked back at the anchor, Ike found a way through the patch and took off at a dead run, still clutching the knife.

"Come here, kid, you can't get away!" Jim yelled as he started the pursuit.

But Ike was smaller, quicker and more nimble, and he opened up a big gap. Soon the man started to tire, and he slowed to a walk. Ike continued to run until he almost stepped on a big gator, guarding the eggs in her nest. Ike jumped over her, grabbed a low-lying limb of a gum tree and pulled himself up. He dropped the knife to grab the limb, but he concentrated on getting as far from the double danger as he could. When he was 20 feet off the ground, he saw the man coming. He looked over at the knife in the gator nest, and then looked back at his pursuer.

Jim was slowing down, looking around, following his trail, when he heard the gator's warning call. He froze. He took another step and looked on the ground in front of him and there, five feet ahead, was the nest with the big gator. They saw each other at the same time. The gator lunged at him as he turned and ran, squealing like a little girl. The gator caught a piece of his pants leg, tripping him. But he tore it loose and got up and ran again, the gator right behind him. In a panic, Jim retraced his steps back to the bayou. The gator, having sensed the danger to her nest was over, stopped and opened her mouth with a hiss, revealing rows of teeth as a parting warning. Jim jumped in his boat, where Lucius was waiting.

Once Jim was safely aboard, he turned and growled at Ike, still hidden in the foliage: "Kid, if you say anything – I mean *anything* – to anyone about this, I'm gonna come after you and drag you back here and skin you alive. Then I'll feed you to that gator. You hear me? I'll get your family, too. I promise! I know you can hear me!"

"Come on, Jim, let's get outta here," Lucius pleaded, starting the motor. "Did he get a look at you?"

"Yeah, but I'll get him later. I know where to find him. He's scared," Jim muttered, putting a rag on his bleeding wrist.

"I know where you live!" Jim shouted as the boat turned around and headed back downriver.

"I know where you live!" echoed off the trees as the boat disappeared around the bend.

CHAPTER 32

When the gator returned, she didn't notice that the knife was missing. Ike was already down at the water's edge, having used a different route to get back to the boat. When he got there, Crip was hovering over Doug, trying to assess his condition.

"How is he?" Ike panted anxiously.

"He's not breathing. He's barely got a pulse. We've got to get him to a hospital right now!" Crip said as he began CPR, carefully working around Doug's wounds. "Start the motor!"

"I gotta get the anchor in," Ike shouted. "It's all the way up into the bushes!"

Crip looked at Ike, then the bank, and then he jumped up and pulled his knife and with one swipe cut the anchor rope.

"Now start the motor and get us upstream!"

Ike started the motor and pointed the boat upriver. Crip strained at the cable, stretching it up high enough for the boat to pass under it.

"Stay in the middle of the river and slow down for the blind turns!"

Ike did his best to maneuver the boat through the darkness while Crip worked feverishly on his brother.

"Did you get a good look at them?" Crip yelled.

"I don't know. Kind of," Ike stammered.

Crip noticed that Ike was shaking, and asked, "You all right?"

"I, uh… guess so."

Just then they almost hit a downed tree, and Ike turned the wheel at the last second, sending them off balance and against the side of the boat.

"Focus! Focus on the river, Ike. Come on! Forget about what just happened!"

"I can't!" Ike yelled.

"Yes you can. Keep your bearing!"

"I'm trying!"

Crip looked back at Doug's still, bloody face.

"Stay with us, Doug! Stay with us!"

In 15 minutes they were at the dock; 20 minutes more and they were at the hospital. Crip passed Doug to the ER crew and gave them all the necessary information. When he had done all he could, he was pushed out of the emergency room. Crip went to the phone and made three calls: one to Victor Gonzales, one to Doug's wife, and one to his pastor. By midnight, they were all huddled in the waiting room, along with a few more close friends and family members. They prayed and talked in low tones throughout the night.

At 5:30 a.m., a doctor came in with a long look on his face. He walked up to Crip, who was holding Mary's hand. They all stood in anticipation of the bad news.

"I'm sorry. There was nothing we could do," the doctor said solemnly. "His head trauma was too severe, and he'd lost too much blood. We couldn't save him."

Mary let out a long, pained moan, and then broke into tears. Everyone pulled up into a group hug as the doctor excused himself.

They cried.

CHAPTER 33

Ike was the only one who didn't join in the hug. He felt all alone. He couldn't cry. He just retreated down into himself.

Three days later, at the funeral, there was standing room only. The whole tribe had come out to pay their respects. Not only was Doug popular within the tribe, he was a celebrity outside the tribe, as he was their spokesman to the outside world. He was friends with the leaders of Springfield, having cooperated with them to create good programs for young people. It was the young men who were the most shaken, as Doug had been a coach, fundraiser and leader for more than 30 years, after he returned from the war. Many Choctaw who had left the reservation and found success had returned to pay their respects to Doug, who had influenced them greatly.

Overflow rooms had been set up in the Lions Club and VFW halls to broadcast the live video feed of the service from the funeral home. Many businesses in Springfield shut down and displayed American flags at half-mast, with a lone, black ribbon tied to the flagpole, below the flag.

It was the biggest military funeral ever held in south Louisiana, with a detachment from Fort Polk serving as the color guard, with full honors. Many in attendance wore little American-flag lapel pins on a black background.

After the preliminaries, Doug's pastor got up to speak. He shuffled his notes, held them up to read, but a wave of sadness overcame him and he had to put the papers on the podium and take a handkerchief out of his pocket to wipe his eyes. He regained his composure and started to read. But he couldn't. He made a couple of unsuccessful starts as he fought back the tears.

"Come on, Pastor, you can do it," one of the deacons stated from the first pew. A few others chimed in their encouragement. The pastor nodded and looked at his notes again. After a few tension-filled moments of silence, he broke down again. His wife got up from the front pew and ascended the steps to join him. She put her arm around him and began to pray.

"Heavenly Father, I ask You to give Mike the words and the strength to speak them. You have us all here for a holy moment of remembrance and perspective. Please bring Your divine purpose out of this tragedy. In Jesus' name, amen."

Pastor Mike turned and gave her a hug, and then took his notes up one more time. He stared at them for a few seconds, but then put them down. He folded them back up and slipped them into the inside of his coat pocket. Then he sighed and looked at the ceiling, and then at the faces in the crowd, and he began to speak.

"The Springfield band of Choctaw Indians is like a big magnolia tree. It has grown from where it was planted by God many, many years ago. It has scars from the difficulties and trials it has faced over times past, but it has survived. It has been blown over but not down by hurricane-force winds of change. It has suffered the drought of economic hardship but has lived. It has been assaulted by the disease of evil ideas that tried to take the Choctaw off the true path. It has been attacked by the saws of greedy men, but still stands. The tree has grown through the fall of decline, the winter of want, the spring of promise and the summer of plenty. It has provided shade, food and refuge for its young and old, orphans and widows, sick and weak. There have been many beautiful, white flowers that have sprung from this magnolia, but none more sweet in fragrance, rich in color, and big in generosity than Doug Simon."

When he said that, a wave of unrestrained grief swept over the church, an eruption of moans of deep anguish and cries of pain, even from big, brawny men. People leaned upon one another and bawled, trying to comfort one another at the same time. Pastor Mike paused and let the expression of loss run its course for a couple of minutes. Then he held his hands up to bring them back to attention before he continued.

"As is the course of nature, the flower gives off its sweet aroma, makes the transfer of pollen to ensure new life, then dies. It falls to the ground as a seed. In one of the great mysteries of God, the flower must die to make the seed that produces the beginning of new life. Doug is a seed that will bring forth a new, healthy tree of sustenance for those to follow. Just as our Lord died was buried, and then rose again in resurrection power, so too must we die to our self-centeredness and selfishness to make room for the resurrection power of God in us to produce a seed of new life, which will grow into a new tree that will also be a blessing to those around us. What you will see in the coming months and years is new life from Doug's seed; new commitments from people to pick up the mantle of Choctaw leadership in our community. New programs will spring forth to help this people. There will be new ideas and resources to fulfill Doug's dream of bringing our people into a new era of modern living, where our families are secure and healthy and our children are equipped for life and work. This, as you know, was Doug's passion: the young people being guided, encouraged and equipped for life as successful adults. Let us all look within to what we have, then without to what we can do, and up for the power and direction to do it. Let us look at Doug Simon's life as an example of a life well lived, a man who made a difference in his generation, his mission accomplished. Let his life inspire us to new heights of service to our fellow man."

Then pastor Mike gazed out across the sea of faces.

"Let's pray.

"Father of all compassion and love, Giver and Taker of life, Architect of the universe, we ask for Your will to be done through this time, in our lives and in our community. You were not taken by surprise, You have everything under control, but help us to see it. Give us *Your* perspective. Help us to view this from *Your* eternal understanding. God, they meant this for evil, but *You* can bring *Your* good and perfect will from this. Give us the faith we need to deal with this. Give us the hope we need to move on. Give us the strength to get through this trial. We pray for these men that are blinded by evil, that You would discipline them and save their souls. Please give us the grace to forgive, and become victors instead of victims. We entrust Doug into Your loving arms and look forward to the day when we can be reunited with him in the new heaven and new earth. In Jesus' holy name, amen."

There was a deafening silence as Pastor Mike left the podium. Everyone was still processing this message. The funeral director cleared his throat, looked over at the ushers, and stood up to give the final instructions. Ike didn't remember anything else that was said. He only remembered the emptiness he felt as the pallbearers rolled the casket out the side door to the black hearse. Mr. Gonzales put his hand on Ike's shoulder and gave him a gentle shake. Then he reached over and hugged Crip, who appeared to be in shock. The family began to file out at the head of the line to the waiting car.

A long procession made its way to Carter Cemetery. There, Doug was buried with a 21-gun salute. There was not a dry eye in the crowd as the color guard handed the carefully folded American flag to Lacey. He thanked her on behalf of a grateful nation.

Ike pondered all these things in his heart.

CHAPTER 34

The next week was a blur for Ike. It was as if he were sleepwalking through a nightmare. Even though his mom, Mr. Gonzales, Sam and her dad had come up to spend a few days, Ike had raised his emotional walls higher and was isolating himself more and more. One by one, each tried to talk with Ike about his grief, and reason with him about getting back to training, about riding, but to no avail.

"I don't care about motocross anymore," Ike would say; then he would go get a canoe and paddle out into the swamp. He would be gone all day, and sometimes into the night.

One evening, as the sun was setting, Ike was sitting in the canoe against the riverbank, paddle across his knees, his head in his hands, crying. Suddenly a pair of wood ducks that had been swimming cautiously nearby exploded out of the water, flapping their wings in alarm as they slowly gained altitude and disappeared over the cypress trees. Ike looked upriver and squinted his eyes, looking for the cause of the alarm. Then he saw Crip come paddling around the bend in Doug's pirogue. Ike quickly wiped the tears away and sat up.

"I thought I'd find you here," Crip said as he glided up next to Ike's canoe and grabbed the gunwale to hold the boats together. "You all right?"

"Yeah, as good as could be expected," Ike replied, looking away to hide his red eyes.

"Hey, I've been crying, too. Real men cry – at the right times. You *should* be grieving. It's healthy to get it out. The soul has to bleed."

"I know, it's just – it doesn't make sense. Why Doug? Besides Mr. Gonzales, he's the best man I ever knew."

"I've been asking that question, too. Some things we won't know the answer to this side of heaven. Maybe Doug had lived his life so well that he graduated."

Ike cast him a questioning look.

"Graduated? From what?"

"From life," Crip stated simply. "See, we all have a purpose in this life. We were put in this generation, in this time in history, to fulfill a certain purpose. Our life is a growing, changing puzzle piece. Maybe he grew to full maturity for his purpose, fulfilled it, and finished his life at a young age. Not everyone lives to be 70."

"But that's not fair. There were so many people that were depending on him. So many lives were changed. He had so much more to do."

"Maybe the growth of our tribe had plateaued because Doug was doing all the work. Now that God has removed him, other people will step up to fulfill *their* purposes. I know there were potential leaders being lazy, and letting Doug do all the work. I am one of them."

Ike looked at Crip. A tear was rolling down his cheek, but he made no move to wipe it away. It was as if he wanted Ike to see it.

"I should have been here, helping him with these kids," Crip lamented. "I've been knowing it. But I've been running from it for years."

"But why?"

"Selfishness."

A flock of geese flew across the sky in a V formation, honking as if to tell Ike and Crip to notice the sunset, which they did. They stared at the purple and pink cloud swirls for several minutes.

Crip swatted a mosquito from his face and said, "It's God's pruning shears."

"What?"

"Did you notice that fig tree in front of Doug's house?"

"The gigantic one that the birds are in all the time?"

"Yep. Doug planted it 15 years ago. A few times a year, he would go out with shears and cut off branches. Some of the branches were bearing fruit, but he cut them off anyway. You know why?"

"No, why?"

"To make it more fruitful. God does that in our lives, too. He takes things away. He removes things that are bad and things that are good for a reason. He is helping us mature to bear more fruit in our lives."

"But that's not fair, to take our stuff away."

"Life's not fair. Get over it!" Crip scolded gruffly, his voice rising; then, slowly, the expression on his face calmed, became more peaceful. "God is God, not you, not me. He knows everything; we know very little. But one thing I've learned: He's good, He loves us and we can trust Him to do the right thing for our long-term good."

"Has He ever let you down?"

"Never," Crip sighed; after thinking about something, he added, "But there were times when I sure was confused about what He was doin'."

"Like now?"

"Like now."

They watched the last remnants of the sun disappear over the marsh, amid the chattering of the ducks and birds around them.

"You have unfinished business here," Crip observed, looking Ike in the eyes.

"What do you mean?"

"You know what I mean. You still haven't named it and faced it."

"Named what?"

"Look deep inside of you. It's been driving you for years. It's almost near the surface, so now is the time to flush it out and deal with it."

"What? I'm just grieving, like you said."

"No. There's something more. Unless you deal with it, you've wasted your trip. Unless you defeat it, you'll never race or jump with the freedom and courage you need to succeed. You'll never reach your dream, or fulfill your purpose, while it lingers in your soul."

"What is it, Crip? Just tell me!" Ike demanded, his voice rising.

"I can't. Only you can."

"What should I do then?"

"Stay out here in the swamp until it surfaces, then nail it. Name it, confront it, conquer it. But you can't do it with your own power. You must turn it over to God, completely. Let Him handle it. You must be willing to turn your whole life, future and even your dream over to Him. Then, if He lets you keep it, if it is still on your heart, then you have the power to reach it – His power. Because then it becomes His battle. Then you can rest in His purpose for your life."

"How long will it take?"

"Depends on how prideful and stubborn you are. It took *me* a week."

"A week? Out here with no food and water?"

"There's food and water out here. You know that."

Crip dropped a gallon of fresh water, some insect repellent, and his knife into Ike's canoe, and then pushed off, picking up his paddle and turning back upriver.

"So that's it, just like that?" Ike called out.

"It's between you and God," Crip called over his shoulder.

"But what if it gets cold, or it rains?"

"In June?" Crip snorted. "Rain, maybe. But no cold. I did mine in January. You wouldn't want to try that."

"But you're a man!"

"You are what you think you are. I think you're a man, too," Crip called back between paddle strokes.

"How do you know if you're a man?" Ike called out.

"I'll tell you the measure of a man when you come back in," Crip called back over his shoulder as he disappeared around the bend.

"Okay?" Ike asked sarcastically as he looked down at his meager provisions.

CHAPTER 35

Three days later, Ike paddled up to Doug's dock with a serene look on his face. He put the canoe away, went into the trailer and showered, and then went to bed. He slept better than he ever had before. He woke up the next day to the smell of bacon and coffee. He stood up, stretched, and put his clothes on. He walked into the kitchen, where Crip was making breakfast.

"Slept good, didn't you?"

"Yep, best ever."

"Then you named it," Crip said, and turned to look at him.

"Yep."

"What was it?"

"What do you think it was?" Ike asked as he poured a cup of coffee.

"Fear – but I don't know of what," Crip answered as he turned off the stove and put the breakfast on the table.

"Fear of losing control and what others think of me," Ike confessed, as he looked out the window into the bright sunshine of the new day.

"You turn it all over to Him?"

"Yep."

"All of it?"

"Yep."

"Your past, present and future?"

"Yes, I did. Did you?" Ike replied, turning the questions back on Crip.

Crip was caught off guard.

"Sure, at that time, but it's also an ongoing process, as I make mistakes, and get forgiven and give it up to Him, then take it back, then suffer consequences, then give it back."

"I was wondering how that worked with imperfect people like me."

"… and me," Crip chuckled. "Let's eat."

"Yeah, two imperfect guys, just eating eggs and bacon," Ike smiled.

"Two men, spilling coffee, eating too fast, burning their mouths."

"Making a mess on the table."

"Slopping food around the kitchen. But it's all right."

"Yeah, you'll clean it up."

"No, I cooked, so *you* clean," Crip continued, eating the eggs with gusto.

"Crip?"

"Yeah?"

"So what's the measure of a man?"

"What do you think it is?"

"Well, some of my friends think it's how big or strong he is, how well he can fight or put others down or curse, smoke, drink, or how much money or stuff he has, or how pretty his girlfriend is."

"None of that," Crip noted. "I know lots of big baby boys that have all that stuff."

"Then what is it?"

"What do *you* think it is?" Crip asked, looking Ike dead in the eyes.

"I think..." Ike looked at the ceiling, stopped eating and waited. Then he stared out of the window for a long moment. "The amount of sacrifice a guy is willing to make," Ike finally said, and then looked at Crip for a response.

Crip stared at Ike, silently signaling him to go on.

"You know, the responsibilities he is willing to take," Ike added.

"For who? For what? You're getting close," Crip replied, trying to lead him further.

"For his dream?" Ike guessed.

"No. 'Cause some dreams are purely selfish and can be bad, like a drug lord or an evil dictator wanting more power or money," Crip explained.

"What is it then?" Ike asked.

"Jesus said the greatness of a man is not the number of people who serve him, but the number of people he serves," Crip reflected. "So, once a man exchanges his agenda for God's, then he has a divine purpose for his life that God designed him for."

Crip put his fork down and leaned forward for emphasis.

"Then that man will sacrifice, pick up responsibilities and work hard toward his dream. God will then get behind it and help."

Ike reached for another biscuit and buttered it. Then he put it in his mouth, chewing on the thought in his mind as he chewed his biscuit, pondering the implications and how this all related to him. They ate in silence for a full two minutes. Ike was first to break the silence.

"So how does a man stay focused on his dream?"

"Audience of one," Crip answered.

"What?"

"Audience of one," Crip repeated. "It simplifies everything. Instead of trying to please all the people around him, which confuses him..."

"…and is impossible," Ike interrupted.

"Right. Confusion also leads to hesitation and indecision," Crip added. "But audience of one means you just relax and live your life out for God. It's so much simpler that way."

Crip grabbed the last biscuit and began to put butter on it.

"Take lying, for instance. It may be tougher to say the truth, in love, but it simplifies everything."

"I like that. Audience of one!" Ike declared joyfully, raising his milk glass for a toast.

"Audience of one!" Crip seconded, toasting with his coffee cup, grinning broadly.

They both drank heartily, then put their drinks down hard for emphasis. Ike stuffed more bacon into his mouth while pouring some milk. Crip let out a monster belch that caused Ike to look up from his food with alarm.

"Crip! You could have given me a warning," he teased.

"Life don't give no warnings," Crip laughed, and he reached over and grabbed the milk carton and began to pour some into his glass. This time Ike let go a sharp, loud belch that caused Crip to over-pour and miss the glass. He set the milk down and glared at Ike.

"What goes around, comes around," Ike announced with a broad grin.

Crip squinted his eyes and pointed to Ike as if about to give a warning, but he had nothing to say. Then they both broke out into howls of laughter.

CHAPTER 36

Sam convinced her dad to let her spend another week with Lacey, to be closer to Ike, fearing that he might do something stupid. Ike's mom and Mr. Gonzales wanted to stay another week, but Crip wouldn't hear of it.

"Why let your business go down?" Crip reasoned with Mr. Gonzales. "I'll cover Ike."

"But *you're* grieving, too," Tricia pointed out. "Besides, I want to be close to my son."

"I understand, but the closer you get, the further he'll move away right now. He needs some alone time to get his head together," Crip pressed.

"But too much time alone is bad for him, too," Mr. Gonzales stated. "He can start thinking wrong without someone to correct him."

"And watch him," Tricia added.

"I understand, but I'm tellin' you, if I were in his shoes, I'd slip out into the swamp so I could hear myself think. I wouldn't want anybody to do my thinking for me," Crip said, as he started sharpening his knife.

"I have an idea," Sam spoke up, holding up a finger. "Why don't we ask Ike who *he* wants to stay?"

They all looked at each other and nodded.

"Not a bad idea. Where is he?" Mr. Gonzales asked.

"He's chopping firewood," Crip said, nodding toward the woodpile.

"I'll go get him," Sam volunteered, jumping up and grabbing her sandals. Before anyone could protest, the screen door slammed and she was skipping off the porch.

When she got to the woodpile, Ike had a good-sized pile of split wood next to him. He looked up and she saw his red eyes, with sweat pouring down his temples and forehead. He went back to splitting wood with a vengeance, working with machine-like efficiency. Sam took a seat and watched him for a while. Finally, Ike sank the maul deep into the chopping block and wiped his face on his already soaked shirt. He took a pull from his water bottle and eyed Sam suspiciously. Finally, she spoke.

"That's good."

"What is?" he asked.

"What you are doin', working out."

"You mean working out my body, or working out my anger?"

"Both."

Ike took a seat on a chunk of wood, and then drank some more water, pouring some on his head.

"Got a question for you," Sam began.

"Yes?"

"We were just in there, discussing who should stay and who should go home."

"And the question?"

"Who do you want near you?"

"I don't care."

"Ike."

"What?"

"We all feel like we should stay."

"No."

"'No' what?"

"'No ma'am'?"

"Funny. Do you mean 'no' to everyone staying?"

"Yes."

"So you want everyone to leave."

"They should get back to work. *I* should get back to work," he stated uncaringly as he got up to grab another piece of wood.

"Ike?"

"What?"

"Do you still want to race?"

Silence.

"Ike?"

"I'm thinking."

He pulled the maul out of the stump and placed a piece of wood on it. Then he paused, wiped his hands on his pants, and then came down with a crushing blow. He went to pick up another piece of wood and placed it on the stump. Then he paused, looked up into the sky.

"Do *you* want to race anymore?"

Sam wasn't ready for that. She thought for a moment, and finally stammered, "I… uhhh… don't know either."

"Neither do I. Not right now."

He went back to chopping wood.

"What are your plans?" she asked.

"I want to stay here, with Crip. This is my new home."

"Ike?"

"What?"

"What makes you happy?"

Ike kept working. On the third piece, he paused again.

"I guess... I guess riding with Skeeter. That was fun. Actually..."

"What?"

"You would like it, too."

"So, you want me to stay."

"I didn't say that."

"In a roundabout way, you want me to come back with my bike," she teased, starting to smile.

"You can do what you want. I'm just sayin' you would like it."

"But I don't really... I mean, I don't like the swamp."

"Why not?"

"I have one word for you: mosquitoes, snakes, bugs, mud, poison ivy..."

Ike interrupted, "*One* word?"

"It's all the same thing."

Ike smiled.

"We have the best training tracks around, and the best jumps and the best riders in the state."

Silence.

Ike went back to work.

"Ike?"

"What?"

He paused in mid-wind-up.

"Does this place have a mall?"

"...Sure does." He smiled and kissed his maul. "A good one that will keep you busy all day."

CHAPTER 37

A week later, Tricia, Mr. Gonzales and Sam's dad went back home, and Sam had her bike and gear up at the Simon homestead. Lacey put her up in the house, while Crip moved in with them at Lacey's and Ike's insistence, to make them feel more secure. Ike had an ulterior motive: He wanted to be alone in the trailer.

Crip let Ike drive the truck out to the bicycle trail and to Skeeter's house so they could train and ride on schedule. This gave Crip more time to go through Doug's things and help Lacey settle up his estate. But every day, Crip would make time to go out scouting for the pirates in the swamp, using a different route and different boat each time, so as not to become predictable.

Sam had trouble keeping up with Ike on the bicycle, but Ike had trouble keeping up with Sam on the track, except for the flat track. Ike attacked the flat track fearlessly, since there were no jumps and he was so adept at sliding his bike around the turns at high speed.

Soon the other riders joined the trio, and they pushed one another, the spirit of competition and camaraderie spurring them on to go faster and jump higher, in a fun and exciting kind of way. Ike was soon jumping almost everything, and he even tried a couple of the freestyle jumps, though he didn't try doing tricks. Meanwhile, Sam caused quite a stir among the other racers, who had never seen a girl go so fast. Lots of teenagers came out just to watch Sam ride.

The local riders hated being beaten by Sam. She could beat half the boys, which prompted the faster ones to tease the slower ones, which caused them to ride harder to keep up. This caused them to ride over their heads, resulting in more crashes – which caused some parents to complain to Ziptie about the increasing injuries.

"No, injuries are part of it; let 'em ride," he would say, but privately he spoke to his teams about riding under control, and he began to fine them each time they crashed.

It didn't take Sam and Ike long to realize that their desire to race was coming back. As their skill grew, their confidence and speed increased, making them anxious to get back into open competition. Sam's dad came up with the bike trailer and tools to help maintain the bikes. The days turned to weeks and the training routine blended into a lifestyle. All the riders reached new heights in their speed and conditioning.

One day, Crip was at the courthouse, doing some research on the Simon estate.

"What? Who in the world is Turk Matherne?" he wondered, talking to himself.

He hurriedly began to find everything he could on that name and the land transactions. After making dozens of copies, he gathered up the paperwork and headed home.

"Lacey, do you know anyone by the name of Turk Matherne?" he asked when he entered, dropping his briefcase on the table.

"Yes, that's the man who kept trying to buy some of our land. Doug always told him no. It didn't sit too well with him, though. He was kind of pushy. I didn't like him."

"Really? Did you know he's been buying up land all around the swamp? He even leased some land on the reservation."

"But he can't get Choctaw land. It's illegal to sell to white men."

"Sell, yes. But there are ways to get use of land if you have a good lawyer," Crip noted. "Something is not right with this guy. I'm going to Google him."

"Okay, you can use Doug's computer. He may have left you some clues in his site histories."

Back at the pirates' camp, a barge bearing the name *TM Salvage* slipped quietly by, pushed by a small towboat. On the barge were four large diesel-powered water pumps. The boat docked in between two other barges, one piled high with shells, dredged from the lake, the other with a crane and bucket. Men in red life vests and battered hard hats tied up the lines and secured the equipment. Up in the wheelhouse, the radio crackled.

"Just leave it there for now. In about a week, we should be ready to start. We'll bring in another dredge and start at Jones Island with a levee. Other crews will be in sectors A4 and G7. We have a meeting of the superintendents on Monday morning at 8 a.m. at the office. How's your food holding up? Over."

The captain looked over at his mate, who nodded.

"Our food is good," he responded. "We won't have to place an order for another three or four days. Over."

"Okay, we'll coordinate that. The quarter-boat is on its way and ETA is 6 p.m. tonight. The crew boat will bring in the rest of the hands Monday."

"Roger that, 6 p.m. tonight, hands Monday. We'll get it set up. Over."

"Remember directive 56, go over with the crew – the *whole* crew. Over."

"Roger on the directive 56. We're gonna need some fuel. Over."

"It's on its way; anything else?"

"Negative. The horses are in the stall. Over."

"Copy, horses in the stall. Office out."

"P-13 out."

The captain looked over at the mate, who asked, "So we'll start the levees next week. Why are we doin' it?"

"You know better than to ask."

"Are we still under a blackout?"

"What do *you* think?"

"I wonder why?"

"Your guess is as good as mine. I think the boss is trying to time everything to happen at once."

"So he doesn't want to tip his hand?"

The captain nodded, and said, "Yeah, but to who?"

"Hey, as long as I get my check, I don't care if we're working for the devil himself."

The captain just smiled and looked at him.

"What?"

"Nothing, it's just…"

"I know, I know: Don't ask."

They both laughed.

CHAPTER 38

"So how's the pirate case comin' along?" Sam asked.

"I just got a breakthrough," Crip replied. "I found a man who's been buyin' up land all around the swamp, and even getting some use of the reservation. He seems to have dozens of businesses all around here. So he already controls a lot of the reservation's economy. If I could find out a little more, I think we might have a link to what's been goin' on, or at least this man might know something about all this pirating goin' on. I'd be curious to know what he thinks of it."

"Why don't you just go talk to him?" Lacey suggested, sipping her coffee from a hand-thrown mug.

"If I could find him. Trouble is, he's invisible: no records, address, phone number, anything."

"Sounds to me like he doesn't *want* anyone to find him," Lacey stated.

"Yeah, that's what makes me suspicious, besides the fact he wants to buy up so much marsh and swampland."

"Why don't you look at the satellite photos around the swamp?" Sam asked.

"Not a bad idea," Crip said thoughtfully, drumming the table with his leathery fingers. "Might be something out of place, or something hidden way back in one of those pull ditches."

"I'll go pull it up on the computer right now," Sam said excitedly, jumping up and bringing her breakfast plate to the sink.

"Where's Ike?" Crip asked.

"Oh, he's cutting trees," she answered from the hallway.

"For what?"

"He said he's goin' into business. He needs some money."

"What kind of business?"

"Firewood."

"What about all the firewood that's stacked outside?"

"Oh, he already split that. He said he's got three customers lined up already."

"That boy's a hustler," Crip said proudly, looking across the table at Lacey.

"Yeah, he reminds me of someone," Lacey smiled.

"Who?"

"Just go down that hall and turn right, and you'll see," she teased.

"Oh, you mean the picture of Doug?"

"Yep," she giggled, "but there's also a mirror in there."

Three days later, Ike came in waving a check.

"Hey, guys, look," he called out. "It's the first paycheck of my new business!"

"Let me see that," Crip responded, reaching for it with a proud smile on his face.

Ike handed him the check and announced, "It's 300 dollars — enough to upgrade the suspension on my bike!"

"So it is," Crip agreed. "How'd you earn it?"

"Sold two cords of oak to the Warrior Grocery Store."

"But this check doesn't have Glenn's name on it," Crip noted. "This is from TM Enterprises. Who is that?"

"I don't know, but I'm sure it will cash," Ike declared, snapping the check from his hand and showing it to Lacey and Sam.

"Hey, Lacey, you still have that friend down at the bank?" Crip asked.

"Yes, why?"

"Do you think you could get her to follow that routing number on the check, get some more info on whoever wrote it? All that's on there is a P.O. box."

"I'll see what I can do."

"Oh, Crip, did you see the satellite photos I printed for you?" Sam asked.

"Yes I did, got 'em right here," he said, patting his shirt pocket as he turned and reached for his hat.

"Where you goin'?" Ike asked.

"Explorin'."

"Where?"

"Middle Bayou. Saw something interesting there."

"What?"

"Several barges and a few boats. I want to find out what they're up to. I'll be back later. How's the trainin' comin'?"

"Good. We've been scrimmaging on the motocross track," Ike answered. "Those guys are serious riders."

"Ike's been finishing ahead of some of the racing team," Sam announced.

"That's good. So where do you need work?" Crip asked.

"Whoops and rough stuff, especially the ruts. I still haven't tried the big triple. Plus, I'm still not in shape yet."

"Conditioning on the track takes time. But you're doin' the right thing, ridin' with fast guys."

"I think once I get my suspension tuned, I'll be able to pick up my pace."

"How 'bout you, Sam?" Crip asked, turning to her.

"Oh, I'm holding steady at midpack, too. It's fun, and I'm getting faster."

"The guys get rough with Sam," Ike added. "They don't like her being in front of them."

"I wonder why!" Crip laughed.

CHAPTER 39

◗◖

Crip shaded the binoculars from the early morning glare as he read the name *TM Enterprises* on the barges. He heard the towboat's twin diesel engines maneuvering out one of the barges, which had a crane on board. There were men on the bow and stern of the barges, manning the lines. Apparently the man on the bow was having problems with the knot on the bit.

"Get that line loose!" the PA speaker boomed from the wheelhouse.

"It's caught!" the man yelled back. He stepped back as the line tightened on itself and began to stretch and pop.

"Come on, let's go! Dollar waitin' on a dime!" the captain bellowed from above, hands on the wheel.

Suddenly a man came running up the barge, shouting, "Get away from that line!" In one motion, the man pulled a large, shiny knife from his belt scabbard and swung. Crip watched with fascination as the sun glimmered on the blade as it arced down across the rope. The three-inch line didn't even slow the blade's descent; a loud *pop!* and the barge was free.

"Wow, Jim, where'd you get that knife?"

"I made it out of a car's leaf springs. Now get that scrap out the way and bring another line out here, and be more careful."

"All right, let's move it!" the captain ordered from his perch as he began backing the barge out into the canal. "We got daylight burnin'!"

Crip focused in on the man's tattoo.

"Rangers. I should have known," he whispered to himself, letting the binoculars hang from the strap around his neck and picking up the paddle. "Well, let's go see what this Boy Scout is up to."

Crip quietly paddled the small, camouflaged pirogue around the back of the barge with the pumps. He tossed a rope up to the bit and tied it off back to his pirogue. Then he shimmied up the rope and landed softly on the deck. With a glance, he learned that no one was on board. He slipped a life vest on and found a hard hat nearby. Then he proceeded over to the pumps to have a look.

"Hey, you! What are you doin'?" a man yelled from the other barge.

"I left my gloves over here. I'll be right there!" Crip answered with a wave, buying some time. He looked the tools and fuel cans over carefully, searching for clues. A man stepped out from behind one of the pumps.

"Lookin' for somethin'?"

"Yeah, I left my gloves over here," Crip answered, turning to check the distance to the edge of the barge. When he turned back, the man was on him in a flash, knocking him down with a tackle, sending his hard hat rolling across the deck.

"So, you wanna play ball?" Crip taunted, slipping out of his grip and securing him in a headlock from behind. "Okay, this is cabbage-ball," Crip chuckled. "Your head could break loose and we could use it for the ball. But we'd need a bat, wouldn't we?"

As Crip loosened his grip, the man gasped for air. Before he could take his second breath, Crip had him in an arm bar.

"Here's the bat. You still wanna play?" Crip asked in a baby voice.

"Let me go, you dirty Injun."

"Why?"

"So I can burn your teepee and scalp your woman," his adversary moaned in pain.

Four more men appeared, each armed with weapons of opportunity.

"Let him up!" the big one with the chain demanded; the others began to circle around Crip.

"Uh oh," Crip breathed, as he watched from his captive's back.

"'Uh oh' is right, you swamp-boy! Now let me go!"

Crip snapped the man's arm and sprang to his feet. In the moment that the others realized what had happened, Crip grabbed the man closest to him with his left hand and pulled him into a side kick that broke ribs. Then he used the disabled man to block the other three and circled to keep them from getting behind him.

"Get him, Jim! He broke my arm!" the man on the ground yelled as he rolled over in pain.

"Get behind him!"

"I'm tryin', but he keeps circling!"

The man with the crowbar stepped in to swing, and Crip moved his new captive under the blow. He caught it on the head, and he dropped like a rock. Crip turned around and threw a roundhouse kick to the man with the wrench, who instinctively raised it up to block, but Crip continued his turning momentum with a turn kick that caught the man's unprotected solar plexus, knocking the wind out of him. He raised his wrench for a strike at the incoming Crip, but Crip reached up, caught his wrist and, turning, used the man's momentum against him and, between his leg and hip, flipped him to the deck, sending the wrench over the side. Crip finished him with a reverse punch to the nose and then turned to the man with the chain. It was already on its way as Crip was turning. He managed to catch it three-quarters of the way and hold on, but the end of the chain still swung up and smashed him on the chin, sending blood and teeth in different directions. His knees buckled, but Crip fought the urge to drop. He saw stars, but he held on to the chain for dear life. He spit gobs of blood out of his mouth.

The man pulled a knife with his other hand and tried to thrust, slicing Crip in the arm. The bigger man was slinging Crip's light frame around like a rag doll, and laughing about it.

"You got him, Jim!" the man with the broken arm yelled; the other two were still out cold.

"Come on! Come on!" Jim challenged Crip with a savage growl. "I'll stick you in the eye like I did that other Injun in the boat!"

"What… what'd you use?" Crip demanded, circling, hanging on to the chain, trying to buy time to get his senses back.

"An anchor! Ha ha ha ha!" Jim laughed in defiance.

Crip's eyes opened wide as he realized he was tied up with Doug's killer. His right hand found his KA-BAR and, turning and pulling on the chain, he sliced the tendons behind Jim's right knee, sending him sprawling to the ground in agony. Before the man hit the deck, Crip had wrapped the chain around his throat. He put the knife to his back and paused.

"I could end your sorry life right now. But that would be too easy. You're goin' to jail for murdering my brother."

"No, he's not," objected a voice from behind him.

When Crip turned around, he was staring down the barrel of a carbine.

"Why not?" Crip countered, turning the man between them.

"Just stop right there. Because you are going to let him go."

"But you'll just shoot me if I do that."

"Might. But you're out of options."

"Nope. Nobody's shootin' anybody," Crip insisted, inching closer to the edge of the barge.

The gun fired, wounding Jim, who crumbled in Crip's arms. Crip raised his arms slowly.

"Just one question."

"What's that?" asked the man with the rifle.

"Why an M1? That's an antique."

"It was my dad's," the man replied. "Kind of special, don't you think? Being shot with an antique?"

"Already been shot with an M1. Right here," Crip said, slowly pointing to his right hand. When the man stepped to look closer, Crip flipped his knife into the man's shoulder. The gun lowered. Before the wounded man could change hands, Crip was over the side and gone."

CHAPTER 40

That night, as Lacey was dressing Crip's wounds, Ike and Sam were peppering him with questions.

"So how'd you get away?" Ike asked.

"Move number 612," Crip answered.

"What's move number 612?" Sam asked.

"Misdirection."

"Misdirection? You mean like a fake?" Ike guessed.

"Yeah, a fake. I faked swimming out away from the barge, dove deeper, then swam back under the barge."

"Then what?"

"Move 43," Crip stated flatly.

"What's that?"

"Borrow their boat."

"I thought you had your own boat."

"First I had to take them on a 612."

"Misdirection again?"

"Sure. You can use more than one 612 at a time, you know," Crip chuckled with a smile.

"Which way did you go?"

"The opposite way from where my boat was."

"Then what?"

"96."

"96?"

"Yeah, 96. You know, abandon the boat."

"Okay, you left their boat."

"But with a twist."

"Let me guess: a 612?"

"You are so sharp. I jumped out of the boat and left it running wide open out into the marsh. Then I circled around to my boat, and here we are."

"Here we are," Sam repeated joyfully.

"Oh, I got the info on TM Enterprises," Lacey said as she cut the bandage and taped it up. "There, all done."

"So let *me* guess: Turk Matherne?" Crip asked.

"That's right. Who else?"

"So why would he be buyin' up all this land?" Ike questioned. "What would he use it for?"

"Whatever it is, it has something to do with this Matherne guy making more money or gaining more power," Crip said with a grimace as he sat up and adjusted his new bandage.

"But what about those big pumps? And the shells and crane?" Sam asked.

"I heard there's a council meeting this week, with a presentation for a major work project in the swamp," Lacey said.

"What night?" Crip asked.

"Thursday."

"We've got to get more evidence before then. Otherwise, they'll be legally covered to do what they want. That's probably our man."

"Hey, did I tell you guys I got four more orders for firewood?" Ike announced.

"Cool. Who for?"

"The general store, the convenience store, the grocery store, and one for delivery to a boat."

"To a boat? You mean for shipment by water?" Crip asked, trying to put the pieces together in his mind.

"Who ordered it?" Lacey asked, looking at Ike.

"A man named Slug. He said if he liked that wood, he would have more orders," Ike explained.

"Any idea who he works for?" Crip pressed.

"No, he's pretty secretive about it. I mean, he doesn't want to talk about his boss."

"He doesn't? Well, isn't that too bad? We're gonna find his boss anyway," Crip boasted.

"Sounds like you got a plan," Sam guessed.

"I'd say a need, not quite a plan," Crip answered.

"Hey, I'm in this time. No way you're goin' without me," Ike protested.

"We'll see. How far will he let you bring the firewood?" Crip asked.

"He's supposed to take delivery at the dock."

"We have to follow that wood and see where it goes," Crip proposed.

"I could hide inside it, like the Trojan horse," Ike suggested.

"No, too dangerous," Crip objected, casting Ike a disapproving look. "But we could go without goin'…"

"A camera?" Sam exclaimed.

"A camera *and* a GPS," Crip clarified. "What day do they expect delivery?"

"Tomorrow."

"I'll have it ready. We'll put the tracking device in the wood. We're about to hit pay dirt."

"I'll say. He'll have 300 dollars for me upon delivery."

"Hey, how come you guys aren't ridin' today?" Crip asked.

"My shock and forks are in the shop, getting tuned up."

"...and I just wanted to see how you were doing," Sam added.

"Get out there and ride your bicycles. You're not getting' a day off just 'cause I got a scratch. Now go!" Crip yelled, picking up a shoe and throwing it at them as they giggled their way out the door.

"Don't you think you're being too hard on them?" Lacey asked sweetly.

"They'll thank me later," Crip mumbled. "Can I borrow your car?"

"Sure, if you have it back by noon... wait. Are you about to do what I think you're about to do?"

"Depends on what you think I'm about to do."

"I think you're about to get into trouble again."

"Nope. Just goin' fishin'," he said, grabbing Doug's camera as he walked out the door.

"For what?" Lacey called after him.

"Big bottom-feeders," Crip called over his shoulder.

CHAPTER 41

Crip eased up to the boat launch at Ruddock. He attached the telephoto lens to the digital camera, rechecked the power level and memory, and then began taking shots of all the vehicles and license plates. When he finished there, he went up to the Manchac launch and did the same, even getting photos of the boat trailers. After he had covered all the launches and docks between western Lake Pontchartrain and Lake Maurepas, he headed to New Orleans to see a friend in law enforcement.

After a brisk bicycle ride, Sam and Ike headed over to Skeeter's to unload their dirt bikes.

"You guys ready for a race today?" Skeeter yelled from the garage.

"I can't wait, and Sam's always sayin' she's born ready, or some such stuff like that," Ike teased, looking playfully over at her as she was getting her gear on.

"You're just jealous 'cause of my speed," she said, throwing her head back and tossing her hair off her shoulders as she pulled her racing socks on over her pants.

"Hey, if I had your experience, I would be National Champion by now," Ike boasted playfully, pulling the gas can from his tank and looking inside to check the level.

"If I had raced the regional qualifier, I would be competing for the Championship next month. I just didn't want to," she said as she buckled her boots. "And it's too late to qualify for this year. But I may go to the National Championship to watch and check out the competition. Have you ever gone?"

"No, just heard about it. They say some of the riders are goin' faster than some of the pros."

"They are the fastest amateurs on earth, competing not just for a championship but to earn a factory sponsorship, 'cause all the pro scouts are there, looking for fresh talent. Anybody who is somebody at the highest level of racing will be there. Plus, it's a great family vacation for the fastest motocrossers in the nation, and even some from other countries."

Ike leaned against his bike, staring at Sam, transfixed by what she was saying.

"What?" Sam asked, standing up and flexing in her boots.

"I belong there," Ike said, matter-of-factly.

"What do you mean?"

"It's part of my destiny."

"But you can't race this year. You have to go through the qualification process. You have to prove you're in the top 42 in your class, by beating the competition at an area qualifier, then a regional."

"Oh, I can do that," he stated confidently. "Don't you worry about that."

"Maybe you can," Sam said as she studied him. "But you didn't... yet."

"Hey, guys, come on', we're runnin' late. We don't want to keep Ziptie waitin', believe me," Skeeter chuckled knowingly as he buckled his helmet.

When they pulled up at the track, the riders' meeting was already under way. Ziptie was talking to a group of about 50 racers, all standing around in their gear, some with water bottles or sports drinks in their hands, listening intently.

"So this is not a sanctioned race," Ziptie explained. "There will be no trophies, no cash payouts. This is more like a glorified scrimmage. Real racers don't need trophies; they race because they are racers, like my little friend Ike Hebert so eloquently stated earlier this month."

He pointed to Ike at the back of the crowd, causing everyone to turn and look. Ike looked like a deer caught in the headlights; he lifted a hand for a faint wave. There was a stir of mumbling as some of the riders asked the others who he was.

"I'll tell you what," Ziptie continued. "I'll put a bounty on anybody who can beat any of my team riders today."

"What do we get?" one rider called out.

"You can come train here with the team for one week. If you keep looking good, then – well, we'll see," Ziptie smiled. This caused a stir among the riders, as they all wanted to be on the top team in the state. "We'll only have two classes today, 250 and 450. All skill levels will race together."

"But I'm a beginner," one boy complained.

"You ain't a beginner," another rider chided. "You been racing for over a year."

"But I can't beat those guys," he whined.

Ziptie heard that and announced, "If you're just here as a trophy hunter or sandbagger, then you're at the wrong place. And you can leave now." He paused and looked around. "Otherwise, go over to the table and give the scorekeepers your names and numbers, and let's race. The gate will drop for the 250 class in..." he looked at his watch, "about 15 minutes. Remember to obey the flags. No passing on a yellow flag, pull off if we black-flag you, and race to the checkers. Remember, the white flag is a courtesy flag only, and you may see it twice or maybe not at all, 'cause we make mistakes, too."

"How many laps?" Sam asked.

"Good question, I almost forgot: 20 minutes plus two."

The whole group groaned.

"Hey, you need stamina to be a champion motocross racer, and we build champions. If you're here for a joyride, you might want to go sit in the stands and watch real racers from behind the fence. Any questions?" he asked a little louder. "Good. Get signed up."

As the group broke up, Ike turned to Skeeter.

"What about practice?"

"Hey, we missed it. I told you to come on time. Besides, you already know the track."

"We had to get our workout in," Ike said defensively.

"You worked out *before* this race?" Skeeter gasped, looking incredulously at both of them.

"Yeah. Why, is that a problem?" Sam questioned.

"No, no problem for me. Hope not for you, either," Skeeter smiled as he grabbed his helmet.

"Who are all these new people?" Ike asked, nodding toward the crowd.

"They're local riders that like to come and scrimmage with us. It shows them where they are in their speed and training. They're also hoping to get Ziptie's attention and maybe get some sponsorship help, or even get on the team."

"Well, I don't need a sponsorship or a team. Ike and I are on the Calais MX team," she stated as she put her hand on Ike's shoulder and shook him playfully.

"That was last year. But I'd sure like to get on the team," Ike said, staring off at the race rig, where Ziptie's team was getting ready.

"Ike, you already have Ziptie's attention," Skeeter said. "You just need to prove you belong, where it really counts."

"I know, I know – on the track, during a race."

"That's you," Skeeter smiled. "Come on, let's go sign up."

CHAPTER 42

Ike reset his tear-offs and pulled his goggles on as he sat nervously on his bike at the noisy, crowded gate. He had never raced in the same class with Intermediate and Expert riders before, and he was feeling intimidated. The bikes were spewing the remnants of condensation out of the pipes as riders turned the throttles while going through their prerace rituals. The rider on his right nodded to him, and the rider on his left mumbled a "Good luck" that was barely audible over the noise of the engines. The four team riders were set to start behind the field and facing backward, to spot the challengers a head start.

Sam gave Ike a thumbs-up from halfway down the line. Ike felt the surge of adrenaline as the starter stepped out onto the track with the sign. The starter began to point down the line as the riders nodded their readiness, and the noise of the engines grew louder.

Ike loved this part. This is where the world went away and he slipped into "Dirt Bike Ike," the character he had forged in his mind in response to the years of being the social outcast of Calais Junior and then Senior High. All the put-downs, the disappointments, the discouragements and the disillusions were pushed so deep into the recesses of his soul that they may as well be gone, for there was no room for them now. He could feel the excitement wash over him as the sign turned sideways. His whole world was focused on one place: the gate right in front of him.

He could not wait for the gate to drop. He revved his Honda over the rev-limiter and began easing out the clutch while holding in the front brake. The riders on both sides were also trying to anticipate the start, and one dumped his clutch too fast and pinned his front tire hard against the gate. An instant later, the gate dropped, leaving that rider's section still jammed against his wheel. That's all Ike remembered as he dumped the clutch and moved into "survival mode," reaching up for the shifter with his left foot while trying to keep the front end down with his weight forward. The rider on his left moved into him, but Ike had room on his right because of the missing rider they'd left behind on the gate, and he used the open line to his advantage as he went through his gears.

The other riders seemed to creep ahead of him, but he held it on longer into the turn, catching back up and even moving into the front five as they put their legs out for the left-hander. He tried to ignore the bumping from riders, handlebars and tires as he held his line through the turn, trying to stay as tight into the inside as he could. The outside riders came flying around, some too hot for the turn, going over the berm, and one of them flipping over a hay bale.

It was all instinct through the first three turns as the panicked game of "chicken" gave way to speed skills. Not wanting to give up a place, Ike was forced into lines he didn't want all the way through turn four. By turn five, he had earned fifth place, and could start using more of the track and start thinking.

'Okay, that's Sam in third, and I'm faster than this guy. Hey! Stop taking up the whole track, bozo! Okay, you wanna block the inside, I'll just take…'

Ike drifted around the outside of a sweeper and then pitched his bike down, tapped the rear brake, breaking the rear tire loose, and then shifted his weight forward and accelerated around the turn, making a quick pass. Then he settled into his game of accelerate, brake, accelerate, brake…

'No coasting, no coasting! Come on, a little quicker on the throttle out of the turn. That's it!'

He could see Sam's jersey in front of him, entering the next turn.

'Gotta catch Sam!'

By the third lap, Ike had not closed the gap on Sam. In fact, she was slipping away from him.

'How is she goin' so fast?'

Suddenly a bike came up behind him. He turned and glanced back on the next jump, just as one of the team members passed him in the air, sailing higher and further than he had on the tabletop. Ike fell in behind him and copied his lines and speed. It was thrilling to start going faster by following an expert rider. Then he heard another rider come up behind him.

'Oh no, you're not!'

Ike matched the rider's speed down the rough straightaway, but as he toed his bike into fifth gear, the Honda started getting squirrelly. Then the front and back end started swapping, sending him off balance and off the track and behind the berm of the next turn. Two more riders went by!

He took a look behind him and, seeing no riders, blasted back out onto the track. Ike slowed back down to his own pace and fell into a groove for the rest of the race. No one else caught him. When the white flag came out, he picked up his pace to finish strong, and that's when he began catching Sam. This inspired him to go full out, and in three turns he caught her. But she slowed and waved him by!

'That's *no fun!*'

As he passed her, he turned a palm up, as if asking 'What's wrong?' She took her left hand off the grip and shook it out, signaling that she had arm pump, so Ike pulled away and got back on his pace. In two more turns, he had caught up with another rider who was tiring, and he made quick work of him.

With only a couple of turns to go, he saw the fifth-place rider and made a run for him, but he sped up to beat Ike to the checkered flag.

Ziptie was waving the flag and pointed to Ike with a smile when he came by, which made Ike feel proud. He pulled up to the rider in front of him and knuckle-bumped his gloves with a nod, then went back to the shade tree, where Skeeter was already sitting down with a wet towel on his head and a bottle of water in his hand.

Ike pressed the kill button and put his bike on the stand. He took off his goggles and then peeled off his gloves. By the time he had his helmet off, Sam was puttering up. She pressed the kill button and coasted up to Ike.

"Catch the bike!" she moaned. Ike grabbed the handlebars just as Sam tried to put her foot down. The bike began to fall, but Ike held it up as Sam tumbled out of the saddle and fell to the ground in a bundle of exhaustion, gasping for oxygen. Ike rolled her bike over to the tree and turned off the gas. He went over to the ice chest and grabbed two waters, and then tossed one in Sam's direction and dropped down to join Sam and Skeeter.

"I am *soooo tired!*" Sam breathed hoarsely, as she tore off her goggles and then worked on removing her gloves.

Ike and Skeeter exchanged smiling nods.

"Somebody's not in shape," Ike cackled, looking at Sam; she just raised her arm in admittance. Ike and Skeeter started cracking up.

"What place did you get?" Ike asked Skeeter.

"I won. You?"

"I think I finished sixth. That's one place in front of Humpty Dumpty," he nodded in Sam's direction, bringing forth more laughter.

"Okay, you can laugh now," she panted, catching a breath, "but when I get back in shape, I'm gonna burn your toast."

"Whooooooaaaa," both guys wailed in mock fear.

"You'll see. The Bayou Cat will be back!" she declared, raising both arms up in victory, though wearily.

"First you gotta get that helmet off," Skeeter teased.

"Yeah, with that arm pump, it's not gonna be easy," Ike chuckled.

"And then there's the second moto," Skeeter laughed, prompting a high-five from Ike.

"Not gonna be a second moto," Sam breathed hoarsely.

"Whadaya mean?" asked Skeeter.

"I'm done. I rode a bicycle 20 miles this morning, remember?"

She sat up and started unbuckling her helmet.

"I did, too," Ike countered.

"Yeah, but you've got weeks of training on me."

"That's right, and if I keep on training, I'll keep being ahead of you in training, as long as I want!"

Ike and Skeeter celebrated with another high-five.

Just then Ziptie rode by in the water truck and honked the horn at them. Using two fingers, he pointed to his eyes and then at Ike and Skeeter, sending them the "I'm watching you" signal, accompanied by a wide grin.

"So you finished sixth?" Skeeter asked, turning to Ike.

"Yeah, or fifth."

"Do you know who you beat?"

"No."

"Two of our team members and almost the rest of the class," Skeeter said in virtual shock. "And you're a novice, you say?"

"Yep, this is my third race."

"Third race? Are you kidding me?! Nobody goes that fast in their third race."

"I do," Ike smiled.

"Dude, if you can repeat that performance in the second moto, you'll probably make the team," Skeeter proclaimed. "Can you?"

"Can I what?" Ike responded.

"Repeat the performance, numbskull," Sam interjected. "And yes, he can do it."

Ike just pointed to Sam, turned his palms up, and looked back at Skeeter in a "I just can't help but be fast" kind of way, inferring that it would be easy.

Ike repeated his performance in the second moto, this time taking third place, two places behind Skeeter.

At the end of the day, Ziptie strode over to them as they were loading the bikes.

"Hey, Ike."

"Sir?"

Ike turned and looked over his shoulder.

"That was some good riding today."

"Thanks."

"You, too, Skeeter, Sam," Ziptie added, nodded approvingly at them. Then he turned back to Ike.

"You know what I like the best?" Ziptie asked.

"What?"

"Consistency. Putting it all together, braking, accelerating, starting, turning, whoops, reading the track, stamina – all of it, lap after lap, in both motos. That's how winners work. Most guys out here can do most of that stuff, part of the time, but you did it all lap after lap, with minimal mistakes. Once you get past the basics, then winning is all up here," he explained, pointing to his brain.

"Thanks. That's what Crip told me, too."

Ziptie took him aside and asked him a question in private.

"Would you like to practice with the team?"

"Would I? Of course!"

"Good. Be here at 8 a.m. tomorrow and we'll start formal training."

"Okay, uhhh, well, can I ask you something?"

"Shoot."

"Sam and I are already on a training program."

"Oh, yeah. Well, Crip is the best MX coach around, so I'll make an exception. But you'll need to start blending in with our team, too. How about you come tomorrow, just to see what we do? Then we'll let you get back on your regimen."

"Can Sam come, too?"

Ziptie studied Sam carefully and rubbed his chin.

"Let's not do that just yet. I'm not sure her head's really back into racing, and she may be a distraction to the team."

"I understand."

"Tomorrow at 8?"

"Tomorrow at 8," Ike agreed, shaking his hand.

CHAPTER 43

❦

"A 'distraction'! Are you kidding me?" Sam was incensed. "Here comes that 'You're just a girl so you don't belong in motocross' stuff again. I mean, when will men get it? We belong in the sport, too!"

"It's not that you don't belong. He doesn't think your head is actually back into serious racing yet. I think he wants to see what you do the next couple of months," Ike suggested.

"Sam, listen," Lacey interjected. "Maybe you don't realize it, but... Well, teenage boys are so distracted by pretty girls. And you are pretty, anybody can see that. I think he thinks it will take the team's mind off of training."

"So does that mean if I weren't so pretty, I could be part of the team?" Sam fired sarcastically.

Crip and Ike just looked at each other in exasperation.

"So if I were extra ugly, would I be a distraction the other way? It's just another way to exclude women from the sport!" she ranted, pushing her breakfast plate away.

"Women are not excluded from the sport. There are ladies' classes, girls' classes, and they can race with the boys if they want," Ike said, grabbing another slice of bacon.

"Yeah, but we still don't get the respect we deserve," Sam shot back.

"Well, I know how you can solve that," Crip replied.

"How?"

"Just go beat 'em!" Crip advised with finality, as he got up and grabbed his electronics sack.

Sam, Ike and Lacey looked at one another as if a light had gone on, and they nodded approvingly.

"Come on, guys, we've got work to do. No training today," Crip ordered.

"Cool," Sam said, as she raised her fists in thankfulness.

"Wait a sec. I'm supposed to start trainin' with the team today," Ike remembered.

"And deliver your firewood?" Lacey asked.

"Whoops," Ike responded, shrugging his shoulders.

"I'll call Ziptie; he's in the loop anyway," Crip answered. "He's just itchin' to help with this case. Sam, I need you to do a search on these license numbers. Lacey will help you with access to the database. Ike, I'm gonna show you how to plant a bug and a GPS transponder."

"Sweet!" Ike exclaimed, jumping up out of his chair. "You mean in the firewood delivery?"

"Exactly. We've got to get the proof we need before tonight's council meeting. Our window of opportunity to stop this scheme is closing fast."

Three hours later, the bugged firewood was on a barge on the Natalbany River, where it empties into the Tickfaw. The barge was headed to the secret hideout. Crip and Ike were on Doug's motorboat, with the electronics tuned in, monitoring the barge's progress.

"Hand me the map, please," Crip requested, as he powered down to idle. "My guess is, they'll turn off somewhere in the marsh before they get to Lake Maurepas."

Ike unfolded the map and placed it next to the computer screen. Crip put his reading glasses on.

"Look, they're turning," Ike observed, putting his finger on the screen to follow the barge.

"I didn't know there was a canal there," Crip stated, his eyes glued to the screen. He pulled the map next to the computer and found the spot. "There's *not* a canal there! At least according to this map."

"How can that be?" Ike asked.

"They just dug it recently, in the last year, while I've been gone. Something really fishy is goin' on. I tell you what. We are going to take a short cut."

"Out here? How?"

"Move 491."

"491?"

"Creative marsh-trekking."

"You just made that up," Ike teased with a playful smile.

"Just using my God-given creativity," Crip smiled, studying the map. Then he looked at Ike. "That's one of the things that separates us from animals."

"But animals make nests and stuff," Ike countered.

"That's just instinct. They just do it 'cause it's in their DNA. We actually plan and think and solve problems and such. For instance, I have a friend that likes to restore old cars. He pulls it all apart and paints each piece and puts it back together, better than new, but with his design in it. He changes a lot of things on the motor, in the interior, the paint scheme, wheels, etc."

"Oh, like Mr. Gonzales and his vintage bikes."

"Exactly. And he enjoys doin' it. I call it the 'Eden factor.' People are trying to recreate the Garden of Eden around them. That's why so many people clear their land, plant flowers, gardens and trees and such. Some of them are spectacular."

"So they enjoy the work, then sit around and enjoy the result."

"Right. Like you did when you restored those old motocross bikes with Mr. Gonzales. You have no idea how much he enjoyed that."

"Really?"

"Oh, yeah. He was so excited the night ya'll built that '82 Elsinore race bike. He called me up that night, at midnight!"

"Midnight? I left at about 11:30, so that was right after I left."

"Yeah, we talked for two hours. You sparked some kind of new life in him. After you guys solved that crime, he called me to come down and help him start up the new shop. So, in a way, you were responsible for getting our friendship back together."

"What? Me?"

"Yeah, you never can tell what good you do for someone, how it will affect others, then others, then others."

"Like a ripple in a pond."

Crip put his arm around him and gave him a man-hug.

"Ike, there is no one in the world like you."

"Better not be."

"No, I mean it. No one in the world walks like you, talks like you, enjoys the exact same things as you, laughs like you, works like you, rides like you and plays like you. No one has your ambitions, skill set, experiences, desires and your specific dream."

"But lots of people talk kinda like me, ride like me, have the same dream as me..."

"True, but not the same overall package. Therefore, God created you to fulfill a purpose and interact with a certain set of people that He brought into your life and have an influence on people that need you so they can succeed."

"That's kind of heavy."

"Yeah, and that's why we believe that life is so valuable. Life is a gift from our Creator, for a purpose. That's why people are worth saving and helping. We participate with God's plan to save people and help them fulfill their destinies."

"Why are you telling me all this?" Ike asked suspiciously.

Crip checked his watch. "I don't know. I guess I have a bad feeling about what I'm about to do."

"What *are* we about to do?"

"*You* are about to drop me off and wait to pick me up. *I* have to get into the boss' head and find out what he's attempting to do. I have a vague idea, but I need proof."

"What are the odds you'll succeed?"

"You don't want to know." Crip turned away and pulled out a snack bar and opened a sport drink.

"Try me."

"Okay," Crip retorted sharply, angrily turning to face Ike. "Fifty-fifty I come back out alive."

"*Fifty-fifty!* Are you crazy?! You have a bad feeling about this and you're still gonna go through with it?"

"Have to. Feelin's don't count. Maybe with women and their intuition, but sometimes a man has to do what he has to do. And I know I must do this today to help my people. It's part of *my* destiny. All of my experiences have prepared me for this. I'm the only one who can do it."

"But what about me and Mr. Gonzales and Lacey and Sam?" Ike was pleading now.

"It's especially because of you guys. You are my peeps. But unless these criminals are stopped, there'll be no end to their destruction. Their blind greed and violence will not stop, 'cause they'll always want more. No, it has to stop here. Take me down that canal right up there."

Crip sat down and began to strip off his shirt and shoes. Ike watched him in disbelief.

"Go on, I'll tell you where to turn," Crip said. "Now toss me that gear bag and start the motor."

Ike picked up the bag and shoved it up under the bow.

"What are you doin'?" asked Crip.

"You're not goin'."

"What?" Crip gasped.

"I'm not lettin' you go. It's too dangerous. You'd be throwin' your life away," Ike contended.

Crip cocked his head and read Ike's face. "You're serious, aren't you?"

"Dead serious."

Crip stopped undressing, looked to the side as if deciding something, then looked back at Ike. "Okay."

"Okay?" Ike looked surprised.

"We'll just leave it alone and go back home," Crip conceded. "But let me tell you a story first."

"Is it true?"

"Just listen, then decide if you think it's true."

"Agreed."

Ike sat down and folded his arms.

"There was a doctor who worked in a hospital in Iraq during the Gulf War invasion. One night he finished with his last patient, then walked down the hall to get his wife, who was a nurse working in another room. He had planned to get her and their children away from the fighting, to safety. As he walked past one of the rooms, he heard some yelling. He walked in and saw four of Saddam Hussein's secret police beating a woman. She was a captured American soldier."

"I think I heard about this," Ike said, listening with interest.

"The Iraqi doctor made an instant decision," Crip continued. "He decided to risk his life, and the safety of his family, to help her."

"Why?"

Crip ignored the question. "He got in his car and drove through a battle and across the lines to the Americans to tell them about her. They questioned him for a long time until they were sure he was telling the truth. Then they asked him to return to the hospital and gather more information that would help them send a rescue team in to save her."

"Did they?"

"Yes, they did."

"Did the doctor make it out, too?"

"Yes, but not before losing one eye and almost getting killed."

"So what does this have to do with us?" Ike asked.

"You asked me why he did it. In the story written about his life, he said he wanted to help that girl because he saw her and the American soldiers as saviors of his country. He said the Americans left their families, came across the seas and put themselves in grave danger to help his people from a cruel dictator."

"Wasn't he scared?"

"He said he feared for his family, but the risk was worth it. He said it *was the right thing to do.*"

"I remember that story now."

"The soldier's name was Jessica Lynch," Crip stated.

"So it *is* a true story."

"Ike, sometimes a man's got to do what a man's got to do and leave the results up to God," Crip explained tenderly. "The doctor was perfectly positioned to save her life. The shrapnel that took his eye was from a car being blown up behind him while he was returning from the Americans. You know who happened to be in that car?"

"No, who?"

"The Iraqi secret police, who were following the doctor."

"So, if that car hadn't blown up..."

"The good doctor's plan would have been discovered," Crip finished.

"... and the Americans wouldn't have the information," Ike said, putting it all together, "and his family would have been killed."

"So God was watching over him," Crip reasoned. "All a hero is, is an ordinary man that does something extraordinary because he is perfectly positioned to help someone in need."

Ike stared at Crip.

"You know what heroes always say?" Crip asked.

"What?"

"Anyone would have done it, if they were in my position," Crip said, and then he paused and put his hand on Ike's arm. "And Ike...?"

"What?"

"I am perfectly positioned in this moment in time to fulfill my mission."

They sat there thinking. Then Ike got up, grabbed Crip's gear bag and tossed it to him.

"I think you're gonna need this," Ike muttered, and then he started the motor and pointed the boat south, toward the pirate camp.

Thirty minutes later, they were in position. Crip pulled out his scuba gear and strapped his knife to his calf. He attached the first stage of the regulator onto the air tank and opened the air valve. After pushing the second stage of the regulator a couple of times to test the air pressure, he reached down and grabbed the tank harness and then flipped it over his back, letting it come to rest on his shoulders. Then he buckled the harness' belt around his waist. He reached over to the weight belt and swung that around his waist.

"What I am about to tell you is *very* important. You must follow it to the letter if we have a chance of succeeding. Do you understand?"

Ike stopped coiling the line and looked intently at Crip.

"Once I leave here, you are to take the boat over here and wait," he said, circling a location on the map. "If I'm not back in an hour, you *must* leave without me."

"But Crip, I'm not... I don't understand why I have to leave."

"I'm not asking you to understand. I'm asking you to trust me. You *must* trust me. Otherwise, you could get hurt."

"I'm not scared of getting hurt," Ike lied.

"It's not about being scared or brave!" Crip insisted emphatically. "It's about being smart, thinking and acting with a disciplined mind, and anticipating what might happen!"

Crip looked Ike dead in the eyes.

"Promise me!"

"Okay."

"With or without me, you are to go back to the house and get ready for tonight. Lacey has some proof we can use as a last resort, and Sam may have found something more. You *have got* to take the girls to the meeting and let Lacey talk. But, Ike..."

"What?"

"Watch your back. We will be tipping our hand tonight, and these goons will stop at nothing to get what they want. And we'll be a threat to them. Do you understand?"

"Yeah."

"Good. Now get ready to hand me my fins."

Crip put the mask and the regulator in his mouth and purged it with a push of the button. He covered his mask with one hand and grabbed the bottom of the tank with the other. Then he flipped over the side, coming up with one hand on the boat and the other outstretched for the fins. He slung the fins over his wrist, and then dropped below the surface. Ike watched him disappear into the murky water.

Something big splashed nearby, causing Ike to look over, trying to find the source of the noise. All that was left were some bubbles popping on the surface of the water. He thought he saw a swirl of movement, and then two beady eyes popped up, not 30 feet behind the boat. Then another noise caused Ike to jump and, looking over, he saw Crip come walking up out of the water on the other bank with mud and sea grass dripping off of him, reminding Ike of the *Creature from the Black Lagoon*.

Crip slogged his feet up through the mud to drier ground and turned to wave. He took the regulator out of his mouth momentarily to say, "Go on, I'll be fine," with a smile not unlike the one he used when he took that first bite of ice cream after supper. Then he turned and began his trek across the marsh toward his rendezvous with danger.

CHAPTER 44

When Crip got within sight of the pirates' camp, he squatted down to take a picture with his small camera. Then he pulled out a tiny spotting scope and studied the building. It was less than 10 years old, with wooden walls and a tin roof, built about 12 feet off the ground. A flight of stairs connected the ground to the front porch, which wrapped around the whole structure. Windows overlooked the swamp on each side, while a metal chimney protruded from a steep roof, which overhung the porch by four feet. The ground level was used for storage, and the dock had several boats and a barge out front.

When Crip saw the men talking out front, he put the earphone to his ear and began to listen to the transmission from the electronic bug.

"Jake, get that firewood unloaded. I need the barge," Jim commanded.

"I'll be done in a minute. Where's the boss?"

"He's taking a shower. Got some important presentation tonight."

"You goin'?"

"Of course."

"I wanna go."

"Nope. He doesn't wanna walk in there with a posse. Just me and him tonight."

"But you have a bullet wound."

"It went clean through. I'm all right. But you can't go," Jim stated.

Jake thought for a moment, and then began to tie off the barge.

"That's all right by me. 'Dancin' with the Stars' is comin' on tonight," Jake said as he tied the barge up next to the dock.

Jim just looked at him in disbelief.

"You're kiddin', right?"

"No, I'm not kiddin'," Jake said defensively. "George Hamilton might get voted off tonight."

Jim just shook his head and turned on his heels. In four strides, he was up the steps and through the door, letting the screen door slam behind him. Crip had already coiled up the headpiece and put it back in the Ziploc bag with his scope. In 15 seconds, he had the fins, mask and snorkel on and the regulator in his mouth. He pressed it one quick time to clear it and then disappeared into the muddy water.

Five minutes later, Crip was out of the water and on dry ground under the camp building, stripping off the diving gear. He listened under each room for a moment and then began moving toward the back corner of the camp. Then he stopped and sniffed the air.

"Uh oh."

Alarmed, he immediately scanned the ground at his feet. Suddenly a water moccasin struck at him from underneath an old tire. He caught the snake in midstrike, and twisted off the head and tossed it aside.

"Nasty things," Crip muttered under his breath.

He went over to the plumbing and listened for running water coming through the PVC pipe. Then he climbed up the creosote pilings on the outside wall until his head was even with the window. Bypassing the fogged bathroom window, he went to the next room. Scanning the room, he saw the desk, a chair and file cabinets. Raising himself up on the floor joists, he tried the window. It was locked. He removed his knife from its sheath and jimmied the latch. It finally gave way.

After opening the window, he pulled out the screen and dropped it quietly on the ground. Sheathing his knife, he pulled himself up onto the sill. He took off his wet booties and rubbed the water off his feet. He leaned into the window and, with a stealthy flip, using the desk for support, came up inside the room on his feet, facing a big map.

After studying it thoughtfully, he pulled out his camera and stepped back to take a couple of shots. He could hear the water still running through the bathroom door. He turned to the computer and tapped a key. When it came on, he studied the folders. Reaching into his Ziploc bag, he pulled out a flash drive and inserted it into the slot. After a couple of clicks, the download began. Next, he went to the file cabinet and opened the top drawer and began running his fingers over the files. Suddenly the sound of the running water stopped!

Crip froze and listened. He heard the man singing Frank Sinatra's "I Did It My Way," so he continued his search. He saw nothing of interest in the top drawer, so he closed it and opened the second drawer. Again, nothing of interest — just bills of lading, shipping receipts, grocery, utility and tool bills. When he opened the third drawer, he *did* find something of interest — deeds to property, all around the reservation. Just as he reached for them, the bathroom door opened. In one quick movement, Crip closed the drawer and faded against the wall behind the cabinet.

Doc walked in, still swabbing water out of his ear and singing. He went over to the closet, but then he stopped short. He saw the flash drive in the computer. He continued to sing as his eyes scanned the room suspiciously. Then he noticed a wet spot on the floor near the window. When he reached into the closet, he grabbed a gun and began to search the room, still singing. As for Crip, all he could see was the computer downloading to the flash drive, and sweat began to roll into his eyes. He reached for his knife and stepped out, right into the business end of a 9mm automatic pointed at his face.

"So, you came to visit? Actually, I was expecting you," Doc said evenly.

"How so?"

"Drop the knife and raise your hands – now!"

Crip dropped his knife and raised his hands slowly, trying to read the intentions in Doc's eyes. He still felt good about the situation as he studied the little man's face and shaking hand.

"Jim! Come in here," Doc yelled through the door. Then he calmly turned back to face Crip. "Forgot something?" Doc asked Crip sarcastically, as he reached for the flash drive and yanked it out. "It's gonna take more than this to stop us now."

Doc dropped it on the floor and crushed it with the chair. Crip, in that instant, lunged for the gun. He grabbed it and turned it in Doc's hand, making it discharge into the wall. From somewhere, iron came down on the back of Crip's head, and that was the last thing he remembered.

Ike paced back and forth in the boat, looking at his watch.

"Come on, Crip!" he yelled at the trees. Suddenly he heard the shot. Ike listened hard. He could hear men yelling.

"We got him! We got Crip!"

Ike turned and started the boat. Then he pushed the throttle forward and disappeared up around the bend toward the Natalbany River.

When he got home, he filled in Lacey and Sam, telling them everything, including what Crip had made Ike promise to do.

"But we gotta go back and save Crip!" Ike fumed.

"Ike, the best thing we can do for Crip is to stick to our part of the plan," Lacey reasoned.

"But he needs us," Ike argued.

"Crip works better alone. And if you haven't figured it out yet, he can take care of himself."

"Then what's all that talk about teamwork and people needing each other?" Ike countered.

"That's true, but he's trying to protect you from danger. Can't you see that?"

"I don't need protection!"

"Yes, you do. You need protection from goin' over there and doing something foolish," Lacey explained. "If they catch you, then they have a big bargaining chip, or worse, you get hurt. Crip is a highly trained Marine with combat experience. We're gonna have to trust him."

"She's right, Ike," Sam interjected. "I know you love Crip, but we've got work to do. You should see what I found today."

"What?"

"Some interesting stuff that can prove those guys don't deserve the permits they want. Come see."

Ike followed her over to the computer.

CHAPTER 45

At 7 p.m. on the dot, the mayor pounded the gavel and announced, "This council meeting will come to order."

The jabbering died down in the overcrowded council chamber as everyone took their seat. The room began to feel stuffy, and some of the women were fanning themselves with their programs.

"We're gonna take them down here, tonight," Lacey whispered to Ike and Sam, who were seated next to her in row four.

After the pledge of allegiance, a prayer, and some opening remarks by the mayor, the business started. Lacey looked down at her program. Old business, something about the park, was first, then a question about insurance, then refinancing. There were other items of no interest to them. She glanced down to the new business and scanned the list. Her eyes stopped on the one about building permits for TM Enterprises.

"Where are we?" asked Sam, peering over her shoulder.

"Here," she tapped with her finger, showing her the program.

"And we've got to get to where?"

"All the way down to here," Lacey whispered, sliding her finger down to the bottom.

Sam moaned. Ike looked at the program with interest.

"What?" he asked.

When Lacey showed Ike where they were and how long they had to wait, Ike grew impatient and slouched down in the chair, folding his arms with a sigh.

An hour later, the representatives from TM Enterprises were called forward to give their presentation. Doc Matherne waddled up to the microphone and opened his briefcase while Jim connected a laptop to the projector.

When Ike saw Jim, he froze in terror. He'd had nightmares about Doug's killer coming after him, and now he was in the same room with him! He slid over behind the big man sitting in front of him, hoping that he wouldn't be seen.

"Ladies and gentlemen of the council, good people of Springfield, Louisiana, Honorable Mayor, I'd like to submit a project such as never been seen in Springfield before," Doc began. "I represent an association of investors who are ready to build a city within a city. May I introduce 'Spanish Moss Estates' – a development that will turn useless swamp and marsh into an upscale community that will make the town of Springfield comparable to Hammond in size and sales tax. This project will inject 50 million dollars in revenue into the town and create over 6,500 jobs, and it won't cost you a dime!"

Doc extended the last word for emphasis and let it hang in the air.

A murmur broke out among the crowd as the council members looked at one another in shock. The mayor raised his hand to signal Doc to go on.

"Furthermore," the little man continued, as he began to swell with pride and feeding off the drama of the moment like a ringleader in a circus, "as my esteemed colleague will show you with the following slides, our plan has three phases."

He nodded to Jim, who proceeded to the next slide – a shot of a map labeled "Phase 1."

"Phase 1 will cover 200 acres, from Highway 22 to Dog Ear Road and the McMann farm to the Old Mill Road," Doc explained. "This will be five-acre lots zoned for single-family dwellings, with underground utilities, a sewage-treatment plant, and a park, complete with a playground and a pond for fishing."

Doc again nodded to Jim, who advanced to the next slide, which showed a virtual community of finished homes with landscaping, viewed from the air.

"We already have pre-sold 18 lots – pending your approval, of course – and have contractors lined up to begin in 60 days. Phase 2," he continued, nodding to Jim, who advanced to a map of Phase 2, "will encompass another 235 acres on the east side, bordering the Tickfaw River, that will consist of two restaurants, one grocery, two convenience stores, three strip malls, and a new theater. It will have a neighborhood of one-acre lots. Ground has even been set aside for a church. Over half of this is in swamp, and we intend to drain the swamp and haul in dirt fill to raise the level."

Jim flipped through the next three slides to show pictures of what it all might look like, eliciting a gasp from the crowd. Doc smiled and raised his voice an octave, brimming with confidence, working his magic like a snake-oil salesman in a western town.

"In the next slide, you will see a map of this phase that includes part of the Choctaw reservation that will be part of the project, complete with a casino, a retirement community and a five-star hotel. The Choctaw nation has already approved this phase and will be positioned to receive over 6 million dollars a year in *new* revenue."

He nodded over to the Choctaw leaders, who nodded approvingly.

"And finally, Phase 3," he said, nodding to Jim, who clicked to the next slide, of a big, colorful title that read, "Maurepas Preservation Project." The next slide showed a map of the completed project, but with the Manchac Swamp added within the red boundary lines.

"Ladies and gentlemen, the Maurepas Preservation Project!" he announced. "This will be a combination wildlife preserve, state park, retirement community and entertainment complex. It will feature a campground, a water park, a museum, two marinas, and a hotel overlooking Lake Maurepas."

When the next slide displayed the virtual project, the crowd broke out into spontaneous applause.

"Thank you, thank you, ladies and gentlemen. But we are just humble builders who want to invest in the great town of Springfield, Louisiana," he said, taking a bow as he withdrew from the platform.

Jim picked up the slide projector and unplugged it. As he turned, he locked eyes with Ike. A big, evil smile began to cross Jim's face as stood and winked at Ike. Then he strutted confidently back to his seat. Ike felt like he had been shot through the heart with a deadly icicle. Fear gripped him so hard that he couldn't move or think. He could feel the hairs stand up on the back of his neck. All he could do was grip his seat.

Meanwhile, the crowd was so noisy that the mayor had to pound the gavel to regain order.

"The Chair opens up the microphone to anyone who wants to speak for or against this… magnificent project," he stammered, nodding a "thank you" to Doc. "You will have three minutes."

Ike, Sam and Lacey cast nervous glances at each other. Then the rush started. People from the town got up to speak for the project in gushing terms. The businessmen, attorneys, doctors, plumbers, carpenters, electricians, teachers, police officers, reporters, mechanics and realtors were all heaping praise on TM Enterprises for bringing Springfield into a "new era" of success. The line formed all the way around the room of people, each wanting to add their voice.

After 45 minutes of the love-fest for the project, the mayor pounded the gavel and stopped the next speaker before he could begin.

"Now that we've heard from those who are in favor of the project, is there anyone here who opposes the project?"

Ike knew he should do something, but he didn't know what exactly it could be. He concentrated on acting like everything was normal. Sam and Lacey looked nervously at each other as the people who hadn't had a chance to speak went back to their seats. Suddenly an elderly gentleman in overalls got up and shuffled to the front. He cleared his throat and tapped the microphone.

"Ya'll all know me," he uttered. "I been a farmer here for nigh on 60 years, providing milk and beef to yall's kids, parents and grandparents. If something looks too good to be true, it prob'ly is. Now this man says he's gonna put a bunch a money in yall's pockets and not take nuthin' from ya. Gonna put a city in a city. Says he's gonna pay fer it all hisself. I'd like for him to explain how."

He put his thumbs in his suspenders and stepped back from the mic to look at Doc, who stepped forward and looked at the mayor.

"May I?"

"Please do," the mayor responded, waving his hand toward the microphone.

Doc stepped to the microphone with a big, phony smile on his face.

"Farmer, uhhh, what was your name?"

"Tafton. Ernie Tafton."

"Mr. Tafton, I understand your concerns and can appreciate your apprehension. Let me assure you, we have spent the last two years pulling together the best businessmen, accountants, architects and community planners available. And the funds to finance this project will come from the people who will benefit from the services. The homeowners will pay for the neighborhoods, the people who use the retirement homes for the retirement home, the people who use the hotels for the hotels, the people who use the water parks, and so on. I'm sure you get the picture."

"Yep, but it takes money to start up a project. And I don't know no investor who don't want more money give back to 'em than the money they handed over. Somebody's got to pay."

"Well, uh, Mr. Tafton, you say you're a farmer. If I wanted to start a farm, I'd need to borrow money to buy land, cows, tools and a house. Am I right?"

"'Course, unless someone handed it down to ya, say, in an inheritance."

"True," Doc conceded. "But let's say a man starts from scratch. So the lending institution – say, a local bank – loans the money. The bank not only wants a little more money back in interest, once the farmer starts selling his milk, but he also gets a new customer that comes back later for other needs, even putting his money in the bank. Plus, the town grows and others benefit, needing more services from the bank, helping it grow. I'd call that good business, wouldn't you, Mr. Tafton?"

The crowd nodded in agreement. Mr. Tafton looked down at his mud-splashed boots and looked up at Doc and held his glaze for a moment as if sizing up the little man.

"So these investors, are they the local banks?"

"Well, of course not," Doc chuckled, backpedaling. "Your local banks don't have this kind of money."

"Do you?"

"Well, not yet – I mean, not me personally."

"What do you mean 'not yet'? What's in this for you?"

"Well, I plan to be paid for my vision and services, too..."

"Like maybe cuttin' down the cypress trees and sellin' all our timber?" Tafton asked, interrupting him. "You ain't from around here, are ya?"

"No."

"Where ya from?"

"Well, I'm from all over – I mean, I've lived in different places."

"Where was you born?"

"New Jersey. Uh, Mayor Tompkins, I don't see the need for this to go on any further," Doc said, pleading with the mayor to rescue him.

"Thirty seconds, Ernie, get to your point," the mayor warned.

"Well, when you bring a new man into your outfit, you get him to fill out a job application. Find out how he did at the last three jobs, see what kinda man he is, what he's done."

"Mayor, I don't think I need to submit a job application here," Doc complained. "I'm not applying for a job. I'm making jobs, thousands of them!"

The crowd burst into applause.

"Thanks, Ernie," the mayor said, dismissing him from the microphone. "Anyone else want to speak against the project?"

The crowd went silent and everyone began looking around.

Ernie Tafton started back to his seat, but then turned around and went back to the microphone for a final comment.

"History is repeatin' itself," he warned. "Out-of-town speculators takin' out the rest of our good timber for profit. You'll be sorry if you let this go through!"

Then he shuffled back to his seat looking everyone in the eyes on his way back. No one got up.

"Well," the mayor concluded, "if there's no one else..."

"I will!" Lacey chirped, springing to her feet.

Everyone turned and looked. Sam and Ike felt like sliding down in their seats.

"All right, Lacey," the mayor consented. "Step to the mic and state your peace."

Lacey grabbed the folders from Sam's shaking hands, straightened her blouse, and walked to the front, keenly aware of all the eyes upon her.

CHAPTER 46

Crip awakened to the loud drone of a diesel motor, his head spinning in pain. When he reached up to touch his head, he found he was restrained by handcuffs. He noticed blood on the floor; then followed the red trail up his shirt and shoulder. It dawned on him that the blood was coming from his head. He took inventory of his situation: Twin diesel motors, the hum of a generator, the oily bilge below — he was in the engine room of a towboat. Looking around for a tool, the only thing he could reach was a small screwdriver. He stretched with all his might and was able to grasp it just as the engines began to shut down, in stages. He could feel the momentum of the boat slow, and he knew they were stopping.

When the engines were cut to idle, he heard the sound of boots on the metal stairwell. Two men were coming down into the engine room. He slipped the screwdriver into his back pocket.

"We're back!" the first man said mockingly as he reached down and tugged Crip to his feet.

"Yeah, did you miss us?" the second man laughed as he fished out the key to the cuffs. Crip tried to look at them, but they were a blur, as he was still weakened and dizzy from the exertion of getting to his feet.

'I must've lost a lot of blood; feel weak,' Crip thought. 'Not enough strength to fight; must think. What are they tryin' to do?'

"He looks like a little drowned puppy," one man observed pitifully.

"Yeah, drowned in his own blood. He's gonna attract every shark in the lake!" the second man scowled. "Bring him up."

They dragged Crip up out of the engine room and across the deck to the edge of the boat. Crip was trying to regain his footing, but they were dragging him too fast.

"Let's cuff his hands behind his back," one of his captors suggested. "This cat's a survivor. I don't want him swimming back to the shore and comin' after us."

"But shore is three miles away," argued the second man.

"Boss said if we don't do this job right, we'll pay with *our* lives," the first man warned with an evil grimace.

"Okay. He's gonna drown any way you look at it," the other shrugged as he pulled out the cuffs and grabbed Crip's left arm. Crip tried to fight them off, but he was too weak. One of the men punched Crip hard in his kidney from behind, causing Crip to crumple over the edge of the boat, his head hanging over the water. He saw his image in the water and was repulsed by the mass of bloody hair and the battered face he barely recognized as his own. As they cuffed his wrists, he strained his fists to try to keep them from closing too tight.

"Wait a minute. Let's tie this crab trap on him so he can't swim."

"Okay."

One of them slid the crab trap over and tied a couple shackles to it for weight, and then tied it to Crip.

Crip's mind was in survival mode, taking in all the information around him. He saw the plastic milk jug attached to the crab trap at the end of about 15 feet of half-inch line coiled on the deck. Then, when they forced his head back over the side, he watched in the reflection of the water and saw which of the men slipped the key into his top pocket.

"Bye, Crip!" they laughed as they shoved him over, along with the crab pot.

Crip took a big gulp of air as he went over and managed to catch the man with the key by the belt and pull him over, too. Crip held on to the man as they sank, grasping for the man's pocket. The man fought back mightily, trying to tear away. Finally the man's shirt tore off and he escaped back up to the surface.

Crip landed on the muddy bottom in 17 feet of water. The crab pot landed next to him, pinning him to the bottom. In the murkiness, he searched the shirt for the key. It had fallen out of the pocket! Immediately, Crip fished for the rope to the crab pot and found it on the third attempt. He began to pull the plastic jug down from the surface. It got harder and harder to pull as it got deeper. Grasping the jug, he unscrewed the cap. Then he let out a little slack from the rope, still holding it behind his back. When the jug was even with his head, he reached around and bit the bottom of the jug, pulling it around to the front. Then he fell over, slowly, to the bottom, pinning the jug under his head. Just as he was about to pass out from lack of oxygen, his lips found the opening in the jug and he sucked in a welcome mouthful of air from inside the jug. He settled in to catch his breath and relax his muscles.

After a few minutes, when Crip hadn't emerged, one of the men yelled to the wheelhouse, "He's done, Al! Let's go."

The captain put the engines in gear and the boat began to pull away. The other man who had fallen in, shaking some of the water out of his hair, spat out, "If the sharks don't get him, the crabs will."

Crip assessed his situation as he calmed his breathing.

'About four minutes of air in this jug. Hands are cuffed behind my back, legs are tied to the trap.

He reached down with his hands to check the knot on his ankles. They had taken three twists with some three-quarter-inch hemp, not as slippery as mono. Then they'd half-hitched and wrapped and half-hitched again.

'Gotta find that key.'

Crip took another big gulp of air and then began to feel around for the key. He moved around slowly, trying not to stir up too much silt. After two more gulps of air from the jug, he noticed a glint in the mud. He edged over toward it and found the key! After dropping it twice, he managed to get it in the keyhole and twist. The cuffs opened!

With his hands now free, he pulled the jug to him for another gulp of air. Then he went to work on the knots on his feet. The water had made the rope expand, and the knots wouldn't break free. He remembered the little screwdriver in his pocket. He fished it out, and then grabbed another gulp of air from the jug, which by now was almost full of water. He used the screwdriver to force open the knots, and after another minute, which seemed like 20, he'd untied his feet from the trap. He finally ascended toward the surface.

His lungs were burning with the last of the oxygen. He exhaled the rest of his breath on the way up, and when he broke the surface, he got the sweetest relief of his life – a big lungful of fresh air! He laid his head and shoulders back and caught his breath, floating in the pink and purple hues of the sunset. When he'd gotten his bearings, he began the long swim back to shore. And he knew where he had to go – directly back to Doc's camp.

CHAPTER 47

At the council meeting, Lacey was just winding up her presentation.

"So you see that Doc Matherne – alias Don Vladimir, alias Donald Troyav-ich, alias Dorian Reysteyn – has been into a lot of things, before and after his time in prison."

"That's a lie!" Doc interjected. "I'm a businessman who has been a servant of the people for 30 years. I challenge this woman to bring forth any proof to these false charges."

The people in the meeting agreed loudly, clearly behind Doc.

"All you have to do is follow the money trail of TM Enterprises," Lacey countered.

"Lacey, do you have any proof?" the mayor questioned in a serious tone.

"Just what we found on the Internet."

"No, I mean hard evidence: transactions, documents, titles, pictures, re-cordings, or any other documents that will stand up in court?"

"Not those, but I'm sure they could be found," she retorted defensively.

"Lacey, we are all sorry about Doug, and we know you've been through a lot, but these are very serious charges that are unfounded and could get you in a lot of trouble."

"I suggest that the lady withdraws these ridiculous stories immediately, and I won't sue her for libel!" Doc said angrily. "We all know that her late husband has been trying to stop this development for the last four years, to protect the environment. But he didn't understand how we could enhance the environment and preserve it and make it accessible to millions of visitors and residents for generations to come, while providing thousands of jobs and millions of dollars for the tax base of not only Springfield but the surrounding cities and the parish. Mr. Mayor, I move to close the discussion and bring it to a vote of the council, relying on their wisdom and discernment in this most critical juncture in this community's history."

"And I second it!" another man chimed in.

The crowd burst into applause. Lacey's jaw dropped. She scanned the room questioningly, regained her composure and then turned and went back to her seat, shaking her head in frustration.

The mayor had to pound the gavel to regain order.

"Order, order!" he directed. "Okay, the motion carries; and now discussion of the TM development is closed. We are now ready for the council vote. All in favor of moving this project forward, raise your hands."

Six of the eight council members voted for the project.

"All opposed," he continued.

One hand went up.

"All abstained."

The last hand went up.

"Motion passed," he concluded with a tap of the gavel.

The crowd erupted into applause, standing and patting each other on the back and shaking hands. Lacey stood and stepped out into the aisle and pushed her way back to where Doc and Jim were shaking hands. She confronted Doc and blurted out, "When Crip gets back with the proof, you're goin' to jail."

Doc looked both ways to make sure no one was within earshot, and then leaned in and whispered with an expanding, proud, arrogant grin, "He's not *comin'* back."

"Yeah, and you won't find a single piece of him, either," Jim added with an evil laugh.

Lacey lost her composure and slapped at Jim, who caught her hand and squeezed.

"And you'll be next," he swore in a low, guttural tone.

Suddenly two hands went to Jim's hand and peeled it back against his thumb, forcing him to release his hold on Lacey.

"Who do you think...?" he began, turning.

Ike was looking up at him with an intense, angry stare.

"I'm justice and truth, and you're goin' to jail for murder," Ike stated with conviction.

Jim pulled his wrist easily from Ike's grasp and looked around at the people who were watching for his response.

"I never killed anybody. This kid's crazy."

"How about you show us that big knife you got under your shirt?" Ike challenged.

Instinctively, Jim put his hand over the knife.

"It ain't a crime to carry a knife."

"It is in this meeting," the sheriff interjected sharply, stepping in.

"This man killed Doug Simon," Ike announced loud enough for all to hear. "I'm an eyewitness."

The onlookers gasped.

"Now see here, young man, you don't know what you're talking about," Doc stammered, stepping in and putting a hand on Jim's shoulder, trying to diffuse the situation. "Jim is an upstanding businessman and my associate."

"'Accomplice' is more like it," Ike disputed. "I saw Doug slice his left knee during the fight, before this man and another beat him with an anchor!"

The crowd began to look at Jim suspiciously.

"That explains the type of wound that was on Doug's head when he was in ER," explained a woman standing nearby.

"Who are you?" asked Doc.

"A *real* doctor," she replied. "I was working in the emergency room when Doug was brought in for treatment."

Ike went back on the attack. "Ask this man to raise his left pant leg and let's see if there's a scar."

"Oh, this is getting ridiculous," Doc quibbled defensively.

"Raise your pant leg," commanded the sheriff, nodding to Jim.

"I will not. I'm outta here," Jim stated gruffly and turned for the door.

"These false accusations won't stand, and anyone who attacks our credibility will end up in court. I promise!" Doc protested as he grabbed his briefcase and followed Jim out.

The door opened just as Jim was reaching for the handle and in walked Crip, who was holding a box of documents. It was Jim's turn to freeze in terror.

"I thought you were..." Jim spouted on reflex.

"Were drowned?" Crip finished. "In the lake where your goons took me? Not hardly."

Doc turned on his heels and looked for another exit, but he was caught by the men in the crowd. Jim turned and tried to push his way past Crip, but Crip dropped the box and took him down to the floor, using his ground-fighting experience to lock the big man with his arms and legs, while another deputy rushed over to cuff him.

"This man is a murderer," Crip yelled to the crowd. "He killed Doug Simon!"

While Doc and Jim were being handcuffed, Crip picked up the box of evidence and handed it to Lacey.

"Here's what we've been looking for. I hope I'm not too late. I was foolin' with crab traps, and then took a swim in the lake."

"Why am I not surprised?" she smiled as she took the box and turned to face the council.

"I have an order of new business!" she called to the mayor. She brought the box to the council desk and began distributing the papers. "I think you'll find a lot of mischief on this skunk when you see these documents."

The mayor and council members began to read the pages with interest and talked among themselves excitedly.

"Hey, Doc, let's see how *you* look in handcuffs," Crip taunted, rubbing his sore wrists as they were being led away.

"You can't prove anything," Doc mumbled.

"You wanna bet your life on that?" Crip quipped, looking him dead in the eyes. "Do the terms 'money laundering,' 'grand larceny,' 'mail fraud,' 'harboring escaped convicts,' 'racketeering,' 'income tax evasion,' 'bribing government officials' and 'murder' ring any bells?"

"Lies, all lies," Doc muttered as he was directed to the door.

"That's really, really sad," Crip breathed, turning to Ike.

"What?"

"When a man sinks so far down in sin that he even believes his own lies."

The mayor pounded the gavel to restore order.

"Order in this meeting! We have a new order of business."

When the crowd settled back into their seats and quieted down, he continued.

"We have new information on TM Enterprises that has come to light. We now have in our hands the proof that Lacey Simon was referring to earlier, and it looks like she was right about Doc — er, Turk Matherne. We must now take a new vote on the TM development project. All in favor of the project moving forward, raise their hands."

No councilman raised a hand.

"All opposed to the project, raise your hands."

Every member voted against it.

"Let the record show that the TM development project for the Choctaw Indian reservation and surrounding area is now dead," the mayor proclaimed, pounding his gravel to emphasize the finality of the decision.

"Mr. Mayor, may I be recognized?" asked a man in a dark suit near the front of the crowd.

"Certainly. The chair recognizes Parish District Attorney Mark Babineaux."

The D.A. stood and addressed the council.

"As acting Parish D.A., I'd like to take possession of that evidence so the people of Tangipahoa can prosecute this criminal case against TM Enterprises and all parties involved to the fullest extent of the law."

"Excellent idea, Mark. The evidence is yours, and good hunting," the mayor said, sliding the box toward him as he stepped forward.

Crip, Ike and Sam jumped to their feet and shouted in victory. Lacey, overcome with emotion, began to weep tears of joy. Crip pulled her to her feet and hugged her.

"It's over," Crip rejoiced. "Doug's killer's been caught!"

"Meeting adjourned," the mayor announced, pounding the gavel, unable to contain the crowd any longer. Everyone broke out into spontaneous applause for Crip, Lacey, Ike and Sam. Then they began milling around Lacey, putting their hands on her shoulders and expressing their condolences and support.

Ike and Sam let themselves be pushed off to the side by the excited well-wishers.

"You did good, Ike, you did real good," Sam said, giving him a big bear hug.

Ike was surprised by the big squeeze, and somewhat embarrassed.

"I just wanted to do the right thing, you know? Be responsible."

"You *are* responsible, a very responsible young man... and I love you!" Sam said, pulling back to look him in the eyes.

"Those would be my exact words, too," Crip echoed with a smile, and then he pulled Ike in for a man-hug, patting his back with gusto. Ike peered over his shoulder at Sam, and winked.

EPILOGUE

Later that month, Ike, Sam and Skeeter were making last-minute preparations on their bikes before their race at Daytona International Speedway. Mr. Gonzales, Ike's mom and Sam's dad were just finishing breakfast in the camper.

"I'm bummed to miss the National Championship, but this is the next-best thing," Sam said excitedly, tightening up the bolts on her seat.

"Yeah, it's the first year of the Ricky Carmichael Amateur Race, and we get to race the same track the pros raced last night," Skeeter replied. "I wish our whole race team could have come."

"We'll just have to represent for 'em," Ike offered with a coy smile, pulling on his boots.

"Okay, guys, here's your new jerseys!" Mr. Gonzales announced, walking up with a box in his hands.

"Lemme see!" Sam exclaimed with joy.

Mr. Gonzales pulled out a red-white-and-blue jersey, with sponsor insignias all over it.

"Hey, that's Honda colors," Sam whined.

"Like I said, gotta represent," Ike declared with a laugh, nodding to Skeeter.

"Don't worry, we got you hooked up, sweetie," answered her dad, coming out of the camper. "Show her hers, Victor."

Mr. Gonzales reached into the box and pulled out an orange-and-black jersey with the same sponsors.

"But this is your 'real' jersey," he chuckled, pulling out another jersey with "Dirt Bike Ike" printed across the front.

"Oh, no way. I am so not wearing that!" Sam exclaimed.

They all burst into laughter.

"Hey, you said you loved me!" Ike pleaded in mock disappointment.

"Not enough to wear that! Where'd you get it, at Goodwill?" Sam snickered.

"In your closet," her dad teased. "We picked this color scheme out of all the hundreds of other 'Dirt Bike Ike' jerseys you had hanging in there."

219

"Ahhh!" Sam yelled in indignation, and then turned to Ike with a warning. "I am gonna embarrass you so bad on the track today!"

"You mean by wearing *this*?" Ike countered, reaching into his bag and pulling out a pink jersey with "Bayou Cat" emblazoned across the front, over an outline of a cat growling.

"Where'd you get that?" Sam gasped in shock.

"He picked it out of *his* closet, from among the hundreds of others he had just like it," Tricia quipped, who had just stuck her head out of the camper.

"No way! Your dad had it made," Ike retorted. "I'll tell you what: If you can get ahead of me and stay there, I'll wear your lame jersey in the second moto."

"Oh, you did *not* just say that," Sam smiled.

"Oh, I sure did. But there is one catch," Ike added.

"What's that?" Sam asked, snatching the cat jersey out of his hand to admire it.

"You have to wear mine if *I* beat *you*," Ike smiled, pointing to the "Dirt Bike Ike" jersey.

Sam shrugged, unconvinced, and replied, "In your dreams," as she held her jersey up to show it off.

Just then a hopped-up dune buggy came chugging up with Creedence Clearwater Revival's "Up Around the Bend" blasting out of its big speakers. Crip pulled his sunglasses down to look at everyone, as if he were a movie star. Then he turned off the motor and stepped out of the buggy. Ziptie stepped out from the other side.

"You guys ready to do the Daytona rock-and-roll?" asked Ziptie, coming around the buggy and cocking his cowboy hat back on his head with a Texas-sized grin.

"What's the Daytona rock-and-roll?" asked Sam.

"That's where you rock the competition and roll to victory on the roughest track on the Supercross circuit!" Crip laughed, waving someone over from across the road.

"Oh, that's me," Ike replied.

"No, I think he was talking to *me*," Sam argued.

"Hey, you know what they say," Crip joshed, putting a hand on Ike's shoulder.

"Girls rule, boys drool," Sam stated.

"No, to the winners go the spoils," Ike hooted, nodding at Sam, dancing and holding up his "Dirt Bike Ike" jersey in front of Sam to see if it fit.

"Nope. Tell 'em, Ziptie," Crip said, looking at his old friend.

"When the green flag drops…"

"…the B.S. stops," added the man whom Crip had signaled to join them, stepping up just in time to finish the sentence.

"Folks, this here is Trampas Parker," Ziptie announced grandly. "He's the only American still alive to have won two World Championships in motocross, and missed a third by only three points due to bike failure."

Trampas stepped up and shook their hands. "Actually, Donny Schmit did it after me, but he passed away a couple of years later."

Ike and Sam just stood there, mouths open in disbelief, unsure of what to say.

Suddenly a golf cart pulled up with the number four emblazoned across the side.

Ziptie continued, "And this here's Ricky Carmichael. He's hosting this event as part of the MX Sports race weekend."

"What?" Ike stammered, dropping the jersey.

"It's the GOAT," Sam said slowly, in a state of shock.

"Hi, guys," Ricky said. "I'm glad you could race with us this weekend. You like the track?"

"What do ya mean, 'goat'?" Mr. Gonzales whispered to Sam.

"'Greatest Of All Time,'" Sam whispered back.

Mr. Gonzales nodded. "Oh, *that* goat," he said, looking Ricky over with respect.

"I found the track to be rough, but not as rough as last night," Skeeter stated, polishing his goggles.

"We smoothed it out some, 'cause your bikes don't have the suspension that the pros use. But it's as close as you can get to racing at the big show with the stars," Ricky said with a smile.

"What's with the jerseys?" Trampas asked, pointing to Ike's and Sam's joke jerseys.

Ike and Sam just looked at each other, speechless. Mr. Rick answered.

"Oh, it's a challenge," he explained. "Whoever wins between them, the other one has to wear their jersey in the second moto."

"Sweet," Trampas nodded approvingly.

"I might have to watch that," Ricky said.

"Could you guys sign our jerseys?" Sam asked.

"Sure," Trampas said, and pulled a Sharpie out of his pocket as Skeeter, Ike and Sam brought him their jerseys, and the two joke jerseys.

"Well, gotta get back to work," Ricky said, handing the jerseys back. "You guys ride smart."

"Okay," Sam and Ike said at the same time, waving to the men as they climbed back into their golf cart. The group stood in stunned silence for a moment, processing what had just happened.

Two more men came walking up, greeting Ziptie and Crip. After handshakes and a few words, Crip turned to the group.

"Hey, guys, I want you to meet a couple of Hall-of-Famers," he announced excitedly, waving them over. "This is Chuck Sun, who was a National Champion in 1980 and on the first American Motocross Des Nations World Championship team."

Chuck stepped forward and shook their hands.

"...and this is Steve Wise, known as the most versatile motorcycle racer in history, having won championships in motocross, road racing, superbike, TT and Supercross."

"Would *you* sign our jerseys?" Ike asked.

"Be happy to," Steve answered, pulling out a marker. "What are you riding?"

"A 2005 CRF250. But I sometimes race an '82 CR125."

"Hondas, huh?" he replied, turning to Chuck with a nod.

"We used to race factory Hondas, too, and test them for R&D," Chuck added, taking Skeeter's jersey.

"What's R&D?" asked Skeeter.

"Research and development," replied Mr. Rick.

"That's how they developed the improvements for the new models that came out the next year," Mr. Gonzales explained.

"You know the old '82 model that you race sometimes?" Chuck asked.

"Yeah," Ike replied.

"That's the factory bike I won my National Championship on and was the precursor to that model, though I raced a 500."

"Well, you two guys did a great job on helping design those bikes, 'cause that group of Hondas are my most dependable and stable vintage race bikes," Mr. Gonzales said.

"I think that '82 250 was the best bike of my day," Steve explained. "It broke a couple times on me, but they got the bugs worked out before it went into production."

The PA speakers boomed: "All Novice and Women's classes to the gate for practice."

"That's you, get goin'," Mr. Gonzales warned.

"Uh, can you give me a hint about riding my Honda?" Ike asked Chuck and Steve, casting an intense gaze at Sam. "I have an important race today."

"Uh, me, too. I'm riding a KTM," she countered, stepping up to them.

Chuck went up to Ike and whispered in his ear. Steve followed suit and walked over to Sam and whispered in her ear. Ike and Sam looked at each other and smiled and nodded, communicating something silent that only they knew. They started their bikes and rode off to practice, with the others shouting encouragement.

Steve and Chuck waved to the bystanders and started walking away.

"What did you tell her?" asked Chuck, putting a hand on Steve's shoulder.

"To forget about the other riders and concentrate on the track."

"That's what I told Ike!"

They both laughed.

"Come on, let's go encourage some other kids," Steve said, nodding to another pit road.

"Good idea," Chuck agreed, taking off his hat and wiping his forehead.

After having practiced for a few laps to get a good look at the track, Ike and Sam lined up side by side in front of the gate.

"Okay, three laps, winner take all," Ike stated, adjusting his goggles.

"Get ready to wear my jersey!" Sam yelled over the sound of the bikes, putting her KTM in gear.

"You'll be wearin' red!" Ike yelled back, revving his Honda.

They waited for an opening in the line of practicing riders who were coming around the sweeping turn in front of the start, and then dumped their clutches, unleashing the fury of the 250 four-stroke motors. The energy surged through the gears, the sprockets and then the chain, spinning their rear tires, launching them into the next stage of their racing careers!

"'For I know the *plans* I have for you,' declares the Lord, '*plans* to prosper you and not to harm you, plans to give you hope and a *future*. Then you will call upon me and come and pray to me, and I will listen to you. You will seek me and find me when you seek me with all your heart.'"
(Jeremiah 29:11-13)

"The Lord will *fulfill* his *purpose* for me; your love, O LORD, endures forever…"
(Psalm 138:8)

Live Your Life on Purpose!

Other books by Roy Jenkins

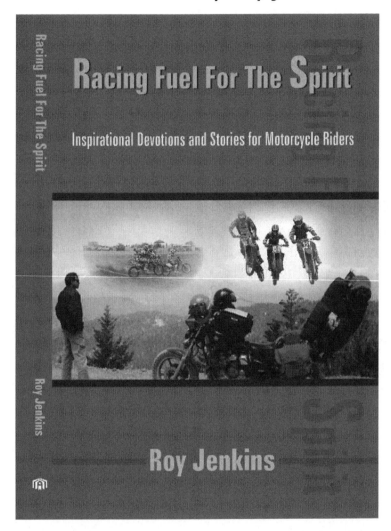

Racing Fuel for the Spirit is a non-fiction, "chicken-soup-for-the motorcyclists-soul" type of book. Each page is a self-contained story with black and white pictures, a scripture verse and a memorable quote to get your day started off right. Think of it as "spiritual vitamins." A topical index helps direct the reader to issues that are of interest. It's the author's way to help motorcycle riders read and understand the Bible.

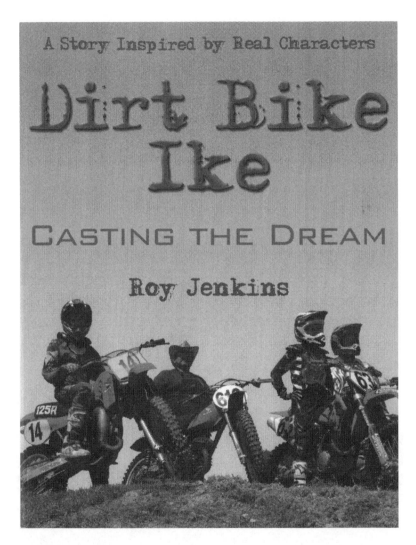

A Story Inspired by Real Characters

Dirt Bike Ike

CASTING THE DREAM

Roy Jenkins

Casting the Dream is the first book in the Dirt Bike Ike series. It is written for the younger teens and is in children's book format. It has a simpler plot and contains color pictures throughout, which give it a "coffee table" look. For more information, links or news on motocross racing in the gulf south, go to Roy's website at www.2wheelcommunications.com.

Made in the USA
Middletown, DE
03 December 2016